Dan McGirt was born in Sylvester, Georgia, in 1967, and was educated at the University of Georgia. He has never been a gun-runner, a nuclear technician, or a high-ranking government official. He has not travelled extensively to some of the most exotic and dangerous locales around the globe and isn't likely to. He enjoys reading, fencing, writing, and acting, and claims to be a perfectly sane, perfectly normal, perfectly behaved young man. *Dirty Work* is his third novel.

DIRTY WORK

Dan McGirt

PAN BOOKS
LONDON, SYDNEY AND AUCKLAND

First published 1993 as a ROC book by the Penguin Group,
Penguin Books USA Inc., New York

First published in Great Britain 1993 by Pan Books Limited
a division of Pan Macmillan Publishers Limited
Cavaye Place London SW10 9PG
and Basingstoke

Associated companies throughout the world

ISBN 0 330 32391 1

Copyright © Dan McGirt, 1993

1 3 5 7 9 8 6 4 2

A CIP catalogue record for this book is available from
the British Library

Printed in England by Cox & Wyman Ltd, Reading, Berkshire

Dedicated to my brother,
Brandon McGirt

1

Back at last! Back to Caratha, the Greatest Metropolis in Arden, the City at the Center of the World, the Fountainhead of Civilization, the Epitome of Bad Zoning and Overcrowded Urban Sprawl! Like stalks of gilded celery, her golden towers gleamed beneath a morning sun that was a ripe, juicy orange in the cloud-garnished autumn sky. Bulging upward like shiny onions, the jeweled domes of the awesome Alcazara Palace dominated the skyline in a sparkling banquet of light. Her leagues-long encircling wall was a great wheel of alabaster cheese with a few bites taken out. The paving stones of the road on which I traveled formed an endless line of meat-loaf slices reaching to the far horizon.

Tough meat loaf, to be sure.

I lacked a metaphor for the far horizon. Some sort of pastry perhaps. With a jelly filling. Raspberry, most likely.

In any event, the road was practically deserted at this hour. Only the clop of my horse's hooves, the creak of the harness, the rumbling of my stomach, and the cries of distant birds broke the morning stillness. Which meant that minus me and my horse, all you would hear were the birds. And if you hunted those down and killed them, you would achieve a scene of perfect silence. If that's what you looked for in scenes.

I rode through this not-quite-perfectly-silent scene toward the fabled Moonstone Gate. Southward spread the gently waving reeds of the Vast Salt Marshes, where the enigmatic Murikolian Marshmen made salt-water taffy in thick black pots. The wetlands gave way to the dark mantle of the deep and mysterious Indigo Sea, dotted with the bright sails of a hundred leaky fishing boats. To the north lay wide fields of grain ripe for harvest, lifeblood for Caratha's teeming millions. Behind me was the road to the sunny kingdom of Raelna, whence I had come, and the wild lands beyond, whence I had also come.

I whistled a happy tune, further disrupting the imperfect stillness of the day. I whistled because it was a beautiful day. I whistled because I was alive and would soon enjoy a big, hot breakfast in my own house for the first time in months. But most of all I whistled because, after much deep soul-searching, I knew what I wanted from life. Within the hour I meant to take the vital first step toward my dream by asking my sweetheart Sapphrina Corundum to marry me.

The thought of her golden hair, her slender sun-bronzed limbs, her vivacious blue eyes, her soft ruby lips, her ready laugh, her keen mind, and her lively manner—none of which I had experienced for several months—made my heart and so forth swell and my blood quicken. Never had I loved any woman so much. Actually, never had I loved any other woman at all, but that was beside the point.

Topping a low rise, I discovered a slight obstacle to my plans. A broken-down cart blocked the road. A domestic model, it was a rickety wooden vehicle that had seen better decades. One of its two wheels lay flat on the ground. The axle was wedged between two pavestones. Half its cargo of bruised purple turnips was spread across the roadway like a knotted blanket. A gaunt ox stood in the harness, patiently awaiting a command to move on.

What touched my heartstrings, however, was the sad-faced old couple in ragged clothes helplessly standing by, obviously too weak to lift the cart and replace the wheel. With them was a young, dirty-faced, fair-haired little girl with a runny nose, eagerly gathering the scattered turnips. She had no shoes and wore only a thin dress of rags. None of the three had a cloak for warmth.

I reined in my horse and gave them a friendly smile.

"Good day, folks," I said pleasantly. "Having some trouble, are you?"

The old couple exchanged hopeful glances and the man, his face a weather-beaten mass of deeply etched wrinkles, shuffled forward with his cap in his hands and his eyes cast groundward.

"We are, milord. I am Ambric. As you see, our poor cart has lost a wheel and my poor wife Myrta and I lack the strength to lift it. Were I a younger man, I would have it repaired in no time, but alas, in my old age my sinews are not what they once were, what with the rheumatism, arthritis, gingivitis, and all. We have come far from our humble farm, where we scrabble out a bleak existence in an unfurnished vermin-infested one-room shack with thin walls, a leaky roof, and no indoor plumbing, to sell these poor turnips so that we might earn a few pennies and buy a winter cloak for our granddaughter. She is the only child of our only son, who was killed in the wars. The variegated fever took her mother last spring and now she has only Myrta and I to care for her, poor child." He sniffled. "It seems we shall never reach the city, though we are in sight of its fabled gates." He looked toward Caratha and sighed. "So near, and yet so far. The market will close and we will not be able to sell our produce and the poor child will shiver and cry through all the long, cold, snowy, freezing, really, really nasty winter which is nigh upon us."

"Perhaps I might be of assistance," I said.

"Oh, we wouldn't want to impose, sir."

"It's no problem," I said. "If I lift the cart, do you think you could set the wheel in place?"

"Probably. But, milord, we could never repay you, for we are exceptionally poor. Very, exceptionally, extremely poor. Abject poverty, I'm talking about. Sometimes we are forced to eat stale dirt for breakfast. When it's available."

"Don't worry about that," I said, swinging out of the saddle and waving his objection away. "I was once a turnip farmer myself, so I'm glad to help you, Goodman Ambric."

The man fell to his knees and pressed the hem of my cloak to his lips. "Oh, bless you, kind sir!" he said. "May all The Gods in Paradise bless you for taking pity on a poor old man and his poor old wife and a poor illiterate little girl who isn't in very good health and has but one dress to wear and never enough food to eat and no toys to play with and needs braces to correct a bad overbite. You are our savior!"

"Yes!" said the woman, kneeling beside her husband. "Oh, tell us your name, kind sir, that we may remember you in our prayers and bless you every day for the rest of our natural lives, which probably won't be that long since we're getting on in years but will hopefully be at least long enough to see our dear little granddaughter raised and properly married."

"My name is Jason," I said, not wanting to frighten them by revealing my full name, Jason Cosmo, a name that struck fear into the hearts of men, women, children, and pets alike.

"Bless you, Master Jason!" they chorused, with tears of joy in their eyes. "Bless you a thousand times over! Nay, ten thousand!"

"Really, it's no big deal," I said, trying to detach them. "I wish you'd stand up. All this kneeling and hem kissing is embarrassing."

"Come, Kara," said Myrta to the little girl. "Come

and thank kind Master Jason, who is going to help us fix the cart so that we can sell the turnips so that you can have a winter coat."

Little Kara dropped an armful of turnips and scampered over. She made a curtsy and lifted her wide, innocent blue eyes to mine. "Thank you, kind sir," she said sweetly.

"You're welcome," I said, patting her on the head and blinking back tears as I gently escaped the grasp of her grateful grandparents. "Now you stand back, sweetheart, so you don't get hurt."

"All right."

Ambric lifted the wheel and made ready to put it in place. I put my hands under the edge of the cart and knelt to raise it. Keeping my back straight, I stood slowly, easing the bed of the cart from the ground. It was a simple feat, for by the light of day I possessed the strength of at least ten ordinary men, possibly more. That was just one of many perks of being the chosen Champion of Rac, the Sun Goddess, Giver of Light, Queen of Daytime.

"Here we go," I said. "Can you get it now?"

"No," said Ambric, dropping the wheel and drawing a long dagger from inside his shirt. "But you're about to!"

Moving quickly for an "old man," Ambric stabbed at the right side of my torso, just under the shoulder. Meanwhile Myrta also developed remarkable spryness and stabbed me under the opposite shoulder blade. Little Kara came at me too, driving her blade against my left kidney.

But rather than the satisfying squish of keen dagger points penetrating flesh, all three killers felt the sudden jolt of keen dagger points snapping in twain.

I dropped the cart, which broke to bits, scattering turnips in all directions.

"I hate it when people take advantage of my good nature," I said.

"Armor?" said Ambric, looking in wonder at his broken weapon.

"That's right," I said, turning and throwing open my cloak to reveal my gleaming coat of mail. "As a matter of fact, it's enchanted armor, forged of the arcane ore miraculum, which, as everyone should know, is far stronger than the strongest steel, and plays hell with ordinary swords, daggers, and such."

"So I see," said Myrta weakly.

"Solid stuff." I gave my chest a good thump for emphasis. "Now this little assault was obviously no spur-of-the-moment thing, and as common robbers don't operate so near the city walls, I can only presume the three of you are professional assassins."

"Indeed," said Ambric proudly. "We are card-carrying members of the Assassins and Cutthroats Labor Union."

"The ACLU, eh? Who hired you?"

"You needn't worry about that."

"Why not?"

"You'll soon be dead."

"How? Your perfidious ploy has failed."

"We anticipated the possibility of failure," said little Kara, her voice growing more mature and her eyes less innocent. "That's why we have a backup plan." She lit a cigarette and took a long draw from it.

"Backup plan?" I asked.

Kara exhaled a mouthful of cancerous, lung-rotting smoke. "Thugs in the bushes. Lots of them."

Fifty, in fact. Armed with maces, cheap swords, cattle prods, pruning hooks, staves, and clubs, they emerged from a large patch of brush beside the road and surrounded me. Leaves, seeds, and small rodents clung to their shabby clothing. Most of them sneered at me. A few didn't have the hang of sneering but managed wicked grimaces.

"I see," I said with a sigh. "And I was in such a good mood."

I looked to my horse, contentedly grazing in the ditch. My sword and shield hung from the saddle, well out of reach. Or so it seemed. I raised my left hand and whistled. The horse did not react.

Ambric sneered. "Trained horse?"

My sword rasped out of the scabbard and flew to my hand. "Trained sword," I said. "Overwhelm is its name."

"Quite a trick," said Ambric. "Forged of miraculum, too, is it?"

"Yes." I smiled dangerously. "So who wants to be first?"

The thugs' sneers dribbled right off the ends of their unwashed chins. They backed away uneasily.

"You didn't say nothing about no magic swords," complained the head thug, a husky man with curly red hair and a bad squint.

"Quit whining, Rostwick, and kill him," said Ambric. "He's only one man."

"I always worry when someone says that," said Rostwick.

"You aren't going to run away, are you?" asked Kara.

"I was thinking about it," admitted Rostwick. A dozen others nodded.

Kara shrugged and puffed smoke. "Suit yourselves. But remember that we know where you live. It would be a shame to wake up with a slit throat one morning."

"Right," said Rostwick. "At him, boys. He's only one man."

They rushed me all at once. It was their best strategy, though they probably didn't realize it. Overwhelm magically analyzed any opponent's technique, recognized the flaws in his attack, and countered them. I just had to hold on and the sword itself would make all the right moves. I'd fought large groups often enough for Overwhelm to have that scenario down pat. Thus I parried with blinding speed and struck with deadly effect, never missing an opportunity to inflict damage. Unfortunately, with these odds even perfection wasn't good enough. For every fatal thrust I deflected, two equally dangerous attacks got past my guard. They didn't get past my invincible armor, of course, but I wasn't wearing my helm or gauntlets and eventually someone would get lucky and divest me of several fingers, a hand, or my head. Furthermore, I might slip on a turnip or fallen foe and go down in the press. Taking all this into account, I decided to change tactics.

"This is fun, fellows, but I've got to run."

I hacked my way through two killers, bounded atop the remnants of the cart, vaulted over the patient ox, and hit the ground running. I could cover a mile in less than five minutes and that was about the distance to the Moonstone Gate. My magic armor was as light as ordinary clothing and wouldn't slow me much.

"After him!" yelled Ambric, before following his female cohorts into the brush. They would let their underlings finish the job.

With my long, loping stride I quickly pulled away from my pursuers. By the time I reached the Moonstone Gate, I had a lead of almost fifty yards.

But something was wrong. Contrary to all custom, the great gate was closed, its gem-studded iron face like a shield sealing the tunnel through the thick city wall. The wall itself was a sheer plane of closely jointed stone blocks rising over thirty feet into the air. I could not hope to scale it. Indeed, the squad of purple-uniformed sentinels manning the ramparts had standing orders to shoot anyone who tried. I was trapped—and I hadn't even had breakfast.

"The gate is closed!" I called to the soldiers as I drew near.

"Yes, I know," said their captain offhandedly, twirling his mustache. I never trust a mustache twirler.

"The gears and pulleys are being oiled. Should only be a slight delay though, and we'll be open for business."

"Can't you see I'm about to be murdered out here?" I waved back at the onrushing thugs.

"Well, yes, why so you are. But I've been bribed not to notice. You know, I think we'll be done with our oiling about the time you're done being murdered."

"How much?"

"Excuse me?"

"How much did they pay you? I'll double it!" I was willing to buy my way out of this mess if I could.

"Look here, now, I'm an honest man," protested the captain. "When I'm bribed, I stay bribed."

"I'll triple it then."

"Of course you will. Why don't you throw in the moon and the stars and the deep blue sea while you're at it? I don't place my trust in the promises of a desperate man."

"You don't think I've got money? *How much did they pay you?*"

The captain coughed delicately. "I dislike discussing personal finances in front of my men, if you don't mind."

"Would thirty be too low?" I knew thirty pieces of silver was the going rate for treachery.

"Thirty!" he scoffed. "Do you think I would abuse my position and violate the trust of my superiors for a mere thirty? What kind of low-life scoundrel do you take me for? Thirty? You insult me!"

"Thirty gold."

That got his attention. "Gold? When exactly was it you wanted the gate opened, sir?"

"Now!"

"Open the—wait a second! This gold—it's all back at the manor house, right?"

I tossed up my coin purse, which the venal captain caught deftly. He inspected its contents and found far more than thirty gold Carathan crowns and Raelnan marks in the bag.

"You can keep the change," I said. "Now open the gate."

The captain grinned. "I am touched by your generosity, but as I told you, I am a man of my word. When I am bribed, I stay bribed, especially when I am bribed by the ACLU, who are known to do unpleasant things to those who double-cross them. But my men and I will drink a round in your honor after our shift. Happy dying."

The thugs were almost upon me. My only alternative to combat was flight into the marsh, and that would ruin my boots. I had no choice but to stand and fight.

Putting my back to the wall, I braced myself to meet the new onslaught. About forty men remained alive, but the run had taken its toll. As my leading pursuers drew near, the last of the band followed by almost a hundred yards. My would-be murderers were clearly unused to this level of exertion.

The first few thugs to reach me could barely lift their weapons to defend themselves. I soon stacked half a dozen bodies at my feet. I noted an inverted process of natural selection at work. The fittest of my pursuers reached me first and died. The less fit collapsed in the road gasping like beached whales and would escape the slaughter to reproduce. I wondered if I ought not go back and finish them just on general eugenic principle.

The main body of attackers reached the killing grounds and stopped to huff and puff and glare at me.

"I guess you fellows want a minute to catch your breath," I said, lowering Overwhelm and leaning casually against the gate. "Let me know when you're ready to continue."

"Thanks," said Rostwick, who was bent over double with his elbows on his knees, his chest heaving like a damaged bellows. "Kind of you."

"Don't mention it. You lead this pack of dogs?"

"I got the boys together, yeah. The little witch said this would be easy money. Hah!"

"What little witch?"

"Kara. You know, the girl. Toughest assassin in Caratha. Who are you anyway?"

"Jason Cosmo," I said offhandedly.

Heads snapped up. Bladders failed. Jaws dropped. Eyes grew wide with fear. The whole lot of them took an involuntary step backward, trembling furiously. I heard the captain on the wall gulp.

"I'll be damned," said Rostwick softly. "I'd have never took the job if she'd told me that. None of us would've. Jason Cosmo. I'll be damned."

"Probably," I said. "Caught your breath yet?"

"Ah, no. Is it true you've killed a thousand men?"

"I've lost count."

"I've heard you're Demon Lord in mortal form."

I shrugged. "You never know. Caught your breath yet? I'd like to finish this soon. I haven't had breakfast yet."

"Well, you see, it's like this—you'll kill us all."

"Probably."

"And if we flee, the ACLU will get us. That puts us in a bit of a pickle."

"Sounds like a personal problem."

Before Rostwick could reply, there was a commotion on the ramparts.

"What's this?" cried the captain, as if just realizing what was happening. "An honest citizen beset by killers! Open fire, you louts!"

The sentries fired their crossbows into the pack of thugs, killing eight of them in the first moments of surprise. The rest of the band scattered, some diving off the embankment into the marsh, others fleeing back down the road to get out of range. Another five took bolts in the back before they were dispersed.

"Problem solved!" I called after Rostwick.

I stepped back and waited patiently as the freshly oiled gate swung open. A platoon of soldiers rushed past me to pursue the escaping killers.

I strolled through the tunnel that pierced the wall. It was wide enough to permit three wagons to pass through side by side, and high enough to give an elephant ample clearance.

I emerged in the section of Caratha called Moontown, which mostly catered to foreigners. Near the gate stood dozens of lodging places ranging in quality from the scroungy Take Your Chances Inn to the homey Gladhearth Hotel. Down the street a bit were strip joints, pool halls, gaming houses, and the Shake Your Bones Saloon, which was all of those rolled into one. Further along were a couple of semi-respectable taverns and nightclubs. Beyond were the shops and homes of tradesmen and artisans, near the Slightly Bazaar, which, though over a mile across, was still dwarfed by the Grand Bazaar on the other side of the city.

Surly traders and travelers ready to leave Caratha stamped and grumbled in the open square near the gate. They did not appreciate the delay in its opening and shouted their irritation to the soldiers in scatological terms that do not bear repeating.

The pale-faced captain emerged from the base of the gate tower and hurried up to me as I stepped into the sunlight. Warily, he held out my coin bag.

"H-here, sir, is the purse which you tossed up to me for safekeeping. I'm sorry we couldn't aid you sooner, but we had to . . . had to put in the pulleys and our weapons all . . . jammed. Yes, that's it! They jammed. I—I hope you understand. Sir."

"What is your name?" I demanded sternly, snatching the bag from his hand.

"Sordin B-Bidlow, sir," he stammered, wringing the sweat from his palms and fighting to keep his trembling knees from buckling.

"Well, Captain Bidlow, I hope this sort of thing doesn't happen too often. I'm a taxpayer, you know."

"Don't worry," he said emphatically. "You won't have trouble at the Moonstone Gate again, sir."

"Glad to hear that," I said, wiping my sword clean on his tunic. "If I do, I'll know where to take my complaint."

"Yessir," said the frightened soldier, surprised but not unpleased that I wasn't carving out his liver and feeding it back to him a piece at a time.

"I'm sure your men will be here with my horse momentarily," I said, dusting a bit of imaginary lint off his shoulder and feeling him tense.

"They wil

"Good. l, I'm eager to get home, so instead of strangling you with your own guts, I'll generously overlook your part in this little episode, Captain Bidlow. You did, after all, do your duty eventually."

"Thank you, sir!" He fell to his knees, though whether in gratitude or shock I couldn't tell. "Thank you! Had I known you were Jason Cosmo, I would not have hesitated to—"

"Yes, of course. Don't mention it. I've had enough groveling this morning."

The soldiers brought my horse and I continued homeward, whistling once again as I passed south of the colossal Consolidated Temple of The Gods, then up the west side of Pantheon Park. My stately little mansion was across the boulevard from the northwest corner of the park, on the fringes of The Estates, where the rich and powerful of Caratha dwelled and dallied.

Six horses bearing the harness of Carathan army officers were tethered out front. Concerned, I dismounted quickly and hurried inside, shouting, "Hello! Who's there?"

The only reply was an alarmed feminine cry from the heated pool out back. I also heard cursing male voices and a lot of splashing. I drew my sword and rushed to the rescue.

A curvaceous young lady with wet blond hair and frantic blue eyes intercepted me in the living room. She wore a damp red robe and had green and yellow stripes painted on her legs.

"Jason!" she cried, flinging herself at me.

We toppled over the back of a couch and she stole my breath with a ferocious kiss that threatened to dislodge my tonsils. Her breath tasted of tequila. Finally, desperate for air, I pried her lips from mine.

"That's some welcome, Rubis!"

"I'm so glad to see you!" she exclai   "It's been so long . . . we thought you might b   . . . I'm so glad you're back!" She punctuated the declarations with a whirlwind of quick, light kisses applied to my entire face.

"I'm glad to see you, too," I said, making a token effort to fend her off. "Where's Sapphrina?"

Her smile went slack for an instant, then she fell to kissing me again. I gently tried to disengage from the clench.

"Rubis . . . please . . . enough."

"All clear!" called someone out back.

Rubis stood. "Come on," she said breathlessly.

"What's going on? Why are all those horses here?"

She shrugged and led the way to the peculiar scene on the patio. Half a dozen dripping lieutenants of the Carathan cavalry scrambled away from the pool, showing every sign of having dressed with great haste: sopping shirts untucked and partly buttoned, jackets missing, trousers not fully fastened, boots unlaced, caps lopsided. Empty beer cans and overturned liquor bottles lay scattered about, along with a couple of riding crops, a body-painting set, and an open bag of Cheez Woozles.

"Halt!" I commanded. The soldiers froze.

Near the pool stood another dripping young woman, the identical twin of the one beside me. She wore a blue towel, broad red paint smudges, and a tight grin.

"Sapphrina!" I said joyfully.

The woman I loved rushed to embrace me. "Jason! I'm so glad you're here!"

"What's going on?" I indicated the sheepish officers.

"Ahem," said one, a finely chiseled fellow with curly black hair, purple paint streaks on his chest, and red paint on his hands. "We were riding by when we heard a cry for help and, rushing in, we found these women here—whom we've never seen before in our lives—drowning in the pool, so of course we leapt in to be of any assistance that we could possibly be of."

"To save them," added a second officer.

"Yes," agreed the other four. "To save them."

"After tying your horses securely out front, of course," I observed.

"Regulations, you know," said the dark-haired one. "Well, our work is done here and we'll be on our way. Good day, ladies. Swim more carefully in the future. Sir."

The soldiers tipped their hats and beat a hasty retreat.

"Are you all right, darling?" I asked Sapphrina. "You seem a bit flushed."

"Flushed? I'm not flushed, dearest. Just a little out of breath. Drowning is hard work."

I brushed the wet hair back from her face and kissed her. "How did you both happen to be drowning at the same time?"

"Actually, I was drowning and Rubis jumped in to rescue me. I panicked and nearly pulled her under too."

"That's right," said Rubis.

"You're usually an excellent swimmer."

"It must have been stomach cramps. Yes, I didn't wait long enough after eating breakfast. Silly me."

"Well, I'm just glad those friendly soldiers happened along in time to save you both," I said. "But let's get inside. You'll catch a chill out here wet. And I have an important question to ask you. The most important question of your life."

2

Sapphrina and Rubis ran upstairs to dress while I tended my horse, ate breakfast, and mulled over the best way to pop the question. I was sure she'd accept, but that didn't make asking any easier. Should I make a big production out of it? Should I slip it unexpectedly into conversation? Did I need to get down on my knees? Was the timing right? Was this the proper setting or should I do it over a fancy dinner? I'd been less nervous facing fire-breathing dragons or marauding ogres.

I finished eating and went to the living room to see what was new on the orbavision. Developed by the technowizard Grammbel, the orbavision receiver was basically an ordinary crystal ball modified to receive images broadcast from a transmitter downtown. It was thus far a novelty for the rich, but since I was last in Caratha, the price per unit had fallen and Grammbel's Orbnet Magicommunications Corporation (OMC) had expanded their offerings to several channels, including the Orbnet Shopping Bazaar, the OSPN sports channel, Music Orbavision, and the round-the-clock Orbit News Network. Also new were broadcast advertisements by Carathan merchants. Orbavision was starting to look more like a revolutionary development than a passing fad. What kind of world it would lead to, I could not say. According to an OMC commercial,

Grammbel's researchers were already working to make the orbaphone and spellfax widely available. These would bring even more change.

Sapphrina and Rubis came down in short clingy dresses, blue and red respectively, and bounced onto the couch beside me, curling their legs under prettily.

"What was it you wanted to ask me?" asked Sapphrina.

"In a minute," I said, overcome with an attack of jitters. I clicked off the orbavision with the remote control. "Tell me about your trip home."

"Fah!" said Rubis. "Zastria is home no more!"

While I was off adventuring, the twins had traveled to their native land to attend the funeral of Dwide Ikanglower, the late Zastrian president. A longtime family friend, he was "Uncle Dwide" to Sapphrina and Rubis, who saw him cut down by terrorists during the infamous Wedding Day Massacre at Rae City.

"Unpleasant trip, I take it."

"If you count the awful storms," said Rubis.

"And the beastly pirates," continued Sapphrina.

"Pirates?"

"Oh, yes," said Rubis. "We were captured by Tannis Darkwolf, the Pirate Queen herself."

"That's foreshadowing if I ever heard it. What happened?"

"She overtook our ship along the Broken Coast," said Sapphrina. "The pirates boarded, killed our crew, and carried us to their vessel."

"How did you escape?"

"Three Zastrian galleys came along and the pirates fled," said Rubis. "We jumped overboard in the confusion. Salt water is bad for the complexion, but better than suffering death, disfigurement, and possible degradation at the hands of pirates."

"What happened then?"

"A galley picked us up and took us on to Kielfa, but they wouldn't let us off the ship," said Sapphrina bitterly. "It seems the Senate elected Father President and he put us on the proscribed list of undesirables."

The twins' father, Corun Corundum, was Zastria's wealthiest merchant, head of the great Corundum Trading Company, whose motto was "What's good for Corundum is good for Zastria." But it wasn't necessarily good for Sapphrina and Rubis. When they refused to go through with marriages arranged by Corun to cement important business and political alliances, he disowned them and they moved to Caratha. They had hoped to reconcile their differences with Corun while in Zastria for Ikanglower's funeral. Obviously, that hadn't worked out.

"You missed the funeral?" I asked.

"Jason, we were put on the first ship back to Caratha and ordered never to return to Zastria on pain of death!" said Sapphrina. "We can never go home again."

Both girls sniffled and the tears started rolling.

"There, there," I said, putting my arms around them and pulling them close. "It'll be all right."

"Jason, that has to be the most inane thing you've ever said," said Sapphrina.

"I agree," said Rubis.

"Sorry."

"Tell us about your own journey," said Sapphrina, laying her head on my shoulder. "Cheer us up."

"Believe me, hearing about my journey won't cheer you up any. Duels to the death, desperate escapes, battles in the wilderness, dragons, ogres, killer vegetables, terrorists, sorcerers, carnivorous sheep—I'll be happy to put all that behind me for good. It's not the life for me."

"What do you mean?" asked Sapphrina, raising her head.

I stood. "I killed over a dozen men before breakfast this morning. Decent people tremble in fear at the mention of my name. My existence is one of constant violence and unending danger. I don't want to live this way anymore. I'm tired of being a hero."

"But you're very good at it," said Rubis.

"Even so, I've decided to exchange my sword for a plowshare. I'm going to discard my riches and return to the simple way of life I know and love."

"You're going to do what?" asked Sapphrina.

"I want to farm again," I said. "I want to be close to the soil. I want to sow and reap and avoid foreclosure, with no concerns more serious than early frosts or long dry spells."

"I see," said Sapphrina. "When are you going to do this?"

"Soon. Before another adventure starts. And I want you to come with me."

"I beg your pardon?"

"I want you to come with me, darling." I paused to gather my resolution. "As my wife."

"Your wife?"

"I'm asking you to marry me."

"So I gather."

The girls exchanged amazed glances and silently communicated on some level only accessible to twins.

"I detect a noticeable lack of enthusiasm," I said at length, feeling deflated by her unenthusiastic reaction. This wasn't what I expected.

"You aren't going back to Darnk, are you?" asked Sapphrina, horrified.

"Oh, no!" I said. My dismal homeland was not called the Armpit of Arden without good cause. "I want to grow actual crops in actual fertile soil, not coax weeds out of the rocks. I think we'll settle in a quiet valley over in the Vesper Hills."

"I see. And I get the impression you aren't envisioning a large estate with a manor house and lots of servants and field hands. You know, the gentleman-farmer setup."

"I had more the yeoman farmer in mind. That's the life I yearn for."

"Just you and me, then."

"You and me."

"I would be a farm wife, then, and do farm things. Shelling peas, plucking chickens, milking cows, churning butter, and so forth?"

"Can't you just see it?"

"Oh, yes, I can see it all right."

"Working together, wresting our mutual livelihood from the ground, relying on none but ourselves, living by the sweat of our brows. Just you and me, with our cozy little farmhouse all to ourselves. Until the children come, of course."

"Children?" echoed Sapphrina.

"Children. Those high-voiced miniature people you see running arour r an where bumping into things."

"I would supply these children, I take it," said Sapphrina.

"We'd work together on it. Am I missing something here?"

"I don't want to live on a farm, Jason."

"Where do you want to live?"

"Caratha. This is where the action is."

"I want to get away from the action, darling. Caratha is grand, but I want a peaceful, quiet, obscure existence where people I don't know aren't trying to kill me all the time. I can't have that in Caratha."

"I don't want to be obscure, Jason," said Sapphrina.

"What are you saying?"

"I'm saying if you want to live on a farm, go right ahead, but I don't think I'll be coming with you. I'm a city girl. I don't milk cows."

"Or pluck chickens," added Rubis. "How gruesome!"

"I see," I said.

Sapphrina smiled brightly. "Now a nice country estate would make an agreeable alternate residence and provide an occasional change of pace from the city. There's nothing wrong with that idea."

"The gentleman-farmer scenario," I said without enthusiasm.

"Exactly. A few hundred acres. A full household staff. Some very profitable estates are available right here in the outlying territory of Caratha. Though what you really ought to do is get Queen Raella to grant you a duchy or something. Then you would own lots of farms."

"And castles," said Rubis. "Castles are very impressive."

"Oh, yes," agreed Sapphrina. "Why don't you do that? I'm sure Her Majesty would give you whatever you ask of her. She likes you."

I threw my hands up in exasperation. "I'm sure she would, but I'm not interested in owning farms. I want to live on one. And I want to be an ordinary farmer, not a nobleman worrying about court and politics and collecting taxes and settling disputes. If I do what you suggest, I might as well stay here in Caratha."

"Splendid!" said Sapphrina. "So you'll forget about this farm nonsense? You can always plant a vegetable garden in the backyard."

"You won't consider my idea?"

"Really, Jason, the idea of grubbing around in the dirt for a living is ludicrous. I am of aristocratic birth, or at least I would be if Zastria still recognized its aristocratic bloodlines. I'm accustomed to a life of wealth and privilege. Why would I want to give that up?"

"For love?"

"Oh, I do love you, Jason, but this is asking a bit much. You want to make a peasant of me. Downward mobility is so tacky."

I pondered this. "Well, I hadn't thought of it that way, but I suppose it would be quite a change for you. The farming life is hard work despite its rustic charm.

Very well, I can compromise and play the gentleman farmer if that's what it takes for you to marry me."

"Did I say that?" asked Sapphrina cagily.

"I thought so."

"Is that what I said?" Sapphrina asked her sister.

"No," said Rubis.

"I'm not sure about this, Jason," said Sapphrina.

"Not sure about what?"

"Marrying you."

"Oh. Well, I know I sprang this on you, but I didn't think it would come as too great a surprise considering our feelings for each other. But if you need time to think, I understand."

"I'm not sure you do understand," she said, visibly uncomfortable.

"Understand what?"

"Jason, we defied our father and left Zastria because we didn't want to get married," said Rubis.

"But those were arranged marriages to men you didn't love. This would be by your own choice, Sapphrina."

"But it's not my choice," said Sapphrina.

"What do you mean?" I felt a horrible, twisting, sinking dread gnawing at my gut.

"She can't marry you," said Rubis.

"Why not?"

"Because I'm Sapphrina," said Rubis.

"And I'm Rubis," said Sapphrina.

"I'm confused," I said.

"It's very simple," said the woman I had been calling Rubis all morning. "I wore the red robe. You called me Rubis. Why?"

"You were wearing red."

"Do you see now why she can't marry you?" said Rubis, whom I had been calling Sapphrina. "You saw me in a blue towel and called me Sapphrina. You can't tell us apart."

"Well, you are identical twins and I hadn't seen you

in months. It was an honest mistake and I don't see what it has to do with you marrying me."

"Well, you just proposed to Rubis," said Sapphrina.

"It was directed to you, dear."

"But I can't marry you if you can't tell us apart."

"I can tell you apart!" I protested.

"Really?" said Rubis. "Then why did you propose to me?"

"I wasn't looking carefully. I just assumed that you were color-coded as usual."

"Maybe we are," said Sapphrina.

"What?"

"Maybe I really am Rubis. After all, I'm wearing red."

"You just said you were Sapphrina."

"Can't you tell who's who?" asked Rubis. Or the one I now thought might be Rubis. She wore blue, so maybe she was Sapphrina.

"Of course," I said, with more confidence than I felt.

"Who's who then?" they both said, standing up.

"You're both who you say you are. I think."

"Are you sure?" asked Sapphrina. At least, I was pretty sure she was Sapphrina.

"Let's put it to the test," said Rubis, who might have been Sapphrina. "Close your eyes."

"Why?"

"Do it," said Sapphrina. Or maybe Rubis. "And don't open until we say."

I complied and heard movement and the rustling of cloth.

"Open," they said together.

Their dresses lay piled in the floor and the twins stood before me in identical black lace undergarments that left no safe harbor for my eyes.

"Can you tell us apart?" asked the twin on the left.

"No," I admitted, feeling extremely awkward. "But what does that prove? I know who I love."

"Do you?" asked the woman on the right. "How can you be sure?"

"Well, you haven't pulled this switching trick before." They were silent.

"Have you?" A note of pleading entered my voice.

"Have we?" they said archly.

My eyes widened. "You're not telling me that . . ."

They exchanged knowing glances. "We've swapped places every day since we met you," they said together.

"Oh, Gods." I shook my head. "Even in . . . when . . . even then?"

"Even then."

"Oh, Gods."

"We really flipped for you when you rescued us in Darnk," said the sister on the left, sitting down beside me.

"And Sapphrina won the toss," said the other, also sitting.

"Whichever one of us is Sapphrina," added the left twin. "Considering your backward Darnkite sensibilities, we didn't think you could handle both of us at once."

"For a while there, it didn't look like you knew what to do with just one of us."

"We decided to let Sapphrina take the lead and let Rubis get her chance by impersonating Sapphrina."

"We could have just as easily gone the other way."

"This is quite a shock," I said woodenly.

"We hoped you would catch on eventually. We planned to tell you after Queen Raella's wedding, but then the Wedding Massacre happened and we didn't have a chance," said the twin on the right.

"You're upset, aren't you?" asked the other one.

"No. Not at all," I lied feebly.

"We didn't want to deceive you, but we both wanted you and this was the only way either of us could have you," said the left twin.

"Otherwise you would have come between us, and we couldn't let that happen."

Both wept. I put my arms around them.

"It's all right. Please don't cry. I'm not angry. I just wish you had told me the truth sooner. I love you still. Both of you." I swallowed hard. "I'll just marry you both."

"You'll do what?" they asked together, snapping their heads up.

"I'll marry both of you. In some cultures, multiple wives aren't uncommon, right? Even here in Caratha, I'm sure it's done."

"Everything is done in Caratha," said the twin on the right.

"I thought I loved one of you more, but if it's been the two of you all along, then a double wedding is the only solution."

"You're very sweet, Jason," said the left twin.

"But we don't want to marry you if you can't tell us apart," said the right.

"If I marry you both, I won't have to."

"No, Jason," they said together.

"It might be different if you'd figured it out on your own," added the left twin.

"We love you very much. You're a decent, honorable, noble man. The best we've ever known."

"But we wouldn't be happy as your wives."

"We don't want to live on a farm. And if you stay in the city for our sakes, then we'd be unhappy because we denied you something you really want. And you would come to resent us. And that would spoil everything."

"I wouldn't resent—" I protested.

"Don't argue. We're women. You can't outargue us."

"But—" I said.

"Besides, childbearing would ruin our figures. We're vain about our figures."

"We're shallow, Jason. Far too shallow for a man like you."

"We don't deserve you."

"We were lucky to have had you as long as we did, but now it's time for us to leave."

"No it isn't!" I cried. "We don't have to marry! We can go on like before!"

"We can't. We've revealed our deception. You've revealed your intentions. You want more than we can give. You deserve more. What we shared can't last any longer."

"Face it, Jason, we're fluff. We're self-indulgent, narcissistic, irresponsible tarts."

"We're prototypical sex kittens."

"What have we added to your life? All we've done is run around half-clad and scream and faint and need rescuing. Sure, we've got great heads for figures—"

"To match our great figures."

"We've given you good financial advice, but that's just a thin veneer of usefulness. We're basically undeveloped characters, interchangeable nonentities who get left behind when the real action starts."

"We're stereotypes."

"In this world, who isn't?" I protested.

"We're the cheesecake factor. We're clear examples of the objectification of women as purely sexual beings devoid of any real identities of our own. We operate solely as appendages of your masculine ego. And frankly, we're tired of it."

"We need to move on. Find ourselves. Maybe switch genres, leave these lightweight fantasies behind, and move up to serious fiction."

"We're not the ones for you."

"Think about it, Jason. You know it's true."

"Good-bye," they said in unison. "We'll send for our things."

They got up and headed for the door. I ran after them.

"Wait! Don't go! We can talk about this!"

They halted and turned. "Don't beg, Jason. This is for the best."

Stonily, I watched them walk down the path to the gate, but followed no further.

"Aren't you at least going to put your clothes on?" I called.

"It's easier to get a cab in our underwear," said one twin.

"And we probably won't have to pay a fare," added the other.

I saw no reason to remain in Caratha any longer than it took to pack a few belongings, saddle up, and ride out the way I had come in. The city had lost its shine. The beautiful parks and temples and palaces held no more luster in my eyes. The theaters and halls and arenas had no spectacle to show me. The shops and markets sold nothing I wanted to buy. The teeming masses, rich and poor, young and old, native and foreign, each with a story to tell, had naught to say that I wanted to hear. The priests and sages could share no wisdom that would make sense to me. The sick had no diseases I wanted to catch. The tricksters played no schemes I cared to fall for. The tax men taxed no taxes I wanted to pay. The jesters had no jokes to make me laugh, the poets and minstrels no verses to uplift me. No, Caratha had Sapphrina and Rubis all over it like flu germs on a sick man's hanky. Besides that, someone in town wanted me dead badly enough to pay the ACLU's exorbitant fees.

I had to get out. I had to go home.

Back to Darnk. Back to Lower Hicksnittle.

3

I stuck to the back roads of southern Raelna, intending to avoid Rae City, ride up through central Brythalia, then cross the northern forest to Darnk. I remembered the Brythalian route from my mad flight through that kingdom months ago with the world's deadliest bounty hunters at my heels.

I wondered if much had changed in Lower Hicksnittle since my departure. It was doubtful. The mottled pig pox going around had surely subsided. Maybe one of the old geezers of the village had kicked off, and perhaps a new baby had arrived if anyone had accidentally figured out how to produce one. Otherwise, the Hicksnittlers were plodding through life as thickly as ever, swilling stale rutabaga beer, gossiping about each other, and having no interest in anything or anyone beyond hollering distance from the muddy village brown.

That category now included me since I had Left for Parts Unknown. Whenever my name came up in conversation the Hicksnittlers would surely cluck and shake their heads sadly and tell each other what a shame it was that young Jason up and Left for Parts Unknown the way he did. Where exactly Parts Unknown was, the Hicksnittlers neither knew nor cared, but one thing they knew for a fact was that No Good Would Come of It. No good ever came of Leaving for

Parts Unknown. Didn't Old Farmer Balfor's second son, the exceptionally slow and ugly one with the clubfoot everybody made fun of, Leave for Parts Unknown six years ago? No good came of that, did it? In fact, poor Farmer Balfor's prize pig drowned in the water trough three weeks later. Proof positive that no good would ever come of dealings with Parts Unknown.

I could attest to the truth of that.

My neighbors would be amazed to see me return. Oh, they'd be suspicious at first, worried that I might bring to the village the taint of Foreign Parts. But since I was a native Hicksnittler, they'd only keep up the ostracism for a few months or so. Then they'd accept me back into the fold as if I'd never left in the first place.

At least I thought they would. No one had ever returned from Parts Unknown before. They might just stone me out of an abundance of caution and be done with it.

Even so, I looked forward to my homecoming. I had missed the shenanigans of our most important holiday in Darnk, the Feast of Groveling, but with luck I'd make it back in time for the Misgivings Eve carnival and the fresh-baked mud pies and moist grubworm tarts of All Famine's Day. I could almost taste the traditional roasted bark with shoe-leather sauce. Yes, it would be good to get back to where I once belonged.

After two meandering weeks on the road, I reached the Duchy of Whitwood in the northeast corner of Raelna. Most of the duchy's territory was covered by a mossy, shaggy oak forest appropriately called Whitwood. There leaves fell from the gnarled trees in a constant shower of color, paving the forest path in red, gold, orange, and yellow. Deer grazed near the trail and rabbits hopped across it. An occasional hedgehog put in an appearance. Migratory birds roosted in the trees, resting before continuing their southward journey. Riotous squirrels chittered and scampered among the high branches and pelted passersby with acorns.

This last feature was annoying, but on my right hand I wore the Ring of Raxx. The leaders of the League of Benevolent Magic had given it to me, probably because no one else would take it. Raxx's identity was uncertain. Who made the ring was unknown. What Raxx did with it was a mystery. How it came to the hands of my distant ancestor the Mighty Champion was a great enigma. About the only thing anyone did know about the ring was that it gave its wearer the power to communicate with squirrels in their own language. Using this power, I asked the squirrels of Whitwood to kindly stop harassing me.

They did. For about five minutes. The ring only granted the power to communicate, not the power to compel obedience. The squirrels didn't care that I spoke their tongue. I was on the ground and they were in the trees. Therefore, I was obviously not a squirrel and that made me fair game.

I met few travelers on the winding forest path, for Whitwood was wild country. Since the untimely death of Duke Rollo the Golden in an unfortunate shaving mishap fifteen years ago, his well-liked widow, the Duchess Leighah, had ruled the territory, though to say so was to use "rule" rather loosely. The Widow of Whitwood was excessively fond of hunting and riding. She spent more time feasting, drinking, and swapping tall tales with her subjects than attending to official business.

Her easy familiarity with the common folk went far toward explaining the Widow's popularity, but her failure to insist on timely tax collections and full enforcement of the laws went even further. As a direct result of her hands-off management style, bold bands of robbers, known as Whitwood Rangers, operated openly and successfully in Whitwood. So long as they didn't seriously kill or maim any ducal subjects, were careful about fire prevention, and remembered to give the Widow a fair share of the take when she dropped by, Leighah wasn't too concerned about their activities.

By sheer coincidence, the duchy's widely famed irregular light infantry and scouts, responsible for securing the borders, patrolling the forest paths, and maintaining order in the land, were also known as Whitwood Rangers. They worked on commission and were thus quite industrious in their securing, patrolling, and maintaining.

On my second day in Whitwood, I encountered a band of these enterprising woodsmen. They dropped down on me out of a tree and cracked me over the head with a blackjack. My only response was to slump to the ground.

When I came to, they had made off with my horse, clothes, and belongings and lashed me to a tree at the edge of a small clearing. It was a chilly day, not good weather for being splayed naked against a tree. I shivered and my teeth clattered.

While shivering, I noticed that my body from the neck down was covered with a thick layer of honey. This brought to mind disturbing images of swarming insects or, alternatively, peculiar amusements down at the Shake Your Bones Saloon.

With my Rae-given strength, I should have been able to burst my bonds and walk free. Unfortunately, I couldn't get good leverage. I next implored the squirrels to come down and untie me, but without the Ring of Raxx, they weren't listening.

As I racked my brain for some clever and heroic alternate means of escape, I heard the unmistakable snuffling of a Great Brown Raelnan Honey Bear. The picture became a little clearer.

Giving a satisfied growl as the scent of its favorite

food reached its nostrils, it emerged from the brush across the clearing and headed my way. I watched in tense silence as it padded purposefully toward me, crunching leaves beneath paws that could fell a charging bull with a single swipe. It drew near and I felt its hot breath on my loins as it sniffed to be sure that what coated my body was indeed the fine quality of Splendid Apiarian Daffodil Honey that finicky Great Brown Raelnan Honey Bears prefer.

Apparently satisfied by the product presented, the beast commenced the intricate and beautiful Happy Honey Dance of the Great Brown Raelnan Honey Bear. I watched the mesmerizing performance with awe. I had seen the dance performed by bears in captivity at the Royal Bestiary in Caratha, but that was nothing like seeing it in the wild. The smiling bear executed an elegant sequence of delicate pirouettes, airy capers, exquisite arabesques, and dainty caprioles culminating in a spectacular *fouetté en tournant* gliding into a full split. The only sound was the crinkle of the leaves. Even that was barely audible, so gracefully did the honey bear dance the Happy Honey Dance.

I redoubled my futile straining against the ropes. The dance ended and the bear approached, lost in the Honey Trance of the Great Brown Raelnan Honey Bear, eyes rolled up in the sockets so that the whites showed. Guided by its sensitive nose, it drew near. Its long, sinuous tongue, which was highly evolved for lapping honey, traced a wet line up my left thigh.

It tickled like anything. I bit my lip to keep from crying out. The slightest sound would disturb the bear's Honey Trance and enrage it beyond all calculation. Helplessly bound as I was, enraging the bear would be unwise. An enraged Great Brown Raelnan Honey Bear is one of the most fearsome foes in nature, more dangerous than the Malravian rock tiger, more bloodthirsty than the thick-snouted liver slug of Denab.

The bear continued its meal, licking and licking with agonizing thoroughness. I bit my lip so hard I drew blood as I fought to keep control, but finally could endure no more. I twisted and contorted as much as my bonds allowed and gave a sharp, loud gasp, quickly stifled. It was enough. The bear ceased its feeding. Its eyes rolled into focus and locked balefully with mine. With a savage snarl, it rose up on its hind legs and lifted a mammoth paw tipped with three-inch claws.

I didn't have time for my entire life to pass before my eyes, so I just hit the highlights, quickly, as the bear reared back for a solid disemboweling swing.

A blazing scarlet streak flashed across my vision and the honey bear's upraised paw burst into flame. A second streak ignited the fur of its back.

With an unbearish whimper, the beast recoiled, dropped to all fours, and performed the Flaming Flamenco of the Anxious Ursine, a wild, uninhibited dance involving much rolling on the ground, snapping at the air, and turning in circles.

A third fiery streak went wild, missed the bear by an arm's length, and hit the trunk of a nearby tree with a shower of sparks. Four riders emerged into the clearing: three scowling men in forest greens led by a beautiful woman with a wild wealth of hair as red as the autumn leaves. My own riderless horse followed on a lead.

The frightened honey bear toyed briefly with the idea of going berserk, attacking the riders, and uprooting a small tree or two, but thought better of it when a fourth streak of fire from the woman's hand scorched a line between its flattened ears. The bear dashed into the brush, whining piteously. As it fled, the flames on its body winked out, having done it no real harm.

The woman halted her horse and regarded me with an amused smile. As I opened my mouth to speak she pointed her hand and sundered my ropes with a precise burst of flame. My release was so sudden that I lost my balance and fell to my knees, as if in gratitude.

I was grateful, but my gratitude was outshone by hot-faced embarrassment. I preferred to wear more than rope burns and daffodil honey when meeting people, particularly women. Placing my hands carefully to preserve what modesty I had left, I looked up at my rescuer. I liked what I saw.

She was in her late twenties, slim-waisted and leggy, with eyes the crisp, dark green of a fir tree in summer. Her face was thinnish and angular, her fine skin the color of fresh cream, slightly flushed. Her cloak was gold, her riding pants black, her jacket russet and green. From her expression, she liked what she saw, too. And she had a more unobstructed view than I did.

"Thanks for the assist," I said. "That was a sticky situation."

She rolled her eyes and sharply commanded her companions, "Give him a towel!"

Her order disconcerted the three Whitwood Rangers. None of them had thought to bring a towel. While they argued over which member of the group was actually responsible for the lack of a towel, the woman returned her attention to me.

"Do you remember me?" she asked.

"You do look familiar."

"We met at the Royal Wedding," she prompted.

"Before or after terrorists crashed the party?"

"Before."

"Most of the people I met that day died when we got to the massacre portion of the program."

"Including my parents," she said bitterly.

"Oh. I'm sorry." Open mouth, insert foot.

"That's some consolation, I suppose." She smiled again, wanly. "You don't recall my name?"

"Could you give me a hint?"

"Solana of Sweetfire."

"Yes. Solana. Now I recall. Raella's cousin, aren't you?"

Her smile broadened. Like anyone, she was glad to be remembered, even with prompting. "Yes."

"I didn't recall that you were a sorceress."

"It didn't come up."

"Right. Well, I'm sure every detail of this meeting will be etched into my memory for a long, long time."

Solana laughed. "I don't doubt it." Her approving gaze lingered on me for just a moment more, then she snapped at her companions. "Where's that towel?"

The rangers came up with a worn saddle blanket, which didn't do much toward getting the honey off me, but went far toward adorning me with horsehair. It would take a good soapy scrubbing to get me clean. For now, I wrapped the blanket around myself and knotted it into a crude toga.

"So," I said, feeling more self-confident now that I was slightly less naked. "How is it that you happened along just in time to save my hide in grand melodramatic fashion?"

"I have sought you for six days at the Queen's behest," said Solana.

"You were looking in the wrong place. I haven't been near the Queen's behest."

She favored me with a peculiar look.

"I don't think her husband would like that," I added.

Ignoring me, she continued. "I met up with these louts not an hour ago and they kindly consented to direct me to you." Her voice oozed scorn.

"Please accept our most humble type of apologies, sir," said one of the rangers, wringing unaccustomed meekness from a gruff voice more suited to shouting "Stand and deliver!" "We hope you'll not take offense at our little prank. No harm was meant by it. 'Twas all in good fun."

"I could have been killed," I pointed out. "That wouldn't have been much fun at all."

"But you weren't killed," countered the ranger hastily. "That's important to remember."

"Her Majesty does not look kindly upon brigands, whatever the Widow may condone," put in Solana coldly. "This man is a personal friend of the Queen and Champion of Rae to boot. You may be sure that he will—"

"Not give this another thought," I said, cutting off her mounting indignation. The bandits fell to their knees with the same expression of mixed fear and relief that I had so often inspired and so learned to detest.

"Thank you, sir! If we had known who you—"

"Save it."

I freed my horse from the lead and noted with approval that my belongings were tied to the saddle. I loosened the bindings as I spoke.

"Why did Raella send you?" I asked Solana.

"To summon you to Caratha. The League High Council meets to discuss an urgent crisis."

"My, what a totally unexpected turn of events. Funny how it's never a trifling little minor crisis. Thank you for saving me, Lady Solana, but I just left Caratha and I'm never going back."

She scowled. "But you are needed. The League—"

"The League doesn't need me. I'm going home."

I dug out the Ring of Raxx and tossed it to Solana.

"Take that back to the High Council. Tell them to give it to someone else. I'm through." I patted Overwhelm and the divinely forged armor and shield. "Take these, too. And the horse is from Raella's stables."

"What can this mean?" she demanded.

"It means let the League find themselves another hero to do their dirty work. This farm boy is going home to grow turnips."

"Turnips?"

"That's right." I tied my clothes and belongings into a bundle and started down the road. "It was nice meeting you again, milady."

Solana rode ahead and blocked my path.

"You can't just quit! You're the Champion of Rae!"

"I almost forgot." I dug into the pack for my Champion of Rae identification card. "Return this, too, would you?"

"You have duties," said Solana. "Sacred duties you cannot shirk!"

"I really don't care to discuss this with you, milady," I said evenly. "Now if you would kindly get out of my way."

An angry plume of flame flared from Solana's upraised hand like the tail of a misdirected comet and set boughs above us aflame before she got it under control. I jumped back, startled.

"Her Majesty commanded me to bring you to Caratha and that, by Rae, is exactly what I will do! If you intend to abandon those who depend on you, then have the guts to tell them so yourself! I'll not bear a coward's whining back to my queen and High Council!" She hurled the Ring of Raxx to the ground at my feet. "Return these sacred relics yourself, if you're man enough! Look the Council in the eye when you tell them you've become a spineless, yellow-bellied, craven, shrinking violet of a recreant!"

"Yes," I said thoughtfully. "I suppose I do owe them that."

Solana did not hide her contempt for me as we rode back to Caratha. She rarely looked at me, only spoke when necessary, kept calling me a peasant, stayed several feet away at all times, and exuded a general feeling of derision as only a highborn lady can. This was just as well. I wasn't enthusiastic about our journey and didn't have much to say to her, though I did think she was extremely pretty and skillful with magic and she'd be an interesting replacement for Sapphrina and Rubis, which was obviously her role in the story. After all, I could have as easily been rescued by altruistic wood gnomes or an old hermit or even the cantankerous squirrels, but I wasn't. I was saved by a beautiful young sorceress, and nobody was fooled by the sudden dislike she had developed for me. She had "new love interest" written all over her.

Several days later we passed through the small town of Raebush, halfway back to Caratha. We picked up lunch from the ride-through window at the local Burgher Lord and continued on our way. At the edge of town we were waylaid by three prophets.

"Doom!" cried the first, a stern, wild-eyed old man dressed in frayed sackcloth. His hair and beard were unkempt and he had ashes smeared on his face.

"Gloom," sighed the second, somewhat younger and less ragged. He also wore sackcloth and ashes, though he had obviously run a comb through his hair at least once in the past week.

"Grave misfortune," added the third merrily. "And lots of it!" He was about my age and wore a well-tailored burlap suit, no ashes, and had neatly styled hair.

"Stand aside!" commanded Solana. "We are on the Queen's business!"

"You serve the Queen of Raelna. We speak for the Queen of Fate," said the first prophet.

"The Queen of Sorrows," added the second.

"The Queen of Bad Tidings and Poor Stock Performance," finished the third.

"Heed us," said the first. "Heed the words of the Prophets at the Edge of Town: Habukizemiah, Nehemearka, and Kysric the Younger."

"Did The Gods send you?" I asked.

"Not directly, but don't interrupt," said the second.

"We speak in rounds, you know," finished the third.

"Sorry."

"We have no time for this foolishness," said Solana.

"Wait," I said. "This is probably important or it wouldn't be happening."

Solana looked down her nose at me and tossed her head disdainfully, but said nothing further.

"Repent!" said the first prophet. "So speaketh Habukizemiah!"

"Relent," said the second. "So sayeth Nehemearka."

"Think again," said the third. "I'm Kysric the Younger, and that's my advice."

"What do you mean?" I asked.

"What we mean," said Kysric, "is that—"

"Still your wagging tongue, Kysric!" said Habukizemiah. "A proper prophet never explains what he means! Being obscure is part of upholding professonal standards!"

"You know my opinions on that," said Kysric.

"I know that if your father had not been Kysric the Elder, greatest of all contemporary prophets save the Luminous Oracle himself, you would have never gained admission to the College of Prophets, that's for certain! You have no respect for tradition, and tradition is a prophet's stock in trade."

"Tradition certainly has its place," said Kysric reasonably. It was obvious this argument was not a new one. "But such hidebound traditions as never saying plainly what you mean serve no useful purpose that I can see. Most of the time we leave clients more befuddled than before we came 'round to prophesy to them. Small wonder no one heeds us anymore. They can't understand a word we're saying."

"Those who do not hearken to our words shall suffer mightily!" said Habukizemiah. "Yea, their flocks shall sicken, their figs wither on the tree, their buns shall be soggy, their mighty fortresses be cast down in ruins! A blight shall be upon them and the sun shall darken in the sky!"

"Those silly scare tactics are another tradition we ought to jettison," said Kysric. "No one takes these threats seriously. They merely undermine our already-shaky credibility. All this going on about locusts and painful boils and mournful lamentations and rivers turning to blood is ridiculous."

"It's what's expected!" said Habukizemiah. "Dire warnings are what we do best. But I suppose you want to prophesize nothing but bountiful harvests and acne clearing up and pretty butterflies and prancing through sunny meadows in springtime!"

"No, I just want to discard the melodrama and deliver our news, good or bad, in simple, straightforward, plain language that anyone can understand. And we should devote more attention to economic forecasting. That's the future, not all this unintelligible metaphorical gobbledygook about teeth gnashing and hair pulling."

"What rubbish!" spat Habukizemiah. "It's not too late to have you reassigned as a lone voice crying in the wilderness. How would you like to chase butterflies in the desert for forty years, eh?"

"Threats again," said Kysric. "You're so punitive."

"Gentlemen," said Nehemearka, "could we save this discussion for later? We've got a job to do."

"Right," said Habukizemiah. "Where were we?"

"Repent, relent, and think again," I said helpfully.

"A time of great troubles is ahead," said Habukizemiah.

"Many shall perish," intoned Nehemearka.

"Things are tough all over," added Kysric.

"The mighty must choose, and when they choose, choose wisely and well, for in their choice lies the shape of the future," said Habukizemiah.

"The light and dark shall contend, yea, and from their contention shall a new world order emerge," said Nehemearka. "New kings will rise and old kings will fall. Queens also. Great nations shall tremble, fail, and be rent asunder. Jeweled thrones shall be trod under sandaled feet. Widows and orphans shall abound, yea, and tribulations without end."

"Prices will spiral upward," said Kysric. "The major trading partners will experience a mild recession, but should recover by the third quarter. Interest rates will fluctuate, then stabilize. The markets will be somewhat sluggish but remain bullish overall. Service industries should be well cushioned against the downturn, but labor-intensive manufacturing will be hit hard. The resulting layoffs and displacements will send secondary shock waves through other sectors."

"You call that plain language?" scoffed Habukizemiah. "I've never heard of half those words! And what was all that about bulls and slugs? Sounded like old-fashioned metaphor to me. Not that I know what in the Assorted Hells you meant by it! You make no sense at all!"

"Touché," said Kysric.

"Am I supposed to get some message out of all this?" I asked.

"We have spoken," said Habukizemiah. "Ponder deeply our words and heed well our warnings."

"Signs and mysteries will be revealed unto you have you but eyes to see," said Nehemearka.

"The answer to your question is yes," said Kysric. "And now I'm off to Burgher Lord."

"True prophets do not set foot in those dens of foulness and iniquity called cities!" said Habukizemiah.

"Another foolish custom," said Kysric. "And Raebush is hardly a city."

"Farewell, prophets," I said. Solana and I rode on, leaving them to their argument.

*   *   *

"What did you make of all that?" I asked once we were down the road a bit.

"Must you continue pestering me with your puerile mewling?" she said coldly, without bothering to look at me.

"Who else am I going to pester?"

"You are loathsome," she said.

"What is it about me that you find loathsome, milady?"

"Your insolent air, your dereliction of duty, and your shameless cowardice."

"Insolent, yes. Derelict, debatable. Cowardly, no."

"You brand yourself derelict and cowardly by your own actions," said Solana. "A man of courage would not flee from his responsibilities, however dangerous they might be."

"The danger is not the question. The question is whether the responsibilities in question are, in fact, mine. I didn't ask to be a hero. It was a role thrust upon me against my will and I think I fulfilled my obligation when I took on the Dark Magic Society at Fortress Marn and fought to save the northlands from a monster horde at Voripol. I've done my part and I'm ready to go home and let somebody else carry on."

"You are afraid to die."

"Who in their right mind isn't? But it isn't fear of death that rules me."

"What then?"

"I'm tired of being ruled by events. Other people and outside forces have taken control of my life. They decide where I go and what I do. I've just decided to reclaim control of my own fate."

"You would abandon the cause of combatting evil? Leave the task unfinished?"

"It's a task that will never be finished. I can't finish it, so what harm if I leave it to others better suited for it?"

"If that is how you feel," she said, "then why do you ride with me now?"

"I was wrong to leave with no explanation," I admitted. "I was upset when I left and I thought several times about turning back even before you came along, just to hand over the relics of the Champion, but . . ."

"But what?"

"I really didn't want to face Timeon and the High Council."

Solana was triumphant. "That is because in your heart you recognize what a coward you are."

She rode on ahead. We didn't speak again until we reached Caratha and the conical blue tower painted with yellow stars and moons that housed the main offices of the League of Benevolent Magic.

4

"Jason! Lady Solana caught you, I see!"

Mercury Boltblaster strode down the corridor, his hands outstretched to clasp mine. The wizard was a small man with a body as strong and supple as a coiled whip. His skin was deep olive, his eyes a deeper shade of green than Solana's, his beard and hair dark black. He wore maroon garments and a flowing black cape.

"Yes," I said without enthusiasm, setting down my bundle to greet him. "Good to see you, Merc."

He wasn't convinced. "Why this dour face, man? You look as though your best friend died. And that can't be, since I'm standing right here."

"It's his courage that's died," said Solana. "If Your Royal Highness will excuse me, I must report to your lady wife the Queen." She shot me a dark glance and stalked away.

Merc raised an eyebrow.

"She disapproves of me," I said.

"Indeed."

"For now."

"Of course. So why did you leave Caratha so suddenly?"

I shrugged. "I'm tired of Caratha. I want to go home."

"Quitting the hero business?"

51

"Exactly. I never meant to get into it in the first place."

"Are you serious about this, Jason?"

"Yes. Well, just between you and me, I thought it would make me a more interesting character if I rebelled against my situation a little. Just to give me some depth, make me less two-dimensional."

"Good idea, but don't take it too far or you won't fit in around here."

"Oh, I expect some traumatic event will shock me into a realization that I can't walk away from the fight as easily as I'd like and I'll be right back in the thick of things, swinging my sword as always."

"So that's why you left? I thought that Corundum girl might have had something to do with it."

"Well, they both did actually."

"They? The twain in tandem? I didn't think you so sly."

"Neither did I. My original plan was to marry one of them and settle down. But they had other ideas."

"You sound bitter, my friend. I should know, I'm an expert on bitterness. It's a waste of time."

"First girl I fall in love with, only it turns out I unwittingly got two for the price of one, and when I want to make it official, they walk out. What's to be bitter about?"

"Nothing. That's what I'm telling you. They've played their parts, taken their bows, and made their exit. But a new love interest will soon take the stage."

"Scant chance of that," I said.

Merc glanced the way Solana had gone. "I thought . . ."

"Well obviously Solana is my new female lead, but I'm not supposed to realize that yet. Officially, I'm still mooning over the twins."

"Oh, right. You'll need cheering up then. A few words of wisdom from a friend to help you put things in perspective."

"That would be helpful."

Merc cleared his throat and put his arm around my shoulder companionably. "You're a fantasy hero in a fantasy world, Jason. You know the traditions. Along with the high adventure comes an endless succession of heated romances and passionate flings. A few of the women you meet will be extremely beautiful, others very beautiful, the rest only mildly beautiful, but you can be sure they'll all have flawless complexions and shave their legs regularly. Some will fight beside you, others against you. Many will die tragic deaths at the hands of your foes. Others will use you, betray you, walk out on you, only to turn up unexpectedly later. It's the way this business goes."

"Thank you for those words of encouragement, Merc, but I'm getting out of this business. I want what you've got. I want to find my true love, marry her, and live happily ever after."

Merc jabbed me in the chest with his finger. "Face reality, Jason. You're more likely to sprout wings than find true love, and I can cite you the studies to prove it. And what's this happily-ever-after nonsense? Never happens. Sure, I finally married the beautiful princess—after a hell of a lot of trouble—but Raella and I are bound to face more crises. And if you do find true love, I guarantee it won't be with the likes of Sapphrina or Rubis Corundum. They're not the type."

"So I've learned."

He smiled. "Well, at least you've learned then, callow youth. Experience is the best antidote for innocence."

"Perhaps." I scowled. "But enough of my troubles. What are *you* doing at League headquarters? You despise the League."

Merc led me to the levitation disk, which took us smoothly to the second level. We stepped off into a curved corridor with dark red carpet.

"I despise them a little less after the help they gave

us at Voripol. And remember, Raella ranks third on the High Council." He coughed into his hand. "Besides, I need their help to restore my powers."

"Ah. Any progress?"

"No. Dhrakol's spell blocked my arcane potential in some unknown way. We wizards work magic by exerting the will and intellect on the ambient magical energy field that subsumes Arden. My will and intellect remain intact, but my ability to make the connection with the Power Arcane has been shut down. It's not chemical, like Noarcane. It's not a mental block. But it is puzzling. Anyhow, I'm organizing an expedition to Everwhen Keep. I hope the records of the Mnemonic Monks contain a cure."

"You must feel vulnerable without your magic, Merc."

He shrugged. "I've always made a point of not relying on it too much, but we do live in dangerous times."

"That's certain. So what is this big crisis that's got the League all stirred up? I thought the Society was keeping a low profile these days. Not that it would particularly surprise me if they weren't."

"I think the whole thing is just another example of League paranoia. They give too much credence to unconfirmed rumor, irresponsible speculation, and the headlines of checkout-counter tabloids. Still, this isn't something they can ignore."

"Why not? What is it?"

Merc looked uneasy. "I don't want to spoil their presentation. They've done up slides and some nice color graphs."

We paused outside the oaken door to the High Council's conference room. Merc gestured for me to enter.

"Aren't you coming?"

"No. I don't like to be in close quarters with that

crowd. I'll see you afterward. Good luck." He turned
to go.

I grabbed his arm.

"Merc, tell me what all the fuss is about," I insisted.

"Well, all right, but don't let on that I told. It's
been found."

"What's been found?"

"The Superwand."

The Superwand. The ultimate implement of power.
A slender little stick that could bend space, twist time,
warp reality, and amend, if not repeal, the laws of
nature. With it, you could do just about anything you
damn well pleased. Gravity got you down? Reverse
it. Not enough hours in the day? Add a few. Want to
divide by zero? No problem. And it made cheating at
dice a snap.

Even The Gods feared the Superwand. You might
think they'd have better sense than allow the making
of such a dangerous device. But The Gods had no say
in the matter. The Superwand was the creation of the
infinitely omnipotent Bunnies from Beyond, a race of
paradimensional pink Cosmic Rabbits far older and
wiser than mere gods. As the Sacred Scrolls of Syna-
buluum tell it, the wand was forged several hours before the Dawn of Time in the cosmic fires of an
exploding galaxy. It was imbued with the awesome
energies of a million quasars, shaped by the intersecting gravitational fields of a thousand cleverly manipulated neutron stars, tempered by the scalding rays
of incredible matter-antimatter collisions, and buffed
to a high shine with a bottle of Dr. Pembroke's Handy
All-Purpose Soapgloss Powder.

It was then used to light a multidimensional su-
perstring cigar and casually tossed down a gravity well.
The Superwand was, for all its power, only a match-
stick to the Cosmic Rabbits.

On the other side of the singularity, at the bottom

of the wormhole, the wand fell into the foul hands of the Demon Lord Asmodraxas. Even with his diabolical genius, he was unable to unleash its full potential, but he did develop enough proficiency with the thing to conquer all the Assorted Hells, master his fellow Demon Lords, sponsor the Empire of Fear in Arden, and conduct a thousand-year reign of terror. Not bad for a beginner.

The Mighty Champion also found the wand useful. He stole it while Asmodraxas wasn't looking and used it to banish the demon-god to a prison of null space. My ancestor then hid the wand to keep it out of the wrong hands. When the Superwand is concerned, any hands are the wrong hands, even divine hands. The Gods themselves could not be trusted with its power. They were wise enough to realize this and set forth an immutable divine law that no one, mortal or immortal, shall seek the Superwand on pain of penalties too terrible to describe.

Despite this prohibition, many daring souls down through the centuries had quested for the Superwand. After all, whoever found it wouldn't be much worried about the ordinances of The Gods. He'd be making his own rules.

Particularly energetic in their recovery efforts were the wizards of the Dark Magic Society. Infinite power was the sort of thing that appealed to their ilk, though the more altruistic among them merely wanted to use the wand to free Asmodraxas and bring back the Evil Empire. It was the Society's search for the Superwand that first brought me into the hero business. I feared this latest development would frustrate my desire to get out of it. But I'd try anyway.

"Jason Cosmo, welcome," intoned aged Timeon, the most senior member of the Council. A wrinkled little gray man with wispy white hair, he wore a pale blue robe and a legion of liver spots.

I sat across the table from the Council. Overwhelm, the armor, and the Ring of Raxx lay on the polished wood between us. To Timeon's right was blue-skinned Ormazander the Cyrillan. At his left were Episymachus and Valence. Valence still had a broken leg suffered in the battle against Morwen Hellshade at Voripol.

"Raella will join us shortly," said Timeon. "She is speaking with one of her vassals."

"I see." I could well imagine the tone of the report Solana was making to her Queen.

"Your arrival is timely," said Timeon. "The Superwand may have surfaced. We must seize it before the Dark Magic Society does. The need for your services as the Mighty Champion reborn has never been greater."

I took a deep breath. It was now or never.

"Before you continue, I must tell you I have decided to retire as Mighty Champion and go back to Darnk. I'm here only to return these holy relics so you can give them to someone else."

The wizards gaped as if I had just swallowed a live gerbil and chased it with a couple of goldfish.

"Go back to Darnk?" echoed Timeon at last.

"And grow turnips," I said.

"Give up a life of high adventure, thrills, excitement, and gorgeous women to grow turnips?" he said disbelievingly.

"That's right."

"In Darnk?"

"Turnips grow well in Darnk. They're about the only thing that does. Except toadstools and dung lilies, of course."

"This is most irregular," Timeon said.

"Unprecedented," added Ormazander.

"Foolish," said Episymachus.

"Not at all wise," agreed Valence. "Really, Cosmo! Turnips! You are meant for higher things!"

"You can't do it," said Timeon with finality. "The Gods themselves have chosen you to be a hero. They even added your name to the sacred Roll of Heroes. It is your destiny."

"There's no fighting destiny," said Episymachus. "Well-known scientific fact."

"Quite so," added Ormazander.

"So as I was saying," said Timeon. "The Superwand may even now be—"

"I'm quitting, destiny or no," I said firmly.

"Why?" demanded Timeon. "You've done a fine job. Why quit now?"

"I abhor the violence and constant conflict demanded by the role which was thrust upon me. I know I embraced it earlier, but I was afraid for my life and not thinking clearly."

"You've caught a case of idealism," said Timeon knowingly. "Common ailment of the young. Your thinking was fine before. Only now is it muddled. Evil must be resisted, and that means violence and conflict."

"This is the critical decade which will determine the nature of the Coming Age," put in Episymachus. "We seek the establishment of a new world order. But should evil gain the upper hand, the next thousand years will be most unpleasant."

"I know that, but—"

"I hope you're not going to go on about not sinking down to their level and the power of passive resistance and seizing the moral high ground and all that rubbish," said Timeon.

"No, nothing like that."

"Good. Can't stand that drivel. I take it you've simply grown squeamish. After killing hordes of men and goblins and whatnot, you suddenly can't stand the sight of blood."

"It does get tiresome," I said.

"It's not concern for your own skin at work, is it?"

"Well, to a degree—"

"We call that cowardice."

"No, not at all. I don't mind dying if it comes to it."

"Good. So it's only misplaced concern for the merciless butchers, thugs, oppressors, murderers, despoilers, and other foul persons you fight which causes you to balk now? Don't you think that's silly?"

"When you put it that way, yes."

"Anything else?"

"Well, I'm tired of being the most feared man alive. I want to be liked."

"We like you."

"By the general public, I mean. They're afraid of me."

"Then hire an image consultant! Problem solved? May I continue now?"

"Look, all I want is to live a normal life!"

"And you think we don't?" said Timeon sternly. "Young man, I have been risking my life and worrying about the fate of Arden since before your father was born. Every member of this Council wants nothing more than to have time for good books, morning strolls, and puttering in the garden. We all feel the weight of the world on our shoulders. We all do our parts. We all have our tasks to perform. Certain tasks demand a wizard. Certain other tasks demand a hero. And for those tasks, The Gods chose you. End of discussion." He paused. "Ahem. The Superwand may even now be in the—"

"But why did The Gods choose me?"

"Heritage," snapped Timeon. "Heroism is in your blood just as magic is in our blood, just as rulership is in the blood of Queen Raella and the other monarchs of Arden."

"Why? Because somewhere in the tangled branches of my family tree sits the original Mighty Champion? That's ridiculous!"

"Tell him, Valence," said Timeon.

Valence opened an ancient, leather-bound tome. "Your connection with the Mighty Champion is direct and unbroken, as this ancient, leather-bound tome attests."

"What is it? *Fifty Simple Reasons Jason Should Play Hero*?"

"No. The latest edition of the *Book of All Kings* by the Mnemonic Monks of Everwhen Keep, hot off the scribner's table. This instant classic accurately records the genealogies of every royal house in Arden, updating even those lines which sank into obscurity long ago. Thoroughly researched, richly detailed, and cogently written." He paused and patted the preaged parchment pages. "I think you will find the section on Caratha most interesting."

"Why?"

Valence shared the inability of most wizards to get to the point without a lot of buildup. "All know the Mighty Champion was the founder of Caratha. And from sources such as *The Book of Uncommon Knowledge,* Plutarp's *Lives of Famous People Who Lived a Long Time Ago,* and *The Wee Tyke's Illustrated Chronicles of Caratha,* we know his true name was Jason Cosmo."

"Could you just get to the point?"

"Not without a lot of buildup."

"Very well."

"The Mighty Champion was succeeded by his son, the Young Champion. He passed the crown on to his son, the Blue Champion. And so on, father to son, until the seventh and Final Champion, Jorvan, was overthrown by the House of Glentra in the Bloody Revolution and massacred along with his family. This ended the Line of Champions. This ended the House of Cosmo."

"Right," I said. "Does your book say differently?"

"Indeed it does. Unknown to history—to conventional history, that is—one of Jorvan's children escaped."

"A newborn babe smuggled to safety by a kindly nursemaid?" I ventured.

"No."

"Floated down the river in a wicker basket?"

"Far from it."

"An illegitimate child raised by a poor family well paid for their silence?"

"Not at all."

"What then?"

"A bumbling lad named Jolson who, through a series of improbable mishaps, missed being massacred and went on to a moderately unsuccessful career as a goatkeeper in the Bogorun Hills."

"He never tried to regain his rightful place?" I asked.

Valence shrugged. "Apparently the lad had no ambition. He neglected even to tell his own children who he really was. But he did pass on the Cosmo name."

"And?" I asked, intrigued in spite of myself.

"And the *Book of All Kings* chronicles the lives of Jolson's descendants," said Valence, leafing through the pages. "An undistinguished lot, I'm sorry to say. Many trades represented and no success in any of them. Onion sellers, mustard mixers, glovemakers, egg poachers, dog trainers, cockfight promoters. Whenever a Cosmo started to get ahead, misfortune struck. War, plague, famine, economic slump. Never able to rise out of poverty, the family eventually migrated to Lower Hicksnittle where they chopped wood and grew turnips."

"That's in the book?"

Valence smiled. "Indeed. The family is traced right down to Jasper Cosmo, his son Jolan, and to Jolan's son. You. The last entry is your own."

"Let me see that!"

The wizard slid the book across to me and I read the final entry on the page:

"JASON COSMO, b. 968 A.H., Lower Hicksnittle. Only child of Jolan and Janna. Strong, handsome, intelligent, goodhearted, but a little too wholesome to be fully convincing as a character. Due to his mother's influence, one of eight literate people in Darnk and by far the most educated Darnkite of this century. Reads without moving his lips, which is remarkable in any land. Woodcutter, turnip farmer in Lower Hicksnittle until 990, when he became object of massive manhunt instigated by Dark Magic Society. In same year, visited by He Who Sits On The Porch, anointed Champion of Rae, blessed by The Gods at Shrine of Greenleaf, defeated Society's Ruling Conclave at Fortress Marn, and slew the dragon Nightfire. Romantically linked to the Corundum twins, but it looks like the affair has gone bust and Solana of Sweetfire will be his new leading lady. Currently resides in Caratha, though he is considering a move back to Lower Hicksnittle to grow turnips again. The Gods only know why, but his reasons don't matter since even the densest of readers can guess that isn't going to happen. This is an adventure story after all, not the *Farmer's Almanac*."

"Fairly up-to-date," I said.

"The Mnemonic Monks are thorough," agreed Valence.

"So I'm in the book? So what?"

Valence looked at me in disbelief. "Isn't it obvious? You are *directly* descended from the Mighty Champion! Aside from having the blood of Arden's greatest hero, you are the rightful ruler of Caratha!"

It took a moment for his words to register.

"That's quite a revelation," I said.

"Indeed it is," said Timeon.

"It's also rather cliché."

"Can't be helped. Hackneyed things happen."

"I knew coming back to Caratha was a mistake," I groaned, cradling my head in my hands.

"What do you mean?" asked Timeon.

"It's the last place in the world I want to be, so of course I'm its rightful ruler. Do you know how upset the old guard will be when word of this gets out?"

"It will bring joy!" said Valence excitedly. "The legends foretell—"

Timeon smoothly interrupted his younger colleague. "You are correct, Master Cosmo. The current regime may look askance at this news. However, the *Book of All Kings* is not in general circulation and you need not fear Prince Ronaldo in any event. He is a good and just man."

"It's the crowd around him I'm concerned about. They might decide a paper heir needs to be swept under the rug—or to the bottom of the Great Harbor."

"But the prophecy," insisted Valence. "What about the prophecy?"

"Not now," said Timeon sternly.

"What's this prophecy he's talking about?" I asked.

"Nothing," said Timeon. "Entirely irrelevant."

"Valence is sure enthused about it."

Timeon gave Valence a dark look and waved his hand airily. "Just an old bit of nonsense about how in the hour of Caratha's greatest need, the Mighty Champion will return to save her from destruction and guide her to a new golden age and how this will happen after seven princely houses have reigned, one house representing each of the Seven Champions."

"And Prince Ronaldo's is the seventh noble house to rule!" said Valence, ignoring Timeon.

"I never would have guessed," I said.

"The time has come for the restoration of the

blood of Caratha's founder to Caratha's throne!" he continued.

"That does it!" I exclaimed, springing to my feet. "Do you expect me to stroll over to the palace and politely ask Prince Ronaldo to get off the throne and pack his things, I'm dreadfully sorry, but this book proves I should be in charge here, there's this old prophecy, you know? What kind of reaction do you think I'd get? I'd get my head chopped off, that's what! Good day!"

"Oh, good job, Valence," said Timeon. "Master Cosmo, you misunderstand our point. We ask you to be a hero, not a king."

I stopped at the door, but I wasn't listening. "I can't be your messiah! I never wanted to be a hero! I certainly don't want to be King of Caratha! You think I can single-handedly wipe out the Dark Magic Society, the Demon Lords, and maybe poverty, racism, famine, sickness, and poor table manners while I'm at it! I can't! I'm just a Darnkite peasant who's been lucky! Hand that sword and tin suit to anyone and he could do all I've done! And probably a better job of it if you choose someone with the right background! I don't care who my ancestors were! Find another hero! I quit!"

5

My retirement lasted just long enough for me to storm out the door and walk briskly down the hall to the levitation disk. As I stepped aboard, clanging alarm bells and wailing sirens rocked the air. The light globes in the hallway went out, flickered on again momentarily, then made up their minds and went out for good, plunging the corridor into abject darkness. I heard shouts of surprise and confusion from the other floors. The entire building shook as if struck by the mighty hammer of Mita the Maker. I lost my footing and nearly tumbled down the levitation shaft as the disk wobbled to and fro like a drunken gyroscope. I saved myself by grabbing the ledge. It was a mildly heroic action, true, but that was just reflex.

I pulled myself to safety and straightened my clothes. If I hurried and took the stairs, maybe I could get out before the excitement started.

No such luck. A bright green fireball whooshed outward from the conference room, blasting the door to kindling. Vivid purple arcs of eldritch energy flashed along the walls, floor, and ceiling and the air grew thick with ozone. The building shook again, hurling me against the wall.

With a sigh, I hurried back to the conference room. It was probably nothing unusual for a roomful of top-level wizards to explode, I told myself. And earthquakes happen all the time. No need for me to be here, really. But maybe someone was hurt. I'd just pop in, see if I could lend a hand, maybe go and fetch a healer. But no heroics. That wasn't my line anymore.

Luminous yellow sulfur smoke boiled from the doorway. Not a good sign. I heard the wizards casting impressive-sounding spells, which broke off abruptly. Even less of a good sign.

"No heroics," I muttered as I plunged into the foul smoke.

The scene I beheld was horrifying. Where the table had been lurked a glowing brimstone pit, the source of the smoke. Out of it clambered a horde of pop-eyed, bloat-faced, worm-rotted corpses with nooses around their necks. They wore decayed boots, jeans, T-shirts, and leather jackets emblazoned with a gallows symbol and the legend "Hanged Ones." Part of this undead gang had Timeon and Ormazander backed against the far wall, where the wizards defended themselves with glowing staffs. Another group carried Valence, screaming and kicking with his one good leg, toward the pit. Episymachus was nowhere to be seen.

"Good, you're back," said Timeon as he smashed a corpse's face with the butt of his staff. "Be a good fellow and lend Valence a hand. Ormazander and I are fine."

Without hesitation, I leaped upon Valence's captors and bowled them over. Reflex again. I'd have to break this habit of leaping fearlessly into danger now that I was no longer a hero.

Momentum carried us into the pit. We landed in a squishy heap of splitting skins and extruded innards on a barren, nightmarish stone plain. I was no expert on interplanar geography, but the pools of boiling sulfur, quicksilver, and lead, the bleak black clouds blotting out the sky, and the startling flashes of wild green lightning told me this wasn't Happy Valley.

"Valence of Hartemath, you are sentenced to death by hanging!" boomed a disembodied voice. After a pause it added, "Jason Cosmo of Darnk, the same! Hanged Ones, carry out the sentences!"

In the foreground loomed half a dozen somber black gallows. Episymachus swung from one, dead. The corpses dragged Valence and me over for a closer look. The wizard struggled feebly, almost blacking out from the pain in his leg.

"This isn't the way to encourage tourism," I muttered as I was hoisted aloft.

"Do something!" yelled Valence. "I can't get a spell off!"

In this place far from the sun, my strength was lessened and I could not break the determined dead hand grip of my captors. Valence screamed as the noose was tightened around his neck. Then his neck snapped. The ranks of the High Council were thinning faster than a middle-aged accountant's hair.

The implacable corpses dragged me up the steps, wrestled me into position, and lacked only getting the noose around my neck before throwing the switch to release the trapdoor. I managed to get one arm free and bat the rope away while I struggled to reach the platform's edge. But these dead men were strong, not having to worry about muscle fatigue, lung capacity, or other biological shortcomings of the living.

Suddenly one of my foes recoiled in a good imitation of pain, his hand smoking like overcooked bacon. The Hanged One had grasped the golden sunburst medallion hanging around my neck. It had slipped out from under my shirt in the fray. In its center was a brilliant red sun jewel, glowing fiercely. It was a gift from Raella, an amulet blessed by the Goddess Rae herself. Its powers might just get me out of this jam.

All I had to do was remember the magic words.

"Alabathka!" I shouted, giving the command for a flash of True Light. The medallion flared. The Hanged

Ones released me and scurried away, only to renew their attack when the afterglow faded.

"Alabathka!" I repeated while I racked my brain for the word that would bring the sustained light I needed. I jumped off the platform and rushed toward the gateway pit back to the League tower.

Dozens of dead blocked my way, hissing and waving their long grubby nails at me. This did wonders for my memory.

"Luminata!" I cried. The amulet flared again and remained on. The pure rays of True Light opened the way before me and protected my flanks, but my back was still exposed. Not wasting an instant, I darted for the pit.

The laws of interdimensional physics are as illogical as any tax code. You could say this hellish landscape was at the bottom of the pit in the conference room, but you would be mostly wrong. The pit had no actual bottom, but rather two mutually exclusive tops. To get out of Hell, I had to leap into the manifestation of the pit on this end. That is, I would proceed initially in a downward direction. At an indeterminable point between here and there, my descent from this side would become an ascent into the League tower. In layman's terms, I would fall up.

I didn't care if I had to fall sideways. I just wanted out of this place. I jumped for the pit.

From out of nowhere, a heavy black boot hit my jaw and sent me sprawling backward. The sun jewel winked out and the dead gathered around, looking rather mirthful for a bunch of guys with rotted brains and wriggly grubworms hanging from their eye sockets.

"That trinket won't help you here," said the no-longer-disembodied voice. The body had just arrived.

I scrambled backward. He sat astride a scaly, fire-snorting moose with little nooses adorning its antlers. He wore high boots, black trousers, and a hangman's hood from which hideous red eyes shone unpleasantly.

His bare chest was a massive expanse of well-oiled muscle. His biceps were like grindstones. He swung a glowing green lariat over his head and didn't look like the type who missed too often. I stayed low.

"I am Gibbitor, Hangman of Hell," he said. "And this is my Noosemoose. You have been sentenced to die on my gallows. There is no escape. So let's have no fuss about it, okay?"

"No escape?" I said.

"None."

To emphasize the point, a Hanged One held up a posterboard chart that contrasted a steeply rising line of skulls, representing successful executions, with a straight horizontal line at the bottom of the graph, indicating an utter lack of bungled hangings.

"Commendable," I said, continuing to inch backward.

"Thank you," said Gibbitor as the Noosemoose inched forward.

"But don't I get an appeal? Due process? Habeas corpus?"

"I'm afraid not. We try to keep things simple here. Swift, sure punishment. That's the thing."

"What was my offense?"

"You are an enemy of the Demon Lords."

"Maybe at one time, but I've retired now. I have no beef with the Demon Lords. It takes all sorts to make a universe and I'm sure there is a proper place for Demon Lords."

"You happen to be in that place. That means you're trespassing, too."

"Oh, come on! I fell into your hellpit by accident."

"While attacking my minions. Add assault and battery to the list."

"Don't you think the death penalty is a bit harsh for all that?"

"Death is our penalty for everything. Cuts down on repeat offenders, you see. And what do you mean, a bit harsh? I'm only going to hang you. My cousin

Havakkar the Ravager would sand off your toenails, pull your lungs out through your belly button, chew your fingers off a joint at a time, dunk you in boiling coffee, twist your legs off with a monkey wrench, cut your tongue out, stick it up your nose, and spit in your eye."

"Well, that doesn't sound so bad," I said bravely.

"Then he would start the painful stuff."

"Oh."

"With me, it's all over quick as a snap."

"You may have a point. Still, won't you consider two hundred hours community service or something? I could pick up trash, tutor young demons, coil your ropes, whatever."

"What do you take me for? I don't wear this ominous black hood because they were out of pink bonnets, you know. You will hang and that's that."

"Maybe not." As often happened in these situations, a desperate ploy occurred to me. I sent out an urgent mental summons.

Eager as a puppy, Overwhelm emerged from a quicksilver pool and flew to my hand. It had fallen through the hellpit with the conference table and landed nearby. With a cry of delight, I bounded to my feet and weaved a circle about me thrice.

"Upgrade that to assault with a deadly weapon!" boomed Gibbitor, slinging his rope. I sliced it apart in midair. The Noosemoose lowered its head to strike me with its antlers. I lunged forward and beheaded it with a single blow, then dodged aside as the beast collapsed, pinning its rider. "Cruelty to animals, too! You will surely perish now!"

"No, I just got a stay of execution," I said. "A pity I can't stay any longer." I scrambled for the pit, hacking my way through the befuddled Hanged Ones. Rotten heads and other body parts flew in all directions.

"Cosmo!"

I looked back. Gibbitor stood, holding his dead

mount overhead as if to hurl it at me. He looked very fearsome in that pose.

"Surely you're not going to throw a dead moose at me?" I said.

With a bullish grunt, he heaved the body. It came on with surprising velocity, but I dodged it. It fell into the hellpit, taking several Hanged Ones with it. All vanished.

"Take him!" he commanded.

The dozen or so remaining Hanged Ones surged forward. So did a gallows, lumbering like a malformed crab, its strained timbers creaking and popping. The noose snaked through the air like the tongue of a greedy python.

I ran. Only a few of the undead now stood between me and the pit. I rushed past them and dived forward.

My headlong plunge abruptly ended as I was yanked backward like a hyperactive beagle on a short leash. Striking like a gecko, the gallows snared me with its ropy "tongue," lassoing my right leg and reeling me in to dangle upside down.

Gibbitor approached. I tried to sever the rope with Overwhelm, but the demon wrested the sword from my hand and hurled it far across the landscape. I summoned it back, but it did not respond. Apparently, Gibbitor had the power to block the sword's enchantment when he put his mind to it.

"Well, manling, it is as I said. None may escape my noose. Now we will hang you properly. And soon your friends will join you. This has been a satisfying— gakkk!"

"*Desist, foul demon!*"

Gibbitor had little choice but to obey as a bright lace net of light wrapped itself around him, simultaneously crushing and burning him. He staggered, fell to his knees, and thrashed about on the ground. The Hanged Ones scattered. I twirled around and faced the pit.

Queen Raella Shurbenholt hovered above it on a disk of amber light. She wore a tight gold bodysuit emblazoned with a scarlet sunburst. A shining sun jewel adorned her brow and sparks flew from her floating red-blond hair. Hot-lensed sunshades hid her eyes. She held in one hand the cord of light that controlled Gibbitor's bonds. She gestured with the other and the robe around my leg untwined itself. I fell with a thump.

"Your Majesty!" I shouted. "How good to see you! I was getting tired of hanging around here!"

"Come quickly, Jason!" she commanded. "Even Lucilla's Lambent Lace will not hold a Demon Lord for long."

I wasted no time in recalling Overwhelm and joining her on the platform.

"Did you say Demon Lord? He's an actual Demon Lord? I've been roughhousing with a *Demon Lord*?"

"A minor one, but, yes, a Demon Lord," replied the Queen. "You are fortunate to have survived until I could reach you."

"I'll say."

"He will trouble us no further this day, but other dangers remain." She released the end of the Lambent Lace spell and it began to unravel.

"What do you mean?"

"You will see."

The disk sank into the pit, then rose into the League conference room. With a commanding hand pass, Raella sealed the hellpit, restoring the natural floor.

The only light was from glowing staffs and the alarms still wailed. Through the thinning smoke, I saw dismembered Hanged Ones lying scattered about the room along with broken furniture, sulfur residue, a headless Noosemoose, and the scattered pieces of my armor. Solana knelt beside Ormazander, binding up his wounded arm. Timeon leaned wearily on his staff, coughing and wheezing. His robe was torn at the sleeve. He looked at us expectantly.

"Episymachus? Valence?" he asked.

Raella shook her head.

Timeon sighed. "They will be missed. They were good men."

"What happened here?" I asked. The building shook.

"It's still happening," said Raella. "All the magical defenses of this tower failed simultaneously and the Society is taking full advantage. Don your armor, Jason. We have blunted the attack here, but others are in danger."

The tower rocked again, more violently than before. Chunks of ceiling plaster fell upon us. I got busy putting on my invincible armor. Raella turned to Timeon.

"Master Timeon, you must give the order to evacuate," she said.

"Abandon our headquarters?" he replied. "People might talk."

The building shook again, hurling everyone to the floor except Raella, who remained on her floating disk.

"Do it," said Ormazander.

Timeon made a finger gesture and said, "Evacuation sequence."

"Please evacuate the building," said a calm but urgent feminine voice coming over hidden spellcom speakers. **"This is an emergency. This is not a drill. Please remain calm. Please proceed quickly and safely to the nearest exit."**

I completed my arming. I wasn't happy about being thrust into heroism once again, but this was no time for quibbling. As long as I was in the thick of it, I'd do my part. But once this was over, I was through for good.

The building shook again.

"I really think you people ought to get moving. The

building has become unsafe. Please proceed in a safe and orderly manner to the nearest exit. Please avoid the levitation disks. Please use the stairs.

Raella addressed Timeon and Ormazander. "If you are able, sirs, we must see to the upper floors. There are valuable records and artifacts to—"

Timeon raised a hand to cut her off. "I know. Let us hurry."

"Jason, take the stairs to the ground level and get everyone out," commanded Raella. "Solana, go with him."

Solana glanced at me with distaste, then bowed acknowledgment of her Queen's command.

"Come, Darnkite," she said, leading the way.

"How could all the defenses fail at once?" I asked as we picked our way down the corridor toward a dimly glowing emergency-exit sign. The tremors grew more frequent, which made a dicey job of going down the dark stairwell.

"They can't," said Solana irritably. "We have backups ten spells deep. It's impossible for all of them to fail."

"Hurry up, evacuate," said the spellcom voice. **"This really is an emergency, not a drill. I wouldn't kid you. You must leave the building. Do not panic. Proceed in a calm and orderly fashion to the nearest exit."**

"Then how did it happen?" I asked.

"I don't know! This is no time for your inane questions!"

Merc met us at the first-floor landing. The lights were still on down here.

"Where's Raella?" he demanded, pushing past me to start up the stairs.

I grabbed his arm. "She's safe! Come on! We've got to get everyone out of here!"

Most of the occupants of the tower were not wizards, but servants, clerks, secretaries, repairmen,

visitors, and paramagicals. In short, they were work-
ing-class folk who had the good sense to run like hell
at the first sign of trouble, without waiting for carefully modulated feminine voices to give the word over
the spellcom.

The League tower had only two ground-level exits.
The front door opened to the street and the back door
to a narrow alley. The front door, unfortunately, was
not available for use. At least, not without first removing several tons of broken blue masonry and twisted
girders all crackling and hissing with residual magic.
This produced a massive pileup of panicked people at
the rear exit.

"Do not panic. Do not push and shove. Proceed in
an orderly fashion, one at a time. Wait for your turn
so that all may exit safely. Did you hear me? I said,
wait for your turn so that—"

The spellcom broke off after a particularly loud explosion upstairs followed by seven or eight thunderous
secondary explosions. Large chunks of metal, wood,
and stone fell squashingly on the crowd at the door.
The floor, walls, and what was left of the ceiling vibrated like a harp string. The subsonics in my bones
gave me a sudden urge to buy overpriced popcorn,
cola, and chocolate malt balls. I pulled Solana and
Merc to me and protected them with my shield, which
absorbed and magically dissipated the kinetic energy
of the falling debris.

The vibrations continued, rising in amplitude, even
after the aftershocks of the explosion died out. The
darkened light globes flared and shattered. The rum-
ble tumble of total disintegration began. This looked
like the grand finale.

"Get the hell out of here!" screamed the hysterical
spellcom when it came back on line. "The whole place
is coming down right on top of your heads! Run! Run!
Run! It's everyone for himself! Or herself! The rubble

take the hindmost! Get out of here you bloody fools! Get out while there's still time!"

Solana jerked away from me and ignited a ball of handfire to illuminate the area. The flickering light revealed that the outside door was blocked by a heap of rubble and the crowd was much smaller. Nine survivors were trapped in a tiny cocoon of debris. A large girder had fallen so as to shelter us from the rest of what was coming down. Which was everything.

"Too late!" wailed the spellcom, once the rumbling disintegration of the upper levels ended. "Oh, why didn't you all get out when you had the chance? If only you had listened to me! If only you had lined up, taken turns, and proceeded in a safe, orderly manner, you might have escaped. Now you're all entombed alive! It's horrible! Horrible! Everything is falling, and even if you're not crushed, it might be days before they dig you out. You'll suffocate! You'll starve! Oh, how horrible!"

"Can we shut that thing up?" I asked. Buildings had collapsed on me before. I wasn't terribly worried. Yet.

"No," said Solana. "Are there any other wizards here?" she asked the crowd.

"Just me," said Merc ruefully.

"Wizards?" screeched an hysterical maid. "They all died when the front door collapsed! They died trying to save themselves!" She laughed manically. "We're all going to die! We're all going to die!"

"Stop that!" commanded Solana. "We are not going to die!"

"You're all going to die! You're all going to die! You're all—fzzrrk!"

Solana blasted the hidden speaker with a jet of fire.

"I thought you said there wasn't a way to turn those off."

"Not without breaking them."

"You're using up all the air with that fire!" shrieked

the maid. "Put it out! Put it out! Make her put it out!"

"Silence, you silly girl!" Solana shot a streak of fire within inches of the girl's face. "Not another word from you!"

A paramagical restrained the sobbing girl.

"I believe it's up to you, Jason," said Merc.

"Is this the outside wall?" I asked, drawing Overwhelm and willing it to cast its pink light.

"Yes!" said two clerks and a handyman.

"Then everyone stand back."

"Well, it's not like we've a lot of room for that," said a cook.

"What are you going to do?" asked Solana.

"Cut through this wall, of course. This sword slices through stone like raw fish."

"Raw fish won't slice through stone," said the cook.

"No, I mean the sword slices through stone as if it were slicing through raw fish."

"What sort of fish? Some sorts of fish are tougher to slice than others."

"Quiet and let him work!" snapped Solana.

It took several minutes to break through to daylight, which significantly calmed the young maid. It was another few minutes before the gap was large enough for us to slip through. The crowd of gawkers across the street cheered as we emerged. Some of them rushed to help us to our feet.

The dust was still settling. The League tower was nothing more than a pile of blue rocks. Atop the broken mound sat a jagged cone that had once been the proud pinnacle of the tower. But despite the tower's destruction, the surrounding buildings were undisturbed. The earthquake had been extremely localized. Unnaturally so.

Alarm bells rang and fire wagons rushed toward the scene with squadrons of soldiers not far behind.

"It will take days to search through all that," I said.

"Where's Raella?" demanded Merc. "You said she was safe."

"She headed for the upper floors," I said weakly.

"She was still in there?" exploded Merc. "Why didn't you tell me?"

At that moment the remnants of the conical tower top cracked asunder and Raella emerged unscathed, floating on her disk of light and carrying a cloth bundle. She glided smoothly to the ground, handed the bundle to Solana, removed her sunshades, and embraced Merc.

After a few seconds she pulled away from her husband. Her beautiful elfin features grew taut as she surveyed the ruined tower.

"Timeon and Ormazander perished in the explosion," she said tightly. "The Dark Magic Society has gone too far this time. They have begun the final battle of our age-long war."

6

"You can't quit now, Jason."

Raella opened the curtains in the ambassador's office at the Raelnan embassy. She had asked me to meet her there after I washed up.

"I realize that," I said resignedly. "There's no fighting destiny. It's a proven scientific fact."

She turned and smiled. Framed in a shaft of sunlight, she radiated power, beauty, and grace. She also showed a bit more flesh than I was used to seeing on Her Majesty. Dye blue her gauzy, high-slit, off-the-shoulder gold gown and it might have come from Sapphrina's wardrobe; it certainly wasn't typical of the demure Raella I knew. I shifted uncomfortably in my chair.

"Our responsibilities often conflict with our desires," she said sympathetically. "I know this well. My obligation to my kingdom kept me from Mercury for many years. But though the personal price was high, I did my duty. I could ask no less of myself. Neither can you."

"I know," I said. "I was homesick, dejected, disillusioned, and discouraged. But I was reminded today just what the stakes are. I realize now that I can't walk away from the fray. Not while I've got the power to oppose evil and do good. The Dark Magic Society and the Demon Lords must be stopped. As the Mighty Champion, I'm in for the duration."

"I am pleased to hear it," Raella said, beaming. "I knew you wouldn't let me down."

"Never. By the way, could you recommend a good PR firm? If I'm going to be protector of the masses and defender of liberty, I need to shed this negative image left over from the Society's manhunt."

"Indeed you must. And I will have my own publicists attend to it. But for now your undeserved reputation for ruthlessness will serve us in good stead."

"What do you mean?"

She sat behind the ambassador's desk and laced her delicate fingers together. "The attack on the High Council and the destruction of the tower were obviously in retaliation for the destruction of the Society's leaders and headquarters at Fortress Marn."

I nodded. "An eye for an eye."

"I have received reports by spellagram of magical attacks on League members across the Eleven Kingdoms. We are under siege and it is surely no coincidence that this offensive follows the supposed return of the Superwand."

"But Necrophilius doesn't care about the Superwand," I said. "Finding it was Erimandras's pet project."

"Don't be naive, Jason. Finding the Superwand has been the Society's dream for a thousand years. Perhaps Necrophilius lacks enthusiasm for the quest, but if the Superwand has been found, do you truly believe he will stand by and let another claim it?"

"I guess not," I said. "So where is it?"

"Rancor."

"Rancor? The pirates have it?"

Raella nodded. "Our agent there reported that Captain Dread, the most bloodthirsty of Rancor's pirates, recently returned from an expedition to southern waters, bringing with him a powerful magic weapon. Further investigation led our agent to believe it was the

Superwand. Unfortunately, we lost contact with our spy before he could confirm this. He is surely dead now and we have only a fragmentary report to go on."

"Why not use a crystal ball or something like that to get the facts?"

"Crystal balls are not so effective as you might think. Since we lost contact with our agent, a powerful cloaking spell has shielded Rancor from all magical surveillance and communication."

"Sounds bad."

"It is. That is why you must go to Rancor, infiltrate the pirates, get the Superwand if they have it, and bring it back to me."

"Back to you?"

"Of course. As head of the League and High Priestess of Rae I am best suited to safeguard the wand."

"Right," I said hastily. "Of course. So you want me to join the pirates?"

"This is where your fearsome reputation will be useful. You are widely regarded as a thief, a reaver, a slayer, with gigantic melancholies and gigantic mirth. Play the part and the pirates will accept you. Get into Rancor. Get the Superwand."

"I'm no undercover spy."

"But you are, as you say, the Mighty Champion."

"And King of Caratha, too, apparently."

She smiled. "An interesting bit of genealogical trivia which we should keep to ourselves for now. Only the High Council read the *Book of All Kings*. Only they knew your secret. And it is a secret best kept secret."

"I'm glad you think so. I've got enough pressure on me as it is."

"I know I can depend on you, as Champion of Rae, to bring the Superwand to me. Anyone else might be suborned by our foes or tempted to use the wand himself."

"You have complete faith in me, then?"

She smiled winningly. "Of course, Jason. Of course

I do. In fact, when you return, I intend to appoint you Grand Commander of the Knights of Rae. I need someone trustworthy for the post. It is a position worthy of your bloodline. You will be the highest lay official of the Church of Rae, leader of its military arm."

"I didn't know the Church had a military arm," I said.

"It hasn't yet. When we have time, I must tell you about my plans for reorganizing and revitalizing the Church."

Her blue eyes, already too wise and ancient for a woman of her years, shone with a fervor I had never seen in Raella. She was inspiring, convincing, and a little frightening.

"Yes, you'll have to do that."

"I shall. By the way, Jason, in the future I hope you will keep me informed of your whereabouts. The Champion of Rae cannot simply disappear as you did recently. As High Priestess, Daughter of Rae, and her Personal Representative on Arden I must know where to find you at all times. We lost precious days while Solana pursued you."

"Sorry about that," I said. "Anything else?"

"Find a ship and leave Caratha as soon as possible. Lady Solana will accompany you on this mission."

"I'm not sure that's a good idea. She has a low opinion of me."

Secretly, of course, I had been expecting Raella to send Solana with me. Working together would give us a chance to kindle the formulaic flames of romance.

"You may be sure the Society also has agents in Rancor and is aware of the Superwand's presence. You need a magician along, and Solana is the best available in the present circumstances." Raella smiled charmingly. "I think you will find that she looks forward to working with you."

"I hope you're right. It's a long trip to Rancor."

"Believe me, Jason, you've made quite an impression on my cousin. She understands now the difficulties you have undergone. I'm sure the two of you will make an excellent team."

"Perhaps we will."

"Excellent. Before you go, you might find this book of interest. I grabbed it from the League library before the tower collapsed."

"*Working with Miraculum,* by Hildman Oreboggle?"

"Miraculum is so rare that the book never sold well," said Raella. "Few copies remain. But I think it will be useful to you. Take it."

I skimmed the introduction and leafed through the slim book. What I saw intrigued me.

"Thank you, Your Majesty."

"What do you say?" asked Merc, holding up his right hand as we strolled out the embassy gates together. He wore a glove woven of stiff gold traced with silver and set with chalcedony, tourmaline, peridot, and spinel.

"Pricey mitten," I said.

"The Golden Gauntlet of Gandylon," said Merc.

"You're kidding."

"Not at all. This is the same magic glove Gandylon wore when he drove the hideous Kheldrin from Varvara and bested the Demon Lord Blook at arm wrestling. He was the greatest mage of his day, a certified grandmaster, and this was his greatest creation."

"How did you get it?"

"It was in the bundle Raella retrieved from the tower. Apparently it's been gathering dust in the League's attic for the past few hundred years."

"Why haven't they been using it?"

"Forgot they had it." He pulled from his pocket a pair of spectacles with iridescent lenses set in a magisteel frame. "Recognize it?"

"Of course not, Merc. Some arcane eyeglasses, I suppose."

"The Rainbow Spectacles of Mesha, to be precise. You've probably not heard of her, but she was the premier magical scholar of the seventh century. Totally blind from birth, she made the spectacles to overcome her lack of normal sight. Needless to say, these lenses granted her a range of vision that more than compensated."

"League forgot these, too?"

"No. Too holy to use. Kept on exhibit in the Hall of Distinguished-but-Lamentably-Long-Dead Magi. As was my new cloak."

"Is this a new cloak?"

His cloak was long, black, and drawn closely about him.

"Can't you tell?"

"Merc, you change the style and color of your cloak every day. How am I supposed to recognize a new one?"

"My old one was just standard Raelnan textile magic with a pocket universe sewn in. This is the genuine article, a cloak worthy of an arcane master, the Strange and Wonderful Cloak of Misregard."

"Never heard of it."

"Trust me, it's strange and wonderful."

"Can you actually use these relics without your powers?"

"Yes. Remember, my problem is an inability to make the inner psychomystical connection with the Power Arcane. These totems have built-in conduits to the Power. All I have to supply is the controlling will and intellect to utilize their properties. Of course, I'm oversimplifying to spare you an extended technical discussion."

"Thank you. I appreciate that."

"These items do not replace the full range of my powers, but they will serve for now. Obviously, I'm postponing my trip to Everwhen. The danger from the Society is too great for me to leave Raella's side."

"I understand. Speaking of Raella, have you noticed anything different about her since Voripol?"

"Such as?"

"Well, her new look isn't quite queenlike. Or at least it's not what I'm used to. On a queen, that is. Not that I've met many."

"I see," said Merc.

We walked on down Embassy Row in silence. That is, we didn't speak. Obviously our footfalls made some sound and the street was full of traffic noises, the rattle of coaches, the clop of hooves on pavement. As we reached the gate of the Cyrillan embassy Merc spoke again.

"It's her whole personality, Jason. She's more sure of herself and far more power conscious than I've ever known. And she was no shrinking violet before."

"You mean before Rom Acheron's brainwashing," I said. "You don't think she still has some Morwen Hellshade left in her, do you?"

"I wouldn't go that far," he said, shaking his head. "Morwen was an utterly self-serving personality. Raella retains her old benevolent goals, but she's grown bolder in pursuing them. To the point of being opportunistic."

"Strong criticism of a woman you're married to."

"See that it doesn't get back to her. Raella now has more influence in more areas than ever before and she's pulling out the stops."

"Does that bother you?"

"No. Use every advantage, I say."

"So what disturbs you?"

"Things that don't fit the Raella I knew. At Voripol, Goddess Rae turned night to day to save her, then hovered around while she dictated peace terms to the other combatants."

"Right," I agreed. "A strong negotiating position."

"And what does Raella do? Guarantee Orphalian neutrality? Maintain it as a buffer state between the northern powers? No. She carves it up like a roast turkey and gives everyone a slice, obliterates a kingdom with a stroke of her pen. The old Raella wouldn't have done that."

"That occurred to me at the time," I said.

"Back home, more of the same. She confiscated the lands of Thule and his allies. Fair enough, they had it coming. But she's got the rest of the nobility over a barrel too and she's putting the screws to them."

"How so?"

"When a noble dies, his lands and titles revert to the Queen, who regrants them to his heir. In theory, she has discretion to withhold the estate. In practice, the succession is automatic."

"Raella is exercising her discretion," I surmised.

"You might say that. The nobility was all but eradicated in the Wedding Massacre. That means she's got dozens of inexperienced young heirs waiting to be confirmed in their ancestral holdings. Raella is refusing unless they renounce a whole list of traditional noble privileges, give up their tax powers, disband their personal armies, and so forth."

"Is this wise? They could rebel."

"Not after Voripol. I see her point. The nobles have stymied her reforms since her reign began. Now the brakes are off. She can do whatever she wants. She intends to jettison the old fiefdoms and divide the kingdom into administrative provinces run by royal governors. She plans to restructure the courts, codify the laws, and so on. She's moving quickly. Maybe too quickly. She's drawing all the power to herself."

"Don't you trust her with it?"

"Of course I trust her! But she's creating an absolute monarchy and future rulers may not be as benevolent as Raella."

"Since when are you a political philosopher?"

"I worry, that's all. And I can't make her see the danger. She's become so supremely sure of herself. That's what scares me. And it goes beyond the political sphere. More of her subjects believe she actually died and was resurrected. She's encouraging the story and playing up her relationship with Rae."

"Daughter of Rae, and her Personal Representative in Arden," I said, mimicking the Queen. Merc winced.

"Exactly. The people worship her like she's the Sun Goddess herself. She used to be called Raella the Good, the Kind, the Warmhearted. Now it's Raella the Great, or Saint Raella."

"Don't you have to be dead to be a saint?"

"Not if you're Raella. Besides, she was dead, remember?"

"Right. I forgot."

"Now on top of all the rest, she's the sole leader of the League. She already wants to revise the charter and establish a League Academy of Magic. She has to improve everything she touches. Did you know the Treaty of Voripol has an article recognizing the League as a sovereign entity, a state entitled to diplomatic privileges, embassies, and all that? She's negotiating with Prince Ronaldo to add Caratha's recognition, which will make it official. Then she'll wear yet another crown."

"She's a remarkable woman," I said.

"That's a helpful comment," snarled Merc.

"What do you want me to say?"

"I don't know. I don't know. I just hope she can handle all she's taking on. She's a hopeless overachiever."

"That might be a good quality in a monarch."

"Right."

"Speaking of monarchs, have you heard that I'm the lost heir to the Carathan throne?"

"That and ten pennies will get you a glass of ale."

"My sentiments exactly." I paused. "Tell me about Lady Solana."

Merc shrugged. "She's Raella favorite cousin, several years her junior. Quite a talent for fire magic, which fits her hotheaded nature, but she lacks a little for control."

"Of her magic or her temper?"

Merc chuckled. "Both. As you probably know. Solana's a hard charger, eager to make her mark. She idolizes Raella, but I think there's a measure of unspoken rivalry at work."

"Is she good in a fight?"

"I don't know."

"Raella is sending her with me to Rancor."

"Then you'll probably learn all you care to know. I think Raella wouldn't mind seeing a match between you and Solana."

"I see little chance of that. She's too sharp-tongued and hotheaded for my taste. Pretty, though. Hey!"

The rider in a slowly passing coach carelessly fired a crossbow at me. Only Merc's phenomenal reflexes in jerking me aside saved me from a painful shafting. The steel bolt sank two inches into the gatepost of the Ganthian embassy.

"You almost hit me!" I said angrily.

"Sorry," said the crossbowman. "I didn't mean to miss." He took another shot. Merc batted the bolt aside. It struck a chip off the embassy's outer wall and rebounded high into the air.

"What are you trying to do? Kill me?" I shouted.

"Yes, actually. And it would be much easier if your friend would stop ruining my shots. Couldn't you stop that, sir? I've got a job to do here."

"Sorry," said Merc.

I studied the crossbowman's face. "You know, with a little makeup you'd look a lot like an old man who tried to stick a knife in me at Moonstone Gate a couple of weeks ago. Ambric, wasn't it?"

"Oh, you recognize me, do you? I had to pay a steep fine for that botched hit. Most unsporting of you to go wearing invincible armor and then kill all our help. That one incident has doubled the price of thug labor, and that cuts profits. Some people have got no consideration!" He fired again. Merc caught the bolt and dropped it to the ground. "Cut that out!" said the assassin.

"What have you got there, one of those self-winding jobs?" I asked.

Ambric nodded and held up the crossbow to give me a better look. "A beauty, isn't it? It's got these little gears in it, they pull the bow right back. Pop in the bolt like this, aim, pull the trigger—stop that, will you? Gods! It used to be nobody dared interfere with the ACLU! Assassins get no respect these days!"

"So sorry," said Merc, twirling the intercepted bolt in his hand. "But your quarrel with my friend will have to wait. We're having an important man-to-man talk here. Kill him later."

"Later?" said the assassin, signaling his driver to stop the coach. "How long are you going to be in town, Cosmo?"

"Until the end of the week, I think."

Putting aside his weapon, Ambric withdrew his appointment calendar from a vest pocket and leafed through it. "I'm booked pretty solid. Didn't expect you back. Thought you'd fled Caratha in mortal dread of us, never to be seen again."

"Oh, no, leaving had nothing to do with you. It was a personal matter."

"Well, I heard you were back, so I thought I'd take care of you with a quick drive-by shooting. I've got a banker to put down this afternoon. Chapter meeting tonight. Tomorrow's no good, I've got that innkeeper in Moontown. What are you doing Wednesday?"

"I'll probably be in Waterfront all day, buying a ship," I said.

"Waterfront, eh? My favorite. Good for ambushes.

I think I could—drat! I've got a gentleman farmer in the outlying provinces. I'll be out of town all day."

"How about Wednesday night, then? Cut my throat while I sleep or something? I could leave the gate unlocked."

"No, Wednesday is bowling night."

"Thursday, then?"

"My day off. How about Friday? I could pencil you in between the duke's mistress and the Chancellor of the Biscuits. 'Round lunchtime?"

"Iffy," I said. "I may be gone by then."

He snapped the book shut. "That's too bad. I'll have to pass your file on to someone else. I hate to hand you over to someone unfamiliar with the case, but it can't be helped."

"What about that sweet little kid? Kara."

"On special assignment to Pylarum. Won't be back for weeks. And my wife, Myrta, is abed with the flu. You met her at Moonstone Gate, I believe."

"Yes. Give her my best. I hope she gets to feeling better."

"That's kind of you."

"Still can't say who took out the contract on me?"

"Afraid not. Mind if I take a parting shot?"

"Be my guest," said Merc.

"Oh, never mind. I must be getting to the bank. If my schedule opens up, Cosmo, you'll be the first to know. Good-bye now." The coach rattled away at high speed.

"That was close," I said. "It's getting so it isn't safe to walk the streets anymore."

7 _____

Back at the mansion, I spent the evening mind-molding my armor. Oreboggle's book explained miraculum's unique property of reconfiguring its own molecules in response to mental directions. You didn't have to be a wizard to have hours of fun molding miraculum, said the book, as long as you had a strong will, a good rapport with your metal sample, and a sound understanding of the principles involved.

I had worn my armor often enough to establish a mental bond with it, a process something like imprinting it with psychic sweat stains. According to the book, I now ought to be able to reshape it into other forms, so long as I didn't try to change its fundamental identity as a suit of armor. Miraculum is mentally malleable, but a given sample also tends to get set in its ways. I couldn't turn my armor into a sword or transform Overwhelm into a teakettle. The metal wouldn't go along with it.

The process was simple enough. I formed a mental picture of the new appearance I wanted the armor to take and willed the metal to adopt it. It was similar to Raelnan clothing magic, but took more effort. The response was sluggish at first, but after an hour or so I got the hang of it.

When I won the armor from The Gods in the Test of Heroes at the Shrine of Greenleaf, it came to me as a long-sleeved hooded chain-mail coat that hung to my knees, a pair of gauntlets, an open helm with nose and cheek guards, and a shield. This was an effective combination, but it had a cumbersome antique appearance and left gaps in my protection.✸ What I wanted was modern styling and complete coverage.

I started my armorial makeover by melding the interlocking rings of the chain mesh into a smooth and seamless whole. That done, I caused the lower part of the coat to wrap around my legs, molding to my thighs and calves in a steely caress. I fixed the gauntlets to interlock with the sleeves and altered the helmet to attach firmly to the neckpiece. After a bit more tinkering, stretching, and adjusting, I had designed an armored bodysuit that protected me from head to toe and allowed maximum freedom of movement. Unfortunately, it looked like a pair of metal long johns.

I solved this by adding retractable studs, ridges, and plates at crucial points like the chest and shoulders, then finishing off with purely decorative whorls and swirls and martial symbols. These changes made the armor more interesting to look at, but still allowed me to wear it under my street clothes and thus enjoy its protection unobtrusively.

I studied myself in the mirror. I was the epitome of the well-dressed hero.

"Behold . . . the Cosmosuit!" I said, striking a pose.

The suit seemed pleased at the designation. According to Oreboggle's book, getting on a first-name basis with my miraculum would help deepen its bond with me. Over time, a item forged of miraculum would become as loyal as a dog, if treated with respect.

Next I worked with the shield. It had shown a tendency to change shapes when I wasn't looking—going from rectangular to round to kite-shaped. Now I controlled the process, putting it through its paces. I finally settled on a concave disk shape as my favorite. I found I could hurl such a shield like a giant Frisbee and rebound it off objects. Also, like Overwhelm, the shield would return to me on command once it got used to the idea. This combination of qualities made it a useful weapon. After a couple hours of practice, I successfully bounced it off three trees and the garden wall and had it fly smoothly back to my arm. All I needed to do now was paint red and white stripes on it and put a star in the middle. Instead, I dubbed it Gardion.

I went to bed feeling pleased with myself. It always boosts one's heroic self-esteem to have your own personalized tools of the trade. It also helps you make a lasting impression on the public when you have have certain named items associated with you. When people recalled the stories of King Raetheon the Patriot, they always mentioned his sword, Sunstorm. When they thought of Hogar the Malravian, they also thought of his faithful war dog, Spudbone. Dezba the Daring was invariably associated with Gulpy, the magic goblet that never runs dry. Dolman Sureblade had his sword, Liquidator. Fearless Freya had Warhead the magic ax. The duelist Gaspard had Quickdart, his lightning-swift rapier. Eckart the Exterminator carried the enchanted flyswatter Splat.

I had borne Overwhelm for several months, but hadn't much advertised the fact. But now I had three items to link with my name through bold deeds. Henceforth, Jason Cosmo would conjure up images of Overwhelm, Gardion, and the Cosmosuit. I was ready to get serious in my new career and equipped to take and hold my place in the forefront of the heroic profession.

The bad guys didn't have a chance.

Contrary to what I told Ambric, I was bound for Waterfront the next day. Exchanging pleasantries with cold-blooded assassins is all very well, but I saw no reason to be honest with them. Lady Solana's embassy coach picked me up at first light. She wore soft boots, fatigues, and a heavy green cloak. Her hair was pinned back from her face. She smiled as I climbed into the passenger compartment.

"Good morning, milady."

"Master Cosmo, I must beg your forgiveness for my recent boorishness. I know you think me completely ill-mannered and insensitive and I am truly sorry. I should not have questioned your courage or your honor. I hope that we can be friends in spite of—"

"Are you saying you've revised your estimation of me in light of my response to yesterday's crisis and acceptance of the important and dangerous mission on which you and I will soon embark?"

"Why, yes."

"Right on schedule, then."

"What do you mean?"

"Our romance."

"What romance?"

"You didn't like me at first, despite a strong under-lying attraction you couldn't deny. Now you realize you were wrong and want to patch things up. I think you're rash and hotheaded, but that only makes you more desirable, for some reason. Eventually, we'll overcome our foolish pride and prejudices and admit that we love each other. Not that we do yet, mind you, but we will."

"I'm sure I don't know what you're talking about, Master Cosmo."

"Of course you don't. And please call me Jason, milady."

"Jason, then. Call me Solana."

"A name as lovely as its bearer, milady."

She colored slightly. "You are entirely too much."

"I know. So what's the plan?"

"We must have a ship."

"Do you know anything about ships?"

"No. Raelna is a landlocked kingdom."

"Darnk moreso. To Waterfront then. This should be educational."

Below the chipped and bloodstained Low Bridge, the murky River Crownbolt emptied into the polluted Great Harbor, where the dead fish bobbed amid the floating rubbish heaps. An underclass of Floaters eked out a squalid existence on these drifting islands of trash, eating what morsels they gleaned from the flotsam or begged from passing ships. They never set foot on shore except when a colony grew so large as to be a navigation hazard and the navy broke it up and arrested the inhabitants.

On the east shore was the home base of the Royal Carathan Navy, where Ronaldo's huge fleet of pedal-powered purple war galleys and battle carrocks was built and maintained. I supposed in some vague sense the fleet was mine as well, but quickly banished the thought. My forebears had fallen from power eight hundred years ago and I had absolutely no interest in raising their standard once more over Caratha.

Waterfront, the overbuilt league of shoreline that was the pulsing heart which kept the stream of world commerce flowing, was on the west side of the harbor. The district began where the Long Pier jutted a full mile into the water. Further along the shores were the Dockworks, a multilayered megadock with a square mile of upper surface area. Nestled between these architectural behemoths were the famous Carathan shipyards.

South across the water stood the Seagates, portals formed by extensions of the encircling city wall that reached into the very harbor from both shores, surmounting man-made peninsulas and leaving only a quarter mile of open water between the last watchtowers. In the middle of that gap rose the Seaspire. Bristling with catapults, it was the most heavily fortified lighthouse in the world.

The Dockworks were for the exclusive use of the great trading companies that maintained the vast structure. Three Carathan companies—Arden Shipping, Panrock Cargo, and the House of Shane—shared it with the Corundum Trading Company. High fences and heavily armed mercenaries protected each firm's area, not so much from thieves as from each other. We wouldn't find a ship for sale or hire there.

Instead, we rode to the end of the Long Pier where the free traders docked their craft. By the time we worked our way back to the mainland, we were certain to find what we needed. At the very least, we'd know a lot more about ships.

"Shall we buy or charter?" asked Solana.

"Either or both, so long as we get a captain and crew along with the tub. I doubt we could get it out of the harbor ourselves."

"I must confess that as a child I did sail small boats on the lake near our castle."

"You're saying you could get us out of the harbor?"

"I think so."

"And once we passed the Seagates?"

"Let's be certain we get a captain and crew along with the tub."

Our search was initally frustrating. Most of the free traders had already docked their vessels for the coming winter. The Indigo Sea grew choppy and unpredictable in the cold months, and men and women whose entire livelihoods depended on keeping their one ship afloat weren't willing to chance losing it in a sudden squall.

A few shipmasters had a different outlook. These fell into three categories: those so desperate they couldn't pass up any commission, however risky; those so greedy they wouldn't pass up any commission, however risky; and those so crazy they didn't pass up any commission unless it wasn't risky enough.

The mariners in the first category were primarily honest folk several generations behind in the payments on their ship, which was invariably small, named after a revered grandparent, and in bad repair. Rancor wasn't on their charts.

The second group were chiefly dishonest folk who transferred their cargoes after dark, wore tattoos, spat a lot, drank heavily, and coined most of the off-colorful words and phrases for which sailors are so famous. They could probably sail the route to Rancor blindfolded. Unfortunately, they would also probably rape us, rob us, slit our throats, and toss us to the sharks before we got there.

That limited our choice to the seafarers in category three. There weren't many of these. Most didn't live to a ripe old age. Those that did tended to do so on small uncharted islands where they lived in tree houses or grass huts, ate coconuts, and palled around with natives named Friday.

Despite the odds against us, we found a category-three captain dozing in a tilted-back deck chair aboard a weather-beaten little caravel, with his wide-brimmed hat pulled over his face. As we stopped to study his vessel he cocked one eye open. He bit his lip speculatively, then grinned and sprang to his feet. Doffing his hat, he executed a deep bow.

"Captain Malachi Skipjammer—shipmaster, swashbuckler, and sometime smuggler—at your service, sir and lady! If it's a swift and sturdy sailing ship you seek, my *Miracle* is just the very vessel for you!" He bowed again, then bounded down the gangplank, pumped my hand, and kissed Solana's.

Skipjammer wore a billowing green blouse and loose red breeches. His lean face was marked by a long nose, an ironic twist to his mouth, and frenetic brown eyes. His wheat-colored hair was pulled into a single long braid.

He put one arm around my shoulder and gestured grandly with the other. "Indeed, sir, this is the selfsame famous *Miracle* of which you have doubtless heard! Only seven times sunk. Had to lay a new keel, replace the hull, replank the deck, and raise a new mast, but she's otherwise the same old proud lass I put to sea over a decade ago. Built right here in Caratha, home of the finest shipbuilding masters in all Arden! Of course, she wasn't actually built by the finest shipbuilding masters. She was thrown together on weekends by apprentices using cast-off materials. But apprentices to the finest shipbuilding masters in all Arden, mind you! They were going to give her to the navy for target practice, but I bought her cheap. No finer vessel afloat!"

"So I see," I said dubiously.

"You do? I mean, of course you do! You're obviously a man with a perceptive eye for a well-clinkered boat! And you, my fair lady, don't you agree?"

"It looks like the mooring lines are the only thing keeping it afloat," said Solana.

"Ahem. Yes. Well, then. Milady jests, of course." He returned his attention to me. "So what's your cargo, good sir? My rates are reasonable! Higher this time of year, but competitive with the big companies, who can't give you the personal service and high standard of commitment to safe and speedy delivery that I provide!"

"Actually we seek passage for ourselves."

"Ah! Then the *Miracle* is indeed the ship for you! Friendly crew! Cozy private cabins with all the modern comforts of larger vessels minus the unnecessary frills! Shuffleboard! Dancing! Hot meals served regularly! Narrow of beam, so you're never far from the rail if you get seasick! Not too many rats, statistically speaking. Truly a traveler's delight, perfect for that romantic getaway! Whither are you bound, sir?"

"Rancor."

Skipjammer was taken aback. He cleaned his ear out with his finger. "You must pardon my poor hearing, sir! I thought I heard you say Rancor, but of course that cannot be, for no honest person goes there by choice. Where was it you said you wished to go? I'll try to hear clearly this time." He cupped his hand to his ear and furrowed his brow in a great show of concentration.

"Rancor," I repeated. "This is something of a special charter."

He looked from me to Solana and back to me again. "Indeed I would say so, sir! And it doubles my price, sir!"

"You haven't named a price."

"Once I do, consider it doubled."

"You'll take us to Rancor?"

"If the price is right, sir, I'll take you to the very edge of the world, sir!"

"We just want to go to Rancor. How much?"

"Excuse us, Captain Skipjammer," said Solana, pulling me aside for a whispered conference.

"What?" I asked.

"You can't be serious," she hissed. "I wouldn't sail that hulk in my bathtub."

"I think it's the best we're going to do," I said, banishing from mind the appealing image of Solana in her bathtub. "And he seems a good enough fellow."

"He's a windbag."

"That could be helpful on a sailing ship. We won't get becalmed."

"Perhaps Prince Ronaldo will loan us one of his ships."

"Perhaps, but we wouldn't get near Rancor in it."

"We may not get near anything but the briny depths in this *Miracle*."

"A chance we must take." I turned to Skipjammer. "Your price, Captain?"

Skipjammer frowned in calculation. "Considering, sir, that I must have supplies, pay my crew, and make minor repairs, factoring in the inhospitable state of the wintry sea and the danger of our destination, adding the distance involved, and multiplying the whole by—"

"Fifty thousand gold crowns for the round trip, take it or leave it," I said. My offer was several times what his ship would have been worth new, but I didn't want to waste time haggling.

Skipjammer gawked for only a second. "In advance?" he asked.

"Half in advance."

"Cash, check, or charge?"

"I've got Heroes Club, gold Chargemaster, and CarathaBank platinum. What do you take?" I flashed my credit cards.

"Jason Cosmo?" asked Skipjammer, reading the cards.

"Yes."

"Seriously?"

"Seriously."

Skipjammer looked troubled.

"Is there a problem?" I asked.

"No, sir! Not at all, sir! It's just that I'd always thought you'd be a bit taller, sir!"

"You still want the job?"

"Indeed, sir! It will be an honor, sir! And your terms are quite agreeable, sir!" He took the platinum CarathaBank card, as I expected.

"Can we sail tomorrow?" I asked.

"With the morning wind, sir!"

"Good. I'll see you then."

"You're young for a sub-master," I said to Solana as we rode through Lowtide, where the streets were narrow and the unwary at risk from thieves, thugs, and press gangs. Even a coach with diplomatic plates wasn't immune from trouble here. Especially a fancy coach like ours.

"I reached journeymage two years early."

Wizards typically began their training at age twelve, serving a twelve-year apprenticeship before being certified as journeymage. The majority rose no higher in the profession, but those that went on to sub-master rank usually took five or six years to achieve it. Thirty was the target age. The rare few who eventually became arcane masters did so after another ten years of advanced study.

"That's impressive."

"Not really. Raella finished six years early."

"Raella was taught by the great Mage Pencader. She also has the advantage of divine blood."

"I'm her cousin. I share that divine blood."

"I'm still impressed."

"You are the impressive one, if all Raella tells me is true."

"Whatever I've done, I've had a lot of help," I said. "I'd be dead a hundred times over were it not for Merc."

"The Prince Consort is—ulf!"

The coach halted suddenly, throwing Solana forward against me. I instinctively pushed her to the floorboard and covered her with my body as the side window exploded. A firebomb shattered on my back, instantly making an inferno of the coach interior.

We crashed out the door together, our clothing ablaze. I rolled on the ground, more to save my outer clothing than myself, since I was protected by the Cosmosuit.

Solana, once her surprise passed, was literally in her element. She put out the fire on our clothes and took control of the flames on the coach. Spotting the bomb thrower sprinting for the cover of an alley, she directed a blast of fire that incinerated the man instantly. Fluffy black ashes swirled in the air as her flamestrike receded.

"Turn down the heat!" I said, summoning Overwhelm and Gardion from the remains of the coach. "I'd have preferred to take him alive!"

"Sorry. I overreacted."

"Get down!"

Our assailants had blocked the street with stacked crates, stopping the coach. The driver was slumped over with a crossbow bolt in his chest. Now his killer, a rooftop sniper, took aim at Solana. I saw him shoot from the corner of my eye and hurled Gardion to intercept the bolt. The shield flawlessly deflected the quarrel and returned to my hand.

Solana whirled, spotted the crossbowman, and incinerated him too. His half-melted weapon clattered to the street.

"I thought you were going to cool it," I said.

"I'm trying!"

A pair of flail-swinging armored horsemen emerged from an alley behind us. Solana turned to face them, a bonfire in her hands. I laid a restraining hand on her shoulder.

"Er—just passing through!" called the rider. The pair disappeared down the opposite alley. We heard further sounds of retreat from beyond the barricade of boxes. The attack was over.

"The cowards! You should have let me cook them all!"

"They knew they were beaten."

"Who were the curs?"

"The ACLU," I said. "They must have me under surveillance. This is their third try at me, though I don't think they expected you to be so formidable. You were magnificent. Excessive, but definitely spectacular." I touched her arm.

Solana indicated the molten crossbow. "But you saved my life."

"You've already saved mine."

I impulsively kissed her. Taken aback, she gave the slightest hint of startled resistance, then responded with steadily rising intensity, revealing a scalding passion that threatened to raze my flesh to the very bone. At length, we stepped warily back from each other, surprised at what had just transpired.

"We'd best save our energy," I said. "It's a long walk back to the embassy."

8

"Two attacks in as many days," I said angrily. "This has to stop."

"The solution is simple," said Merc. "Let's pay the ACLU a visit."

"A good idea," said Solana.

"It is not so simple as that," said Raella. "This is Prince Ronaldo's domain. We can't indulge in attacks on his subjects, however justified."

"A bad idea," said Solana.

"We have diplomatic immunity, don't we?" said Merc.

"We must not abuse it, dearest," said Raella. "I don't want to endanger my good relations with Ronaldo. Not with a new trade agreement and the future of the League at stake. You're not a free agent anymore. You're my consort. You must consider the political implications of your actions."

"I don't think routing the assassins will cause an international incident," said Merc.

"It might," said Raella. "The ACLU has much hidden influence in Caratha."

"True enough," said Merc. "But it will have much less by the time we're done."

"The ACLU isn't the problem," I said. "It's whoever hired them to ice me. Could it be the Society? I know Necrophilius promised no further action against

104

me and Merc, but with the Superwand at stake, he might make an exception."

"I'd call destroying the League tower an exception," said Merc. "Wouldn't you?"

"Good point."

Raella spoke. "The tower attack also demonstrates that the Society has more effective means of dealing with enemies than hiring common killers."

"Who else would want me dead?" I asked.

"It wasn't long ago that you were the most wanted fugitive in Arden," said Raella. "That infamy may have won you enemies you know nothing about who wish you dead out of spite, fear, envy, or to avenge some imagined grievance."

"You're right," I said. "All the more reason to change my image as soon as possible."

"Meantime, the sure way to smoke out your foe is to follow the money," said Merc. "Right now it's in the ACLU's hands. We'll just persuade them, in a friendly fashion, to tell us whose pocket it came from. No harm in that, Raella."

"I'd rather not take the chance," said the Queen.

"The alternative is that I keep beating off attacks without knowing who's behind them," I said. "I agree with Merc. I'm tired of looking back over my shoulder to see who's there."

"The sooner you embark on your mission, the sooner you'll leave the ACLU behind," said Raella. "You've arranged to sail tomorrow, have you not?"

"That's right," said Solana, before I could answer.

"And you're safe from attack here at the embassy," continued Raella, "so there's no reason to be concerned with the ACLU right now."

"They attacked an embassy coach," said Merc.

"In Lowtide, which is to be expected," said Raella. "I've made my decision. No action is to be taken against the ACLU. I'll raise the matter with Ronaldo tomorrow. We'll let him deal with them."

"I disagree," said Merc.

"Respect my decision, dearest. I am the Queen."

"Of course you are," said Merc stiffly.

"Maybe I'll just visit the ACLU by myself," I said. "I'm no officer of state."

"As your High Priestess, I must forbid it," said Raella. "We can't endanger your mission."

"Are you my High Priestess?" I asked.

"You are in Rae's service, pledged to accept the discipline of her Church. Which means you should respect my decision in this matter, too." Raella stood. "If that is settled, I must consult with Ambassador Brishen now. Chancellor Vannevar is arriving tomorrow to assist me in my talks with Ronaldo. Solana, come with me, please. We must talk."

The two women exited the room. Merc and I stared at each other in silence.

"The back gate, half-past midnight," said the wizard.

"I'll be there."

The Assassins and Cutthroats Labor Union's headquarters was a funeral parlor on Slum Row in the Wrong Part of Town. The building was a fortified mansion in the Grim Baroque style. Stone vultures and grotesque gargoyles glared down from the forest of garrets and turrets on the slate rooftop. Huge grinning skulls framed with a border of dancing skeletons were carved into the torch-flanked double doors at the front entrance, beneath the slogan:

DEATH IS OUR BUSINESS
Open 24 Hours a Day

Raella was right about one thing. The ACLU had a hammerlock on the business of dying in Caratha, and that gave the organization tremendous clout. Aside from their monopoly on murder for hire, the assassins, through fronts and subsidiaries, controlled every funeral home in the city; pulled the strings in the Gravediggers Union, the Alliance of Independent

Casketmakers, and the Guild of Gravemarker Masons; owned several granite and marble quarries; ran the only embalming-fluid plant in town; and operated card and flower shops.

This farflung network of enterprises allowed the ACLU to offer a complete range of services. Not only would they kill your enemy, they'd stuff him with preservatives, dress him in new clothes, fit him in a coffin, and put a wreath on his grave. For a slight surcharge, they'd dance on it, too.

Actually, graves weren't always involved. The Gods had different ideas about how their worshipers should be sent to their final reward. Rae and Frix, God of Fire, preferred flashy funeral pyres. Surflord and Torrent Wetlace liked to receive the bodies into the waters they ruled. Most of the others were happy with a pine box and a hole in the ground. Death, of course, took them any way he could get them. The ACLU was ready to accommodate all tastes, with everything from cremations to deep-harbor specials.

Merc and I bounded up the steps to the doors.

"Shall I knock, or shall you?" I asked.

"Allow me," said Merc. He reached out with the Gauntlet of Gandylon, made a tight fist, then suddenly flung his hand open. The doors flew out of their frames, blasted inward by an invisible ray of force.

"That felt good," Merc said.

A pair of mailed mercenaries armed with halberds met us inside. Merc disarmed and disassembled one with his incomparable martial-arts skills. A leap, a kick, a couple of blazing hand strikes, a twist, a throw, and it was all over for the guard.

I smashed the other with Gardion, knocking him through a wall.

"Nice," said Merc. "And you're not even at your fully juiced-up strength by night, are you?"

"Flimsy wall, I think."

The second wave of defenders arrived. Half a dozen

fighting men wearing hardened leather studded with brass came at us from two directions. They were armed with shortswords and bucklers, which might as well have been toothpicks and saucers against my invincible blade and shield. I disabled two and killed one.

"Watch this," said Merc as he danced and dodged to avoid the trio harrying him. "Nothing up this sleeve, nothing up this sleeve, and—voilà!"

He flicked his wrists and the swirling black Cloak of Misregard stretched to engulf his attackers. I heard muffled screams from within the folds. When the cloak snapped back to normal length, no bodies fell to the floor. The three warriors were gone without a trace.

"What happened to them?" I asked.

"I'm not sure," said Merc.

"Not sure?"

"I think the cloak ate them."

"Ate them?"

"That's right."

"You'll have a hard time getting that thing laundered."

"It's hand-wash only."

We passed into a somberly appointed parlor. Two guards opened fire with mini-crossbows from behind a couch. Merc's cloak flapped around and swallowed the missiles in midflight. I hurled Gardion at the men, stunning them. As the shield returned to my hand Mercury leaped over the couch and landed between them, cloak spread wide. When he turned around, they were gone.

"Really dressed to kill, didn't you?" I said.

"Exactly."

I shuddered. "That cloak gives me the creeps."

"No, I'm giving the creeps to the cloak."

Alarm bells rang throughout the building.

"Party time," I observed.

His vision enhanced by the Rainbow Spectacles of

Mesha, Merc scanned the walls. "There," he said, indicating a section of the back wall. He gestured with the Gauntlet of Gandylon and knocked a man-high hole in the wall. We leaped through into the midst of a squad of surprised mercenaries rushing down a corridor. I smacked and slashed with Overwhelm while Merc kicked, punched, and let his carnivorous cloak do its thing.

"Now what?" I asked, when we had dealt with them all.

"You go left. I'll go right. We'll smash everything in sight and see what we can shake loose."

"As good as any plan we've ever had."

We did a high five and split up. I followed the corridor back to the guard station, surprising fifteen sleepy-eyed mercenaries who were still struggling into their armor. I sent them back to dreamland, unavoidably sending a few even further.

Beyond the guardroom was another corridor. I kicked open a door labeled NIGHT MANAGER. The man inside certainly looked qualified for the job. He was tall and old with a long white mustache, clad in black from head to foot. He hadn't a speck of color about him anywhere. His face was a strong aquiline, with a thin nose and oddly arched nostrils. His massive eyebrows almost met over the nose. His mouth was rather cruel looking, with peculiarly sharp white teeth that protruded over his ruddy lips. His ears were pale and pointed, chin broad and strong, and cheeks firm though thin. His nails were long and fine, cut to a sharp point. His complexion had a deathly pallor. His eyes were intensely red.

"Welcome to my office," he said, sketching a courtly bow. "Enter freely and of your own will. I am Vlad Morbidica. How may I assist you?"

"I'm Jason Cosmo," I said. "I want to see whoever is in charge here."

"I am the night manager. Do you require our services?"

"No. But your embalmers are going to have a lot of in-house work to do soon unless I get what I want."

"You are making threats against the ACLU in our own house? How bold. How foolish."

From the other end of the house came a cacophony of screams, crashes, explosions, and rumbles. The walls vibrated and the floor buckled.

"What was that?" demanded Morbidica. He looked about nervously.

"My partner," I said. "Now where do I find the big boss? I want to see him or her right now or we're going to have quite a bloodletting."

"I'm sure we can arrange a bloodletting," said Morbidica, suddenly leaping at me with his hands curled into claws.

I met his leap with Gardion, intending to smash him back across his desk. Unexpectedly, the shield passed right through his body, which transformed into mist. Thrown off balance by the unexpected absence of my target, I stumbled forward.

Suddenly Morbidica was behind me, snaking his arms around in a wrestler's hold and hefting me from the floor. He slammed me down against the desktop, cracking it. I lost my grip on Overwhelm. The incredibly strong night manager yanked my helmet off and tugged at the armor protecting my neck.

Because of the Cosmosuit's impact-absorbing properties, I was less stunned by hitting the desk than Morbidica expected. I launched my elbow back into his ribs.

The blow had no effect except causing him to lift me and slam me down again. This time the desk gave and we both hit the floor, immediately wrestling each other for advantage. Morbidica hissed at me and tried to bite off my nose with his razory fangs.

In every vampire story I've ever heard, the local

authorities take forever to figure out what they're up against. First they think some kind of wild beast is loose, then a psychotic slasher. Finally an old professor with a funny accent convinces the sheriff that a vampire is indeed working the area and it would be a good idea to stock up on garlic and pointy wooden sticks.

I was a little quicker on the uptake than that.

"You're a vampire!" I said.

"You're dinner," Morbidica replied, snapping his teeth.

"You've got a serious overbite," I said. "But I think we can fix it."

I socked the vampire in the face with my mailed fist, demolishing his teeth. His hands flew to his mouth, feeling the splintery white stubs of his ruined grin.

"Wha haff you dud to ne?" he howled.

"You've been defanged," I said, springing to my feet and calling Overwhelm to my hand. "Hold still and I'll add decapitated."

"Awl keel yew!"

Morbidica leapt at me again, and like a sucker I fell for the turning-to-vapor trick again, swinging Overwhelm through a cloud of mist, only to have the vampire materialize with his hands around my throat. He was much stronger than me, probably as strong as I was in the daytime. Only my armor prevented him from crushing my windpipe.

Thought of the daytime gave me an idea.

"Alabathka!" I cried. The Rae amulet was outside my armor, but under my surcoat. The flash of True Light was thus partially obscured, but enough of the glare hit Morbidica to make him recoil in pain.

"I thought that might work," I said, wasting no time in yanking the amulet into view and shouting "Alabathka!" again.

"Put it away!" wailed the vampire, shielding his

eyes. "I can't wifstan vhe danable light of vhe danable sun!"

"Take a close look, friend. This is the damnable emblem of damnable Sun Goddess Rae and I'm her damnable Champion!"

"Arrgh!" cried the vampire, putting his hands to his ears. "Say not vhat danable holy name!"

"What name? Rae?"

"Aieeee!"

"Rae, Rae, Rae, Rae, Rae, and a drop of golden sun for you! Luminata! Sha-boom, sha-boom!"

The medallion snapped on its continual light effect and I aimed it to transfix Morbidica in the beam. His body smoked and withered. He tried to turn to mist, but could not. Dust was all he managed to become.

"I'll leave you for the janitor," I said, and kicked the pile of ashy fluff across the floor.

More yells, bangs, shouts, and crashes sounded from the other end of the mansion. Merc was certainly enjoying himself. And why not? He had been without magical abilities for weeks. Now that he had three powerful arcane toys to play with, he was making up for lost time.

I recovered my helmet and returned to the corridor. A pair of crossbow bolts whizzed past me. I turned and charged the crossbowmen at the end of the hall, blocking their shots with Gardion as I came.

Halfway to them, a trapdoor opened beneath my feet. I fell fifteen feet or so into a pool of foul water. Laughing, the crossbowmen came to the edge of the pit.

"What do you think of our clever hidden death trap?" asked one.

"A pit full of dirty water? I've seen better."

"Just wait."

An iron grate closed off the top of the shaft and slowly descended. Additional water bubbled up from below at an alarming rate.

"Get it yet?" asked the crossbowman.

"The sinking grate will meet the rising water and trap me beneath the surface, I suppose," I said.

"Yep."

My buoyant miraculum armor kept me afloat with little effort. Radiating unconcern, I whistled impatiently as water and grate slowly converged. The cross bowmen looked perplexed.

"Excuse me," said one. "Perhaps you don't realize the full implications of the situation."

"Which are?"

"When you get trapped beneath the surface, you're going to drown."

"Really?" I said. "That's dreadful."

"General idea of a death trap, you know. Anyway, you might ought to thrash about or something. Scream. Beg for mercy. Struggle a bit. You're ruining our fun."

"You enjoy watching people drown?"

"Yes."

They peered down at me eagerly. I continued my aimless whistling until the grate was in reach. Then I hefted Overwhelm and slashed it open.

"Hey! You can't do that!" shouted a crossbowman.

"Watch me," I said, releasing sword and shield to clamber through the hole, get my footing atop the remnants of the grate, and launch myself up through the air before the guards could stop me. It was only an eight-foot hop from the present level of the grate.

One man kicked me in the face as I dragged myself up to the floor. I grabbed his ankle and flung him into the pit. His head hit the ragged edge of the iron grate with a dull crack and he slipped into the water.

I swung up and gained my feet as the other man shifted back and whipped a long knife from his belt. I let him stab me and the knife broke against my armor, then I broke his arm and tossed him in after.

his companion. I recalled Overwhelm and Gardion from the pit.

"You two can get your jollies watching each other drown," I called.

Yet another squad of mercenary guards charged down the hallway. I slashed my way through them while bellowing war cries I had learned from the fierce Malravian hill people.

"Booga booga yah-booga! A messy death awaits you at my hands! Booga booga yah-booga boo! Raw, I eat a dozen such as you for breakfast each morning, washed down with sour goat milk! Booga yah booga yah booga yah booga!"

Admittedly, it was more convincing when shouted in unison by ten thousand fur-clad tribesmen bedecked with the bones of their enemies and waving nail-studded war clubs. And the full chant went on for several hundred verses. Still, that bit about drinking sour goat milk had a strong effect. The mercenaries blanched. I relented and didn't recite the next verse, the one about after breakfast vomiting the curdled contents of my stomach at my foes with unerring aim. I was, after all, a civilized warrior.

Having routed the guards, I continued unchecked through the mansion, smashing furniture, kicking down doors, breaking windows, knocking over vases, leaving scuff marks on polished floors, and spitting in potted plants. The ACLU would rue the day it signed a contract with my name on it.

I charged up a stairway to the second floor. Several assassins lay in wait for me behind a hastily erected barricade on the landing. Their crossbows did not find the mark, and I plowed through the barricade like a bull through a hedge. The killers fled and I pursued.

Too late, I realized this was just what they intended. A heavy net dropped from the ceiling to entangle me. I stumbled and fell to my knees. The assassins turned and tossed little glass grenades that shattered on impact and released invisible clouds of dormadose sleep gas.

I held my breath and struggled against the net. No sooner had I cut my way through it than a second net fell on me and the killers threw another volley of dormadose grenades. Seven bravos wearing gas masks fell upon me with blackjacks and clubs.

The Cosmosuit absorbed the force of their blows, but the attack hampered my effort to escape the second net. I couldn't hold my breath much longer and one strong whiff of dormadose would put me to sleep for a day. Assuming I lived long enough to wake up again.

A third salvo of gas grenades broke all around me. My lungs screamed for air. Desperate, I did the unexpected. I cut a hole in the floor with Overwhelm and dived through, dragging three of my attackers with me.

The trailing edge of the net caught on a broken timber, halting our fall with a sharp jerk. Overwhelm and Gardion went clattering to the floor. Two of the bravos lost their grip and followed, stunned or killed by the twenty-foot drop. The third thug hung on and we traded kicks and jabs as we swung above an embalming workshop.

Naked corpses in various states of repair lay on slabs throughout the room. The cool air reeked of wax and attar. Shelves and cabinets held dried herbs and oils and perfumes used in preparing bodies for burial. Startled embalmers scrambled for the exits as the new arrivals hit the floor.

I smashed my opponent's face with my fist and he joined his senseless fellows below. Then the timber gave way and I went tumbling after. I rolled as I hit the floor, bounded to my feet, and summoned Overwhelm and Gardion.

It would be disrespectful to the dead to further demolish this room. I dogged the path of the frightened embalmers, bounding through a storeroom and small lounge into a carpeted corridor. A pair of guards came at me with pikes.

"I hope the ACLU has a good health-insurance plan," I said calmly.

"They do," said one guard.

"How are the death benefits?"

They slowed their charge.

"Fairly generous," said the guard.

"But we're not up on the particulars," said the other. "Why don't we go check on that, Harve?"

"Good idea, Wade."

They dropped their weapons and fled.

Merc appeared at the opposite end of the corridor. We started toward each other.

"Hey, Jason, why is your side of the building still standing?"

"I'm working on it."

"Find the big boss?"

"No, but I had a little dustup with the night manager."

"Good for you. I think we've got the assassins routed. Most seem to have fled."

We converged before an intriguing set of brass-plated doors etched with funeral scenes.

"Interesting," said Merc. "Have you been in here yet?"

"No." I tried the doors. "Locked. You can see through the doors, right?"

"Wrong. They're lined with lead, which blocks the magic see-through rays of the glasses. But let me see if I can pick the lock." Merc gestured with the Gauntlet of Gandylon and blew the doors to fragments.

"You've got quite a touch with a lock pick. Ever consider burgling as a new career?"

"I've been thinking about it. Looks like we've hit the jackpot."

The gloomy office beyond was richly furnished in

dark wood, leather, and brass. Behind a large desk sat a gaunt man with a skullface grin and sunken eyes.

"I'm Chale Barrowight, Chief Undertaker of the ACLU," he rasped. "The two of you have made quite a mess of things here tonight. Now we're going to make quite a mess of you."

"Well, Merc," I said. "That sounds like the prelude to a nasty surprise."

"I agree, Jason."

The world exploded in a bright white glare.

9

"Jason, get down!" cried Merc.

I hit the deck. Though mostly blinded by the hot white magnesium flash Barrowight had set off, I still saw the spiral of intense green-blue light that streaked over me, cooking the very air with a subatomic sizzle. It would have vaporized me had it connected.

Merc's eyes were shielded by the Rainbow Spectacles. He saw plainly what I could not: a dark-robed wizard had stepped out of the shadows and attacked while the Chief Undertaker escaped through a hidden passage behind a sliding bookshelf.

Unfortunately for Barrowight's spell-slinging lackey, he was severely outclassed. Merc wasn't called Boltblaster by accident. Though currently bereft of his own spellcasting capabilities, he was the Eleven Kingdoms' leading practitioner of showy, flashy, pyrotechnic magic. He was familiar with every spell of that sort, its dangers, and its limitations.

"The Teal Twistor of Termination?" he scoffed. "You threaten us with that minor stage trick?"

"Minor stage trick!" said the wizard. "That's one of the most horrendously difficult and dangerous attack spells known to modern wizardry!"

"Oh, you find it difficult, do you?" said Merc. "I warm my coffee with that spell."

"Oh, come now! Who do you think you are? Arkayne himself?"

"I'm Mercury Boltblaster," said Merc. "Son of the late Herm Boltblaster, who developed the Teal Twistor. As I said, I believe he worked it out one morning to heat his coffee. Now if you want to see a real spell, let me demonstrate the Raspberry Ray of Radical Ruination."

Merc raised his hands as if to cast the spell. I wondered if he was bluffing, if he could actually channel such a spell through the Gauntlet. Our opponent, however, was unaware that Merc had lost his powers.

"That's quite all right," he said. "I know your reputation. I'm only a sub-master and I have no wish to get involved in a spell duel I can't win."

"You should have thought of that before you attacked us," said Merc.

I caught his exaggerated intonation and picked up my part. It was the old "tough guy/nice guy" routine.

"Wait, Merc. If he's surrendering, let's give him a chance. It's Barrowight we want."

"Even so," said Merc, "he works for the assassins."

"Wait," pleaded the wizard. "All I do is step out of the shadows and blast people while Barrowight escapes through his hidden tunnel. That's all. No assassinations."

"But you're probably a card-carrying member of the Dark Magic Society," said Merc.

"No," said the wizard. "I was forced to join. This is a closed shop. But they drummed me out of the Society for doing charity work to help underprivileged children in poor neighborhoods. I'm really a nice guy. Do you think I like working for the assassins? I only took this job to pay off my student loans."

"So where does the secret passageway lead?" I asked.

"It connects with a network of tunnels that honeycombs the entire city. Barrowight can go anywhere from here."

"Will you stand aside and let us pass?"

"I'll lose my job if I do."

"And you'll lose your life if you don't," said Merc.

"Knowing the ACLU, I could lose both if I let you pass."

"Not if you get out of town quickly enough."

"Good point. I'm persuaded. Hope you catch him."

The wizard departed.

"Can you see yet?" asked Merc.

"Just fine."

"Then let's get to it."

I rolled the bookshelf aside, revealing a narrow stairway that wound downward into darkness. I willed Overwhelm to cast its light. It was an unfortunate shade of pink, but it was enough to light the way.

"We won't need that," said Merc. "I can see in the dark with the Spectacles."

"That's fine for you. What am I supposed to do?"

"Follow me."

I shut down the shining sword. "Lead on."

The stairs were worn smooth from long use. Generations of Chief Undertakers had escaped this way while their minions held off pursuers above. It was a classic big-boss maneuver.

The stairway bottomed out at a blank stone wall. Without discernible hesitation, Merc manipulated a hidden catch and a doorway opened in the wall. We stepped through into a sewer tunnel with walkways along each side and a channel of sludge in the middle. Extremely dim light globes, distantly spaced, provided extremely slight illumination.

"Which way?" I asked.

"Left," said Merc.

"How can you tell?"

"I'm tracking him by infrared. The trail is still warm. He won't get away."

"Unless he wanders through a furnace," I said.

"What?"

"Well, a furnace is very hot, so it would obscure an infrared trail. Wouldn't it?"

"Yes, Jason, I'm sure it would."

Iron grates dropped down from the ceiling before and behind us. Had we been anyone but who we were, we would have been caged in. Fortunately we were who we were and mere iron bars were not much of an obstacle. A couple of good whacks from Overwhelm cleared the way.

"Handy item, that sword of yours," said Merc.

"It's great for opening stuck jars, too."

"On the other hand, it does sap vitality from any attempt at suspense."

"What do you mean?"

"Well, being trapped in a cage down here in the dark tunnels below the city is a situation potentially brimming with dramatic tension. Can our heroes escape in time? What ingenious method will they use? That sort of thing. But when you can slice the bars up like so many cucumbers with your super-duper magic sword, it makes the whole scene something of a farce."

"Sort of like blasting everything in sight with high-energy spells whenever you run into trouble, eh?"

"I can't do that anymore," said Merc.

"No, now you just use your talents as a super-incredible ninja deathmaster kung fu acrobat from hell to demolish fully armed, battle-hardened warriors with your bare hands. Or gobble them up with your eldritch outerwear."

"I can be hurt at least. I take risks. I don't run around like a fortress on legs, fully encased in an impact-absorbing, utterly impenetrable, unencumbering, light-as-air, self-adjusting, mentally controllable suit of magic armor made by The Gods from some miracle metal that also happens to float in water.

That's pretty extreme. Makes it difficult to challenge you without resorting to contrived, artificial scenarios. Ludicrous."

"Preposterous, I'd say."

"I'd agree," said Merc.

"We're both preposterous."

"Yes. But we live in a preposterous world."

"A world that never truly tests us," I said. "We have too many props to fall back on."

"Absolutely," said Merc. "But they do keep us alive."

"Are we truly alive, Merc? Or are we merely puppets on a string, roughly hewn marionettes jerkily acting out a cosmic farce, a divine melodrama scripted by a power we don't understand, staged for the amusement of some unknown, unseen audience which laughs at our follies and smiles at our pretensions to meaning. If we are never fully tested, never endure real trials and tribulations and make hard choices that define our characters and throw in stark relief the hazy contours of our very souls, can we say that we are truly alive? If we risk nothing and lose nothing, how can we ever gain anything? How can we grow? How can we be fully human?"

"Who cares?"

"I care."

"Here, you care? We're trudging through a stinking sewer and you ask these questions?"

"Could not this stinking sewer function as a metaphor for the sordid, tawdry squalor of the human condition? And if so, what better setting in which to ask if there is not something more, something higher, finer, and nobler that we can be, aspire to, achieve? Can humanity crawl out of the sewer in which it lives?"

"I'm sure it can," said Merc. "But it's not likely to climb any higher than the gutter that feeds the sewer."

"You're a cynic, Merc."

"Thank you."

"I thought finally marrying Raella would mellow you some."

"It was more than losing Raella that made me cynical," said the wizard. "It'll take more than regaining her to make me otherwise. I've done and seen too much to believe everything will turn out well in the end."

"It happens."

"Not often."

"More often than not."

"I wouldn't say that."

"That's what makes you a cynic."

An alligator glided past us in the channel and sank beneath the surface.

"I hope we don't have to tangle with one of those monsters," I said.

"If we do, I'll just tangle it in my cloak."

"What was that you said about you can be hurt, you take risks?"

"No challenges here. We'll never develop."

"No physical challenges anyway. We need a good mental or moral challenge."

"I don't. I'm a pragmatist. I don't waste time making fine moral distinctions. You're the goody-goody of this duo."

"I think you've got a heart of gold yourself, Merc."

"Humph." Merc halted and studied the wall. "Looks like another hidden door here. He had his hands in this area, so the catch or lever must be here. Aha!"

He pressed a stone in, there was a grating click, and a section of the wall rolled aside, revealing a ladder in a narrow shaft that stretched both upward and downward.

"He went down," said Merc.

"I was afraid you'd say that." I sheathed Overwhelm, slung Gardion over my back, and mounted the ladder. "Better let me take the lead here." I started down.

"Watch yourself. We're headed for dimlock territory." I stopped my descent.

"Dimlocks?"

"Yes," said Merc, stepping onto the ladder. "Dimlocks."

"I thought they were an old wives' tale."

"Most old wives know what they're talking about."

"By dimlocks, I assume you mean those shambling, blank-eyed cannibalistic folk who live in tunnels deep under the city and only come up to the surface late at night to devour small children who don't eat their broccoli."

"Those are the ones," said Merc. "Get moving, would you? The trail isn't getting any warmer."

The Spectacles gave off a faint light, enough that I could see where to put my hands and feet.

"If these tunnels lead everywhere, why is Barrowight going down among the dimlocks? Surely he's got other hideaways."

"I'm sure he does. But you and I just took apart assassin central. I doubt the security at his other bases is much better. So he's probably hoping to lead us into a trap down here. It wouldn't surprise me to learn the ACLU and the dimlocks have some kind of mutual understanding going. After all, the assassins have a steady source of supply for the dimlocks' favorite delicacy."

"I didn't know that many parents took out contracts on their kids for not eating their vegetables."

"You'd be surprised."

The shaft went down a long way. We passed at least three intersecting horizontal shafts, but according to Merc, Barrowight had not entered any of them. He went all the way to the bottom.

So did we. The shaft ended at a wide, low, damp tunnel.

The dimlocks were waiting for us. Clad in rags,

with scaly gray skin and long black hair, they hissed and growled and waved their clubs and knives and axes and generally behaved like underground-dwelling cannibals.

I willed Overwhelm to its maximum pink glare and shouted "Luminata!" Merc put the Spectacles on wide-angle high beam. The assault of light should have put the dimlocks on the run.

All it did, however, was reveal that they were wearing dark glasses.

"It was worth a shot," I said, and we attacked.

The dimlocks were strong and ferocious fighters, but still no match for my armament or Merc's magic cloak. As usual, it wasn't so much a fight as a rout. The dimlocks retreated, vanishing into their warren of tunnels.

"Can you find Barrowight's trail?"

"Yes," said Merc, "but he can lead us on a merry chase for hours down here and there may be things lurking in the dark none of us wants to meet. I'm getting tired of this."

I yawned. "You're right. It's late, and I sail at first light. Want to call it a night? We've accomplished plenty."

"It would be good to get back before Raella misses us."

"True." I raised my voice. "Barrowight, if you can hear me, we're going home! We've had enough hide-and-seek for tonight! But don't worry, we'll call on you later at a more convenient time!"

"I'd rather we finish this now," said the Chief Undertaker, emerging from a nearby side tunnel. "Another visit from you two would put my overhead through the roof."

"You no longer have a roof," said Merc.

"My point exactly."

"Please hold your hands where we can see them," I said.

"Certainly. Now what is this all about? Storming the ACLU mansion at midnight is most irregular."

"I just want to lodge a complaint," I said.

"Go on."

"Your people have tried to kill me ever since I returned to Caratha."

"So what's your complaint?"

"That's it."

He seemed taken aback. "Surely a man of your prominence expects to be targeted for assassination occasionally? I thought perhaps you were insulted at the way my people have bungled the job so far. Let me assure you that only my most seasoned assassins have been assigned to your case. Their repeated failures are inexcusable."

"I'm not concerned about—"

"After all," continued Barrowight, "we want to give you the kind of death you deserve. Your reputation rides on it, and so does ours. You have my personal guarantee that when we finally get you, you'll go out with style. After all, you're the most important part of what we do."

"I'm flattered."

"That's the kind of dedication that made us number one in this business. Well, that, and killing all our competitors."

"Your people attacked a Raelnan diplomatic coach," said Merc. "That kind of dedication can buy you more trouble than you want."

"I apologize for the loss of the coach, Your Highness. The ACLU will compensate your government for its destruction."

"Fine," said Merc.

"If your government will pay for the damage done to the ACLU mansion tonight."

"Not likely," said Merc.

"I want to know who you're working for," I said.

"I can't tell you," said Barrowight. "We adhere

strictly to a Professional Code of Silence. It would be unethical for me to violate client confidentiality by revealing that information."

"You kill people for a living and talk about ethics?"

"You kill people, too, Cosmo." He indicated the fallen dimlocks. "We're in the same line of work, only I'm more honest about it. I don't wrap it up in sanctimonious pietics."

"I know the difference between us, if you don't. But look, all I want is a name. If somebody has a score to settle with me, I want to deal with him face-to-face, not have assassins skulking in the shadows all around me."

"Thieves skulk. Assassins don't skulk. We lurk. There's a difference."

"The name, please."

"I won't reveal it. Threaten me, torture me, kill me if you like, but I simply will not give you that information. The instant the ACLU violates its guarantee of client anonymity, we lose all the goodwill we've developed over the years. People hire us because they don't want to be personally connected with the deed. We have to respect that or our client base dries up. What you want me to do threatens the very existence of the organization I lead. I will not violate my duty to my fellow assassins."

"Feel strongly about that, do you?"

"Yes."

"I feel strongly about people trying to kill me. Now if you're concerned about threats to the ACLU, you ought to be concerned about Prince Mercury and myself. Tonight was just a stroll in the park for us. If we really get worked up, we can destroy the ACLU from top to bottom, starting with you."

"That would give me something fun to do while I'm in town," said Merc, cracking his knuckles.

"Do you believe me?" I asked.

"Yes," said Barrowight.

"If you can't reveal your client to me, I'll respect that. In return, you call off your killers. One more attack on me or anyone close to me, and Merc and I will be all over you like ants on molasses. The ACLU will be an unpleasant memory inside a week."

Barrowight drew himself up to full height. "The ACLU has never failed to carry out a contract. Our honor demands full performance. Our reputation is at stake."

"Your existence is at stake," said Merc.

"We don't succumb to threats."

"It wasn't threats that brought your house down tonight," I said. "It won't be threats that finish you."

"You don't understand who you're dealing with," said Barrowight, still playing it tough.

"We took out the Dark Magic Society," said Merc. "Your outfit is a bunch of Pup Scouts by comparison."

"Think about it," I said.

The assassin boss did, and forced a smile. "Perhaps you have the right of it. We do sometimes declare certain targets off limits as a matter of policy. Prince Ronaldo, for example. I think it likely your name is on that proscribed list, Cosmo. Indeed, I am sure of it."

"And the contract?"

"Void. I'll inform the client tonight and refund the fee. Please accept my humblest apologies for any inconvenience we may have caused you. To make up for the trouble, I'll send you a gift certificate good for a free assassination. If you ever need to be rid of someone and don't wish to soil your own hands, we'll be happy to take care of it."

I spat. "Don't do me any favors. Just stay out of my way."

"Agreed. Shall we shake on it?"

"Isn't that a poison ring you're wearing?" asked Merc as Barrowight offered his hand.

"Why, so it is," said the assassin, snatching his hand back. "Silly of me to forget I had it on."

"We'll skip the handshake," I said. "Just remember our deal."

10

"You look tired," said Solana. "Did you not sleep well?"

"You might say that."

Our coach rattled and rolled toward Waterfront. Involved in meetings with her staff well into the night, Raella apparently remained unaware of the excursion with Merc. At least, she hadn't said anything about it when the royal couple came to the embassy courtyard to see Solana and me off on our mission. Of course I had no idea what words might have passed in private between Queen and Consort. Raella would find out eventually, but by then I'd be out to sea, and making explanations would be Merc's problem.

"Fancy send-off committee," I said, noting an ornamented green-and-gold stretch carriage with four white horses in harness parked near Skipjammer's ship. It looked out of place on the docks.

As we exited our vehicle a liveried servant approached me and bowed.

"Master Cosmo, my master requests a moment of your time."

Taking a closer look, I recognized the fancy green *S* on a gold field that was the sign of the House of Slash, one of Caratha's most eminent noble families. That piqued my interest.

"Very well," I said.

"This way, please," said the servant.

"What's going on?" asked Solana. "What could Lord Slash want with you?"

"That's what I want to find out. Should only take a minute."

Skipjammer noted our arrival and bounded down the gangplank.

"The carriage has been waiting over half an hour for you, sir," he volunteered.

"Interesting."

The servant held the carriage door, helped me step inside, and closed the door behind me. The curtains were drawn, but the interior was lit by a glowglobe in the ceiling and a shaded desk lamp. The leather seats had thick cushions, and there was a console with built-in orbavision, spellfax, and spellular phone.

A handsome, firm-jawed man in business attire put aside some papers and extended his hand to me. "I'm Damian Slash," he said. "I'm pleased to meet you."

"Jason Cosmo. Likewise." His grip was strong.

"A drink?" he asked, indicating the minibar.

"No thanks."

"I'll get right to the point because I know you're eager to depart on your semisecret mission to Rancor, which I know all about from my private intelligence sources. I head a group of 'concerned citizens' who are very interested in your future."

"That's very flattering. How so?"

"We support Prince Ronaldo. We like his policies. We are disturbed by what we read about you in the *Book of All Kings*. We view you as a threat."

"The *Book of All Kings*?"

"Don't play dumb. We have—had, rather—eyes inside the League. We know about the *Book*. We know who you claim to be."

"I don't claim to be anyone."

"Forgive me. I should say who some claim you to be. The Mighty Champion reborn. We have no problem with such talk in League and Raelnan circles. They can believe whatever they want. But in Caratha, such a claim has political significance. And politics is a dangerous game."

"The sort of game where groups of concerned citizens hire professional assassins to take care of persons they view as threats because of the genealogical speculations in musty old books?"

"Exactly. You see, my associates and I prefer not to believe such claims as might upset the present order in Caratha, and we'd like to deprive anyone else of the chance to believe such dangerous things. Surgical removal seemed the most appropriate means to that end."

"Didn't work out so well, did it?"

"You are as formidable as your reputation suggests," agreed Slash. "Master Barrowight contacted us late last night with the distressing news that he could not honor his contract. That's why I'm talking with you personally."

"When violence fails, try persuasion."

"Exactly."

"Natalia was your sister, wasn't she?" I asked suddenly.

Slash frowned. "She was. The adventurer of the family. My dear sister hunted you for the Dark Magic Society's reward. Had she been more successful, it would have saved me a bit of bother."

"She died fighting at my side," I said. "In the end, she proved to be a woman of honor. I assume that sense of honor is characteristic of all the House of Slash. Or am I off the mark?"

"Our honor is sacred to us," said Slash, nodding.

"Then my guess is you're here to pledge your honor and reach some kind of agreement with me."

"You are about to leave Caratha on that ship. We want your promise never to return. We want to preserve the status quo. Your presence in Caratha, in light of what the *Book of All Kings* reveals, is a threat to the status quo, which must be preserved."

"I don't want to rule Caratha."

"You are wise. But remain in Caratha and you will become the center of a raging storm of intrigue. Rabble-rousers and troublemakers will see you as a rallying point. You will be thrust into the dangerous, dirty game of politics whether you seek it or not. And we will be forced to eliminate you. Far better for all if you simply depart from the scene voluntarily."

"I'm not that easy to eliminate," I said.

"But are you easy to persuade?"

"I don't plan to dwell here any longer, but whether my affairs will bring me here again from time to time I cannot say."

"See that they do not."

"Let's not get into the tired threats routine. If you want to make a gentlemen's agreement, I can assure you I have no interest in Carathan politics, direct or indirect. I support Ronaldo too. I absolutely do not desire, plan, or intend to pursue my supposed claim to the throne. You'll have to be satisfied with that."

"If you keep this promise not to involve yourself in Carathan affairs, my group will not do anything else to harm you. We bear you no personal ill will. Indeed, I admire your accomplishments."

"Thank you. Do we have enough of a bargain to shake on it?"

"We do."

We shook hands.

"If that's all then, Lord Slash, my ship is about to sail."

"Bon voyage."

I exited and Slash's driver snapped the reins. The carriage pulled away rapidly.

"What was that about?" asked Solana. "Anything to do with our mission?"

"No. Lord Slash wanted to ask a personal favor of me."

"I see," she said, in a tone indicating she did not.

"I knew his sister Natalia," I said.

"Oh. Of course. I realize there is more to it than that, but my class and good breeding prevent me from asking prying, personal questions."

"I know."

We boarded the *Miracle*.

"Welcome aboard, sir!" said Skipjammer. "Watch your step, rotted plank there. Allow me to introduce my crew. This is Caleb Topspinner, my first mate." He grabbed by the arm an old man who was about to step off the gangplank into the water. He looked to be about a hundred years old and only vaguely aware of where he was.

"Good to meet you," I said.

"Mumsy prunes and soft-shell clams," he replied, nodding vigorously. "The cats vail and hock lax with good farfel," he added.

"I see," I said. I turned to Skipjammer. "He's your first mate?"

"Indeed, sir! A highly experienced sailor, sir!"

"Maybe a bit too experienced. Now, if I've got this right, the first mate takes command should something happen to the captain."

"Correct, sir!"

"Embowered pokes of girning terrapins are blithing the snorkeled bladderworts," Topspinner earnestly added.

"Well, nice to know the ship will be in good hands."

"Good hands, indeed!" said Skipjammer, wiping a long thread of spittle from the first mate's chin with his handkerchief and sitting the old man down on a bench. "Now this is Patchwork Phil, the bosun."

Perhaps half the age of the venerable first mate, Patchwork Phil was much scarred and well weathered. He had stringy gray hair and muscles like frayed cables. He was missing his left arm and ear, his right leg below the knee, and wore an eye patch.

"How do you do," I said.

"Good to see you again," said Phil, flashing a yellow-toothed grin.

"Have we met?"

"Good to see you again," said Phil, flashing a yellow-toothed grin.

"What does a bosun do?" I asked.

"Good to see you again." He left out the grin this time.

"The bosun is in charge of odd supplies and daily maintenance," said Skipjammer, hurrying us along. "Carry on, Phil."

"Good to see you again," said the bosun.

The captain led us toward a tall, lean, muscular woman with dark skin, darker eyes, and a pearl pinned to her nose.

"This is Coptris of Pharistan, my second mate," said Skipjammer.

"Pleased to meet you," I said.

She spat in my face.

"She hates men," said Skipjammer. "She killed her father, two uncles, and seven brothers in Pharistan before running off to sea."

Coptris glared at me defiantly.

"What a remarkable accomplishment," I said.

She spat in my face again. We moved on.

"This is Old Blue, the best sea cook on the salty sea, sir!"

Old Blue was a fat, grizzled, dark blue Cyrillan with a grin as big as a walrus. He was stirring a thick, chunky liquid bubbling in an iron pot over the cooking fire. The rim of the pot was coated with a thick black crust of sediment from meals past.

"Howdy now!" he boomed. "I done got the lunchtime gumbo mash a-cooking up good and hot, yessir, uh-huh—mmmmm! In here we got some good bacon, we got the spitbeans, we got crawdads, we got the secret Cyrillan herbs and spices that make it cook up good, mmmm-hmmm, yessir, I guarantee that! We got fresh mud lobster from the river bottom, we got fat shrimps, we got the chokefish chunks, and dog gizzards, yessir, it's sure enough good! You cut you up some old mushy vegetables, you get some kewpie squash, you stew up green tomatoes, you put in the red-hot devil pepper and blue kalumba sauce in there with some fine chopped mango. Yessir, heapin' good, uh-huh! Throw in the pig toes for flavor and three cat tails, but you got to done take the fur offa them tails first, yessir! Half a gallon rancid wine, and a pinch of paprika." He sipped a bit of the bubbling brew from the spoon, grimaced, coughed, spat, and regained his grin. "Damn good! Needs salt, though!" He threw in four fistfuls of rock salt. "Just you wait until dinnertime, you can't wait I know, uh-huh, mmmmmmmm-hmmm!"

"This would be the hot meals served regularly that you mentioned?" I asked Skipjammer dubiously.

"As promised, sir! Believe me, when you're out at sea far from any land and it's the only food around, it tastes better than it sounds."

"I don't doubt it."

We mounted the unsteady ladder to the poop deck, where a sandy-haired sailor was slumped against the wheel. Skipjammer shook him roughly awake.

"Whazzit? Where? How? Oh, hi, Cap'n. I must have dozed off."

"I want you to meet Jason Cosmo and his companion, Lady Solana. Master Cosmo, this is Nodkin Blinkbutter, my helmsman."

"Good to meet you," I said, extending my hand.

"It's good to meet—" Blinkbutter stopped in midsentence, asleep on his feet. Skipjammer kicked him in the shin. "—you and the lady," continued the helmsman.

"Does he do that often?" I asked Skipjammer.

"What?"

"Fall asleep."

"Usually only every fifteen minutes or so, sir. But he doesn't stay out long. I'll show you to your cabin now, if you like."

"Cabin?" said Solana. "Singular? One cabin for both of us?"

Our cabin was on the port side, under the poop deck. Two bunks, made up with bed linen and mints on the pillows, stood side by side against the bulkhead that ran along the centerline of the ship. In the middle of the room was a polished wooden table, bolted to the floor, and a pair of wooden chairs. Against the sternward bulkhead was a writing desk, chair, and a couple of brassbound chests. The square portholes were closed, though with the curtains back to admit light. An unlit lantern hung from a hook in the ceiling.

"I hope the arrangement will be satisfactory, sir. If you want separate cabins, I can evict one of the mates or let milady bunk with Coptris."

"This will be fine," I said. Skipjammer bowed and exited, closing the door behind him.

"Fine?" said Solana. "This is somewhat improper."

"I've nothing to hide," I said. "You've seen me tied to a tree wearing naught but daffodil honey."

"You've not seen me in such attire," she said, a little stiffly.

"Nor need I do so," I said. "Appealing though the prospect is. We can work out the details to preserve modesty and propriety, but I think it best for us to share a cabin for the sake of confidential discussions."

"What do we need to discuss confidentially?"

"The mission, perhaps. Or other topics."

I put my arms around Solana and kissed her, once again savoring that incredible smoldering sensation all through my body that I had enjoyed yesterday in Lowtide.

She responded with initial enthusiasm, then jerked away.

"Jason," she said. "Please don't make too much of what happened yesterday. I was carried away by the heat of the moment. You're an attractive man. I have much respect for you. But we have an important job to do and I don't think we should get involved with each other in this context."

"Of course," I said coolly.

"Please don't be insulted."

"Not at all," I said. "I was out of line. Forgive me."

"You understand, don't you?"

"Of course. You're absolutely right. So what do you make of Skipjammer and his crew?"

"The most improbable lot of mariners I can imagine. We'll be lucky to reach the Seagates without sinking."

"The Seagates? What about the end of the pier?"

Outside, a man screamed. This sound was followed by a loud thud and crack. We rushed from the cabin. There was a new man-sized hole in the main deck just starboard of the mainmast.

"Who was it?" called Skipjammer from the forecastle.

"Learson, Cap'n. He slipped from the rigging and fell right through the deck."

"Well, someone go below and see if he's all right! A bother it will be if he's knocked on through the bottom! We're taking on enough water as it is!"

I crossed the deck and called up to Skipjammer. "Are you sure this vessel is seaworthy?"

"We're putting out to sea in it, aren't we?"

"What was that you said about taking on water?"

"Not to worry! Five crew members man the bilge pumps night and day and another four stay busy patching leaks. As long as they don't slack up, we'll stay afloat, sir!"

"Is that standard procedure?"

"On the *Miracle* it is! Ahoy, mates! Let's cast off and sail!"

Two sailors got stranded on the dock when they went ashore to unhitch the mooring lines and waved sadly to their mates as they were left behind. Another crewman fell overboard and never surfaced, though no one seemed to notice. Up above, the bottom fell out of the crow's nest and the sailor on watch fell a good fifteen feet before his foot caught in the loop of a line. He swung helplessly while the crew raised the sails. They rigged them improperly the first three times, but finally got it right after a reproachful lecture from Skipjammer in which he explained which way was port and which way was starboard and how to tell a halyard from a capstan. Helmsman Blinkbutter fell asleep, almost causing us to ram the ship in the neighboring berth, but he awakened in time to avert disaster and we made it into the harbor.

Reading the buoys wrong, we overran a small pleasure craft and failed to give proper right of way to a harbor patrol cutter until they fired a couple of warning shots into our bow with their mangonels. After that we cut doughnuts across the harbor for half an hour, finally making it through the Seagates with a tow and an armed navy escort.

"Open sea at last!" proclaimed Skipjammer.

"Thank The Gods," I said, retching again. My knuckles were white and stiff from clutching the rail for the last two hours and I felt as though I had been repeatedly punched in the gut by an ill-tempered troll.

"Don't thank them yet," said Solana, leaning up from her own violent regurgitation. Her face was an unflattering lime hue. "Is it too late to change our plans and go overland?"

"I think so."

"I was afraid you'd say that."

"You'll live."

She leaned over the rail again. "Yes, but how long?" she said when she was finished.

11

Twelve days out of Caratha, the *Miracle* sailed the rough, wine-dark waters of the Broken Coast, where savage breakers crashed against brooding, red-orange cliffs. The jumbled heights were pocked, cracked, and gouged as if defaced by the picks and hammers of vandalous giants.

That was one theory.

Others held that the Broken Coast was broken by the awesome energies unleashed when The Gods and Demon Lords battled here during the Age of War. The dispute between these camps was fierce. The Royal Carathan Geological Society had heard many thoroughly researched, painstakingly detailed, agonizingly long papers with titles like "Picky, Picky, Picky: Hammering Away at the Discredited 'God and Demons' Theory of Broken Coast Seaward Cliff Features," on the one hand, and "The Undeniable Impact of Divine and Infernal Confrontation on Shoreline Geological Development: New Findings Deal a Giant Blow to the 'Giant' Theory," on the other. The struggle was also hotly fought in public lectures, private confrontations, and the secret proceedings of faculty tenure committees. Which view would eventually prevail was hard to tell. To me they were just cliffs.

Some distance from the shore, leaping kula-kula fish flashed silvery in the sunlight and trilled "kula-kula!"

as they eluded a pack of porpoises. The flesh of the
kula-kula is highly toxic due to the poisonous kula oil
that the fish produce in their poisonous kula glands,
and it is well known that while porpoises often pursue
them, they make a point of never catching them. Why
then porpoises chase kula-kula is a question naturalists
have not yet answered. Either the porpoises are simply being playful, or they do it so that the kula-kula
will leap, flash, and trill, giving passengers on passing
ships something to remark upon besides the crumbling
red-orange cliffs of the Broken Coast.

I was too busy disgorging breakfast over the rail.
Sailing with Skipjammer wasn't as bad as flying, but
my stomach wasn't making fine distinctions. Still, I
wasn't as bad off as Solana, who had been unable
even to stand for the past week. Her strong arcane
connection with fire made her exceptionally susceptible to seasickness. I spent several hours each day tend-
ing to her in her misery.

Otherwise, I occupied myself by helping Skipjammer and his sailors. They needed it. I knew nil about
sailing and the sea, but that put me at no disadvantage
with this crew. I could tie knots, swing a hammer, coil
ropes, and give first aid, all skills much in demand.

I also did everyone's arteries a favor and threw Old
Blue's salt stores overboard. He kept his pot of gumbo
mash cooking at all times, as he had continuously for
the last ten years. He ladled our meals out to us three
times a day, poured the inevitable leftovers back in
the pot, and added whatever he felt was needed to
replenish the stock and improve the flavor. This
mainly meant enough salt to preserve a rhino. I was
convinced Old Blue's tongue was lacking key taste
buds. Everyone else had to drink straight seawater
with meals to wash the salty gumbo taste from their
mouths. I think it was Blue's cooking more than the
motion of the ship that kept me nauseated.

"Feeling better today, sir?" asked Skipjammer, joining me as I wiped my mouth clean.

"Not by much," I said miserably.

"We're making good time with this wind today, sir. I think we'll make up the seven days we lost sailing west because the charts were upside down. I still don't know how that happened."

"One of life's little mysteries. You know, I was just thinking there would be little left of a ship dashed against those cliffs."

"Indeed there would not, sir. And we shall do our best to avoid them, lest we be smashed like an eggshell! I sailed an eggshell once, sir, and let me tell you, it is a trying thing indeed! When the *Miracle* sank the first time, I was marooned on an island where roosted the roc, sir, a bird of rare splendor and immense size. The roc feeds elephants to its young, sir, and soars as high as the sun! Have you ever seen an elephant?"

"A kind of large pig, isn't it?"

"Just so, sir, and a tribe of men couldn't devour one in a week. But the roc, sir, can carry a grown elephant in each talon, at least when it manages to catch two standing very close together. Vicious bird. Ought to be hunted to extinction. It typically lays three to five eggs in its mountaintop nest, but the first hatchling out rolls the other eggs over the edge and sends them tumbling down the mountain. That, sir, is how I came upon an eggshell, sir! It floated well enough, but tended to capsize. It took me eight weeks, sir, to reach safety in Canabrista!"

"Astounding," I said.

"Moreso, it was astonishing, sir!" Skipjammer related all the hardships he endured on his egg-borne odyssey. Hunger, thirst, exposure, storms, boredom, and a pack of man-eating harpsichord seals could not stop him, so great was his will to survive.

When the tale wound down, I observed that if we

were to hit the cliffs—and they did seem to be getting closer—probably no trace of us would ever be found.

"Not so, sir! We·are now in the outer precincts of sunken Aqualon, sir, that fabled land flooded by The Gods as punishment for crimes long forgotten. Not a vessel founders on this coast but that they note and salvage it, sir!"

"I'd rather not be salvaged. Could you perhaps have a word with your helmsman? I think he's asleep again."

Skipjammer followed my gaze to the snoring figure of Nodkin Blinkbutter slumped against the wheel.

"Confound his narcoleptic hide!" he said. "I told him to drink stronger coffee!"

Skipjammer went aft to awaken the snoozing sailor and I offered up yet another prayer to the Sea God, Surflord. I was tempted to walk to Rancor from here. It might be safer.

Because it was late in the season, we did not cross the open water, but hugged the shoreline. Sailing east beyond the Broken Coast, we would pass the associated fishing villages of the Federation of Independent Sea Harvesters. Next we'd put in at the Brythalian town of Nerak. Then we'd enter Zastrian waters, passing Kielfa and Port Kylas, navigating the Spendthrift Isles, and finally rounding the Cape of Good Prospects to sail up Bonerattle Bay to Rancor. If all went well, which it wouldn't, the journey would take no more than a month.

I didn't want to think about what might happen to the Superwand during that time, assuming it actually was in Rancor. Yet overland travel would take even longer and require traversing the treacherous Lumpwad Mountains of southern Zastria. Aerial transit was out because a flying carpet required a master wizard to pilot and the only one available was Queen Raella, who was not exactly available. Riding gryphons or dragons was also impractical, and no one had yet bred a dependable winged horse.

"Ho! Surface man!" shouted a tinkling voice, rousing me from my reverie.

My eyes widened when I realized the speaker was a mermaid a dozen yards out. She easily kept pace with the ship and didn't seem at all bothered by the high waves. Her fishtail was shimmering blue, as was her long hair, and her skin shone like mother-of-pearl. She waved to me. I waved back. She blew me a kiss and vanished into the depths.

Skipjammer returned to my side.

"I just saw a mermaid," I said, expecting disbelief.

"Not surprising, sir! They frequent these waters and often frisk about flirting with sailors. Particularly those of the *Miracle,* sir."

"Why is that?"

"Because the briny blood of the merfolk flows in my veins, sir!"

"What?"

Skipjammer worked himself up for another interminable tale. "My grandmother's sire, sir, was a merman of Aqualon, a noble prince beneath the waves. Indeed, sir, when he wooed the winsome Lady Phaedriope, my great-grandmother, in the moonlit coves of Lyth, he laid pearls and shells and all the treasures of the sea at her feet and bade the dolphins dance and sing for her amusement. Their daughter, my Granny Wetsplash, had skin like fine pale jade, sir, and silky green tresses dark as kelp. She breathed water as easily as air and spent her last years in Aqualon itself, after burying her husband and seeing my fair mother Mydrian married to my sire. He was a far-ranging mariner himself, Amalkin Skipjammer was, and my lady mother with him. Indeed, sir, I was born on the storm-tossed deck of a carrock daring the alien waters of the Eastern Ocean. It's the salty water of the sea itself which flows in my veins, sir!"

"You just said it was the briny blood of the merfolk which flowed in your veins."

"The same substance. And the fact has proved my salvation on many an occasion. I recall the third time the *Miracle* sank. It was off Cape Harakan during the great hurricane of eighty-four. Such a storm, sir, as was never seen before or since! Waves sixty feet high! Winds that bent mountains like palm trees! Whole cities washed away! And I was caught in the midst in full sail, sir! There was nothing to do but run before the wind, sir, wherever it took us! For twenty days, sir, we . . ."

It was six more days and sixty more tales of Malachi Skipjammer to Nerak. We'd thus far had mild weather for the season, but winter officially began in two days and we couldn't expect our luck to hold.

Nerak was a small town at the south end of the Brythalian Corridor, a narrow strip of hilly territory connecting landlocked Brythalia, over two hundred miles inland, with the Indigo Sea. King Rubric, the Brythalian monarch, dreamed of challenging the great maritime powers for control of the sea-lanes. His scheme involved diverting the mighty River Longwash down the Corridor and thus stealing the river trade from Caratha by stealing the river. The digging was already under way, but Rubric's engineers were terminally incompetent and had thus far succeeded in little more than burying hundreds of workers in collapsing trenches and flooding large tracts of prime farmland.

Phase two of Rubric's grand scheme was the construction of a gigantic war fleet. Brythalia was blessed with ancient forests and many lakes. Lured by generous bribes, master Carathan shipbuilders had gone to Brythalia and used the wealth of timber to build a hundred galleys on the forest lakes. And there the Brythalian navy remained, undisputed ruler of those tiny, isolated bodies of water.

Someday Rubric's armada might sail down his grand canal to wrest the oceans from their masters of the past thousand years, but meanwhile Nerak was a place of outcasts. The big shipping companies like Corundum Trading and the House of Shane shunned the port, leaving it to the pirates, smugglers, and slavers who gladly shared their booty with the royal governor in return for a safe base of operations.

The place had a sordid look fully in keeping with its clientele. A haze of oily smoke from a score of chimneys hung over the town, which sprawled over the slopes of three clustered hills like the emaciated body of a murder victim. The wooden buildings, mostly taverns and brothels, leaned this way and that like unsteady drunks. The governor's keep, balanced unsteadily on the least eroded of the hills, looked as though the pressure of the afternoon sunlight might bring it down. The wharves were in poor repair, but ten ships had berthed there anyway. A space was open at the last pier.

Perched on the prow, Skipjammer spread his arms wide.

"Nerak, sir! As vile a den of iniquity as you will find! Nerak! A place of low cunning and black treachery, sudden violence and cruel laughter, rampant greed and gluttonous appetites! Nerak, sir!" He hopped down. "I know the place well."

"Just get us to shore," said Solana weakly. "Please. I long to stand on solid ground."

Patting Solana's arm consolingly, Skipjammer appraised the moored ships. "I must say this is an unusual conglomeration of corsairs for this time of year, sir! I'd expect them to be working the sunny waters of the south, but we have a veritable roll call of infamy here! The *Blackguard* and *Deception* of Lawless Lawler. The *Jaundice* and the *Scurvy*. That's the Malad brothers, Jacques and Louis. Toracan's *Conspirator*. Gypsum's *Sea Demon*. And look there! It's the *Notorious* of Tannis Darkwolf, the Pirate Queen!"

I perked up at that. She was the one who had almost carried off Sapphrina and Rubis. I wanted to get a look at her.

"A million crowns, her head is worth!" said Skipjammer. He turned to me. "A tenth the value of your own, I think."

"True," I said. "But she's done more to earn her price than I did for mine."

"If you say so."

"I must meet these pirates," I said.

"Here?" asked Solana. "Why? Best to avoid pirates until we reach Rancor."

"If I can convince them of my bona fides now, we'll have an easier time in Rancor."

"Too risky," insisted Solana. "The meeting may go sour. We can't take the chance."

"We must," I said. "Captain, can you make introductions?"

Skipjammer followed the exchange with puzzled interest. "Aye, sir," he said. "But don't you know them already? Tales of your pirating exploits are told from Xorth to Praetora, sir!"

"None of those tales happen to be true," I said.

"No? Yet if you are not a pirate, sir, why do you seek their company?"

"To convince them I am a pirate."

"Perhaps I am a bit slow, sir. Did you not just tell me you are *not* a pirate?"

"I did."

"But you would have the pirates believe that you are?"

"Yes."

"Then say no more, sir! Leave it to me!"

Skipjammer escorted Solana and me to the Big Booty Burger Bar. Home of the world-famous Booty

Burger, it was ~~where~~ the top pirates partied when they were in town. To aid our infiltration, I wore a red vest and bright blue pants over the Cosmosuit, and a bandanna borrowed from Skipjammer's sea chest. He was even more gaudily garbed. Solana wore a cloak of plain gray, with the hood up to conceal her remarkable hair.

"You'll wait outside," I told her. "If we get into trouble, you're our ace in the hole."

"Right," She slipped into a recess across the street. Skipjammer and I entered the bar.

The Big Booty was constructed like a great feasting hall with a firepit in the middle. Over a hundred cutthroats ate and drank lustily at six long tables beside the pit. Serving wenches in stylized Spandex pirate costumes aglitter with bangles and sequins kept the platters and mugs full when they weren't being snatched into some lecherous corsair's lap for a rum-soaked kiss and a bit of rude handling.

None paid heed as we entered. We paused by the door, studying the crowd. They were a ragtag lot, scarred and sun-darkened, dressed in bloodstained finery, bedecked with gaudy jewelry. Many were short an eye, an ear, a hand, or some other bit of anatomy. All were visibly armed.

The chieftains drank and argued at the far end table. I started in that direction. Skipjammer restrained me.

"You can't just walk up to them, sir," he whispered. "Let me handle it." He grabbed a passing girl by the arm. "Ho there, lass! Where's a place for me and my friend?"

The girl pointed to an open spot at one of the tables. We sat down with a group of pirates wolfing down goatburgers and fried rat tails with ketchup.

"Ho there, mates!" said Skipjammer affably, slapping a couple of the corsairs on the back and sending what was in their mouths spewing across the table. "Good to see you lads!"

"Do I know you, chowderbeak?" groused one of the pirates, who had a thick jaw, no nose, and a large ruby hanging from his right ear.

"Malachi Skipjammer, my friend! How's the ale?"

"Don't drink ale. We're pirates. Drink rum."

"Rum it is, then! I didn't catch your name, friend."

"They call me Nosy Bill, on account of I got no nose."

"So I notice, my friend."

"I'm sensitive about me nose."

"Indeed, my friend! Though I doubt your nose is too sensitive."

"What? Are you making fun of my nose?"

"Of course not," said Skipjammer. He picked up a rat fry, thought twice, and put it back. "You haven't got a nose. How could I make fun of your nose if you haven't got one?"

"Well, all right, then. You a pirate?"

"Indeed I am, my snoutless friend! I am a pirate most piratical!"

"Good. Thought you might be a smuggler. You've got a smuggler face. We don't like smugglers in here. Just pirates."

"I assure you, I am a pirate. I love pirating! Nothing like it!"

Skipjammer knocked back half a bottle of rum in a single gulp to settle the matter. Nosy Bill nodded his approval.

"Quite a gathering of the greats," said Skipjammer, nodding toward the head table. "What's the occasion?"

"You mean, you don't know?" said Nosy Bill accusingly.

"I'm afraid I don't, friend."

"Don't you read your *Freebooter's Forum*?"

"My subscription lapsed," lied Skipjammer. "I've been working the waters down Khorfa way."

"You must have put in at Rancor on your way back here. So how could you not know?"

"Well, my friend, if you'll tell me what it is you think I don't know, I'll gladly tell you if I know it or not. Then you'll know too."

"How's that again?"

"I shouldn't have to repeat myself, you nostrilless ninny."

"Who are you calling a ninny?"

"You, of course."

Nosy Bill wiggled his fingers in an odd way and tugged his left ear. Skipjammer did not respond. The pirate squinted at him and spat.

"You're no pirate! You don't know the secret sign!"

A hush fell over the Big Booty Burger Bar at Nosy Bill's outburst. All eyes turned to where Skipjammer and I sat.

"He's a bloody smuggler!" shouted Nosy Bill into the silence. "He doesn't know the secret sign!"

The chieftains whispered among themselves.

"Bring him here," said Lawless Lawler, a big, hairy man with a voice low and harsh, like a congested bear. "His friend too."

Two large pirates seized each of us and shoved us to the front of the hall.

"Great work," I hissed sarcastically.

Skipjammer cocked an eyebrow. "You wanted to meet them, didn't you?"

12

The pirates dragged us roughly to the chieftains' table. The six leaders regarded us contemptuously. Lawler's glare would have penetrated plate armor. The dark-eyed Malad brothers fingered their knives. Blue-skinned Toracan swilled wine from his goblet, but kept his unpatched eye on us. Pale Gypsum stroked his chin and adjusted his own eye patch. Sultry Tannis sneered.

"So, you dogs claim you're pirates?" asked Lawless Lawler.

"They're not pirates!" said Nosy Bill.

"We are, sir!" protested Skipjammer. "We are pirates in the first degree! I myself have been a pirate since the age of three!"

"If you're a pirate," said Lawler, "then answer a few questions."

"Gladly."

"Who sets pirate policy?"

"The Council of Free Captains, sir, with their decisions ratified at the biennial Congress of Cutthroats."

The chieftains swapped knowing glances.

"What's a captain's standard share?" continued Lawler.

"A third, with first pick of the booty."

"Penalty for cheatin' your mates at dice?"

"Loss of an ear to the ax."

152

"Secret pirate password?"

"Yo-ho, ho-ho."

"What does *X* mark?"

"The spot."

"What do dead men tell?"

"No tales."

"Yo-ho-ho and a bottle of . . . what?"

"Rum."

"Prisoners we're tired of walk the . . . ?"

"Plank."

"Aha! Gotcha!"

"But that's a trick question," continued Skipjammer. "It's a myth. We don't really make them walk the plank, we just throw them overboard."

Lawler grunted. "Give five synonyms for a pirate. In alphabetical order. Quickly now!"

"Buccaneer, corsair, freebooter, sea robber, and, let's see, privateer," rattled Skipjammer.

"That wasn't in order. And a privateer is not quite the same thing as a pirate, is it now?"

"Close enough," said Skipjammer. "A question of perspective."

"Maybe so. So why don't you know the secret pirate hand sign?"

"I do know it, sir!"

"You didn't respond to Nosy Bill there."

"That's right!" said Nosy Bill. "He didn't!"

"Maybe I didn't want to," said Skipjammer.

"What? Why not?"

"Well, we can't go flashing the secret sign to just anyone, can we? It wouldn't stay secret for long if we did that."

"Well, maybe not," conceded Lawler. "So what?"

"How do I know Nosy Bill here is a pirate?" said Skipjammer.

"What do you mean? Of course he's a pirate!"

"Of course I'm a pirate!" said Nosy Bill.

"How can you tell?" insisted Skipjammer.

"Well, he looks like a pirate," said Lawler.

"Anyone can look like a pirate, sir," said Skipjammer. "All you need are bright clothes, gaudy jewelry, and maybe an eye patch."

"Then why don't you look like a pirate?" demanded Lawler.

"Yeah?" said Nosy Bill.

"I do," said Skipjammer, patting his orange vest and green-and-purple-striped pantaloons. "Who but a pirate would wear these colors together?"

"A smuggler," said Lawler. "You've got a smuggler's face."

"The clothes make the man," said Skipjammer.

"Well, true enough. What's that got to do with Nosy Bill?"

"I'm just not sure he's a pirate," said Skipjammer, shaking his head.

"Well, he sails with us on our pirate ship and helps us rob merchant vessels," said Lawler. "That pretty much makes him a pirate, don't it?"

"It does!" said Nosy Bill.

"Well, if you're convinced," said Skipjammer. "But I wouldn't be so hasty."

"Why not?" demanded Lawler.

"Yeah, why not?" said Nosy Bill.

"Just look at him," said Skipjammer.

Lawler and his colleagues studied Nosy Bill intently. The disfigured pirate squirmed uncomfortably under their scrutiny.

"What about him?" said Lawler at last. "As I said, he looks like a pirate."

"Perhaps too much like a pirate," said Skipjammer.

"What do you mean?" asked Lawler, studying Nosy Bill again in case he had missed something.

"Maybe he's someone who isn't a pirate but wants you to think he is. And it seems, sir, that he has you convinced."

"I am a pirate!" said Nosy Bill.

"Quiet, you!" snapped Lawler.

"Don't you see?" said Skipjammer. "If you weren't a pirate but you wanted to look like one, you'd probably get carried away in putting together your pirate look. Just like Nosy Bill here. He's got no nose! As if he lost it in battle or something! Excessive, don't you think?"

"I did lose it in battle!" protested Nosy Bill. "You were there, Cap'n! I lost me nose saving your life!"

"Quiet!" snarled Lawler. "Yes. Yes, I see. Well, if he's not a pirate, what is he?"

Skipjammer shrugged. "A spy, perhaps."

"A spy!" said Nosy Bill.

"There! We've hit it on the first guess, sir!"

"I'm no spy!" said Nosy Bill.

"You just said that you were," said Skipjammer. "Which is it?"

"Well, if that don't beat all!" said Lawler. "Nosy Bill a spy!"

The assembled pirates grumbled, cursed, and shouted. They didn't think kindly of spies.

"I'm not a spy!" whined Nosy Bill. "I've sailed with you for years, Cap'n Lawler!"

"Been at it for years, has he?" said Skipjammer. "Shameful. Where's he from? Where are you from, Nosy Bill?"

"Zastria, originally," said Nosy Bill. "What's that got to do with it?"

"There you have it, sir," said Skipjammer. "He's a Zastrian spy."

"A stinking Zastrian spy!" growled Lawler. "What do we do to stinking Zastrian spies, boys?"

"We skin 'em alive!" roared all the pirates.

"We do?" said Lawler. "I thought we roasted 'em."

"It's stinking Carathan spies we roast," said Jacques Malad softly. "Zastrians we skin." He toyed with his knife. "Slowly."

"Very slowly," added Louis.

"Then take him away!" said Lawler. "Skin him! Slowly!"

"Very slowly," repeated Louis.

"Yes! Very slowly!" said Lawler.

Half a dozen pirates dragged Nosy Bill from the room while the rest booed and hissed and cursed his name.

"Well, that's done," said Lawler. "Good work, whoever you are."

"Thank you, sir!" said Skipjammer. "Malachi Skipjammer is my name!"

"Any relation to Malachi Skipjammer the smuggler?"

"None at all."

"What's your ship?"

"The *Miracle*."

"Doesn't Malachi Skipjammer the smuggler sail the *Miracle*?"

"He may, sir. I've never met the man. I'm Malachi Skipjammer the pirate. Always have been!"

"And is your friend a pirate, too?" asked whiskey-throated Tannis as her sneer for a doomed prisoner changed to an expression of frank feminine interest in a potential colleague. Jacques Malad noticed her appraisal of me and started playing with his knife again. I had a faint premonition of future plot complications.

"A pirate indeed, fierce lady!" proclaimed Skipjammer. "It is my honor and pleasure to present to you the greatest pirate who ever lived—the one and only Jason Cosmo!"

At the mention of my name, an awed hush fell over the feasting hall. Then the pirate crews rose as one, waved their knives, stomped their feet, whistled, hooted, and cheered.

The captains were more restrained, but startled nonetheless. Their faces bespoke amazement, skepticism, scheming, and hope.

"Incredible," whispered Tannis as her eyes narrowed to speculative slits.

"Impossible," said Jacques Malad.

"Blook's bony beak!" said Toracan. "It's a bloody miracle!"

"I always thought you were older," said Lawler.

"Most people do," I replied.

"And taller. About ten feet is what I heard."

"Been dieting."

"I thought you were a folk legend," said Gypsum softly. "A product of rum-fired imagination. A character in tall tales."

"No, I'm real," I said, thumping my chest.

"Where have you been lately?" asked Lawler.

"In early retirement," I said. "I thought it wise when the big manhunt for me started last year."

Lawler nodded, satisfied. Gypsum was still not convinced.

"Why is it that everything I've ever heard about your deeds is thirdhand or worse?" he asked.

"I've never before consorted with my fellow pirates," I said. "My exploits are so great that lesser corsairs would just be in the way. But I've decided it's time to be more sociable. We pirates should stick together."

The crews responded enthusiastically.

"Is it true you kidnapped the concubines of the Thirteen Oligarchs of Xornos?" called a pirate from the crowd.

I turned. "Yes. But I gave them back."

"Why'd you do that?"

"They were too much trouble to keep around. Besides, I just wanted to say hello to them."

The hall roared with laughter.

"Like you 'said hello' to King Oriones's harem?" called another corsair.

"Exactly," I said dryly.

"How long did it take you to spend the loot from

the Unprecedentedly Large Treasure Fleet of the Padishah?" asked another pirate.

"About two days," I ad-libbed.

The pirates cheered again. Several asked me to autograph their eye patches or peg legs and grumbled when Lawler told them to wait until later. This was easier than I had expected. Apparently the Jason Cosmo of popular legend was a hero to ordinary pirates, who told colorful stories about him around the cooking fires and held him up as a paragon of piratical virtues. Some of the chieftains were dubious, but their crews loved me. It was nice to be appreciated, even by a bunch of cutthroats.

"Let's hear it for Cap'n Cosmo!" shouted a big, beefy pirate with a hook nose. "He'll give ol' Dread what for!"

"Hooray!" responded the crowd. "Hooray for Cosmo!"

"All right, pipe down!" bellowed Lawler, banging the hilt of his dagger on the table. "Back to your swilling, louts! Cap'n Cosmo and we have got business to discuss!"

Chairs were brought up and Skipjammer and I took our places at the head table.

"We've got them snookered good, sir," whispered Skipjammer.

"I just hope we can keep them that way," I replied.

When we were settled, Gypsum asked, "Why have you come out of retirement now?"

"I missed pirating."

"Why should we believe you're who you say you are?"

Before I answered, Skipjammer whispered in my ear, "I would suggest you adopt a more arrogant air, sir. You are supposed to be a living legend."

"What did he just whisper in your ear?" demanded Gypsum.

"None of your bloody business!" I snarled. "Who

are you to question me? I'm a living legend, you
know! You doubt what I say? Why I'll roll your guts
on a spool, you bleached-out barnacle!"

Pale Gypsum grew even paler. "I beg your pardon,
sir. I just had to be sure it was you."

"Well, now you're sure! So let's talk piracy! I've
got big plans! Plans for the biggest haul ever and I'm
going to cut all of you in on the deal! We must go to
Rancor at once and assemble the full Council to hear
my plan!"

"Well, there's a slight problem with that, me
bucko," said Toracan. "Things in Rancor aren't what
they used to be."

"What do you mean?"

"Captain Dread has declared himself Big Goomba
and abolished the Council of Free Captains."

"Well, that was rude of him," I said.

"We think so, too," said Lawler. "Pirates are an
independent breed. We don't want a Big Goomba telling us what to do."

"So what are you sitting here for?" I said. "Go to
Rancor and hang Captain Dread from a yardarm!"

"It's not so easy as that," hissed Jacques Malad.
"Many captains support Dread."

"We are loath to spill the blood of our fellow pirates," explained Gypsum.

"Since when?" I said.

"What he means," said Lawler, "is that we don't
want to get ourselves killed. Rancor is heavily fortified
and Dread has used his gold to hire mercenary Dreadguards to enforce his will."

"Out of work Maceketeers, for the most part,"
added Gypsum.

"If you can't best him by arms, use treachery," I
said.

"To do that we need a bold and brilliant leader to
devise a bold and brilliant plan," said Tannis.

"I'm your man," I said, meeting her eye.

"I feel better already," she said.

"What plan do you have?" said Jacques Malad defiantly.

"I will sail to Rancor, challenge Dread, and kill him," I said.

"Where's the treachery in that?" Louis sneered.

"Well, all right. Suppose I first pretend to be his friend and then kill him when he's not looking?"

"Better," admitted Louis.

I was getting inspired. "In fact, to make it more treacherous, we'll all go to Rancor and pretend to be his friends! We'll tell him he's a fine Big Goomba! We'll laugh, we'll talk, we'll have a few drinks—and then we'll all stab him when he's not looking!"

"Inspired!" said Toracan.

"Brilliant," said Tannis.

"I like it," said Lawler.

"Good plan," said Gypsum.

The Malad brothers said nothing.

"Fine! That's settled, then. Glad I happened along when I did! Now let's all have some ale!"

Their expressions told me I had committed a major faux pas. Tannis looked disappointed. The Malads smiled at my discomfort.

"Rum," whispered Skipjammer. "Pirates drink rum. Straight from the bottle."

"Rum, I meant! Straight from the bottle!"

The captains smiled. The council of war became a celebration. The pirates ate pirate food, drank pirate drinks, sang pirate songs, and danced the pirate jig. Skipjammer regaled the crowd with fabricated tales of my piratical prowess. I signed autographs. Tannis brazenly suggested I should come see how well appointed the captain's quarters were on the *Notorious*. The Malad brothers muttered and glowered.

After imbibing several bottles of pure rum to establish my piraticalness, I too was singing loudly and boasting of my fictional exploits. Shameful to say, I also boldly pinched serving wenches and threw food. The traditional drink of my homeland was stale rutabaga beer, which is so weak it barely qualifies as alcoholic. I usually drank ale or wine, and then only in moderation. Unused to strong drink, I lost my head and caroused as energetically as any cutthroat there. Skipjammer was also soon deep in his cups.

Much, much later, in the wee hours of the morning, the party finally died down. The rum supply was exhausted, as was the beer, wine, ale, and seltzer water. The fire was low, the platters empty, and most of the pirates either snored soundly on the floor or had wandered off in small groups to seek other diversions.

"We ousht to gets back to the ship," I slurred. I stumbled to my feet and the floor rose up to meet me.

I awoke amid satin sheets and thick furs. A gentle bobbing told me I had passed the night aboard a ship, but this certainly wasn't my bunk on the *Miracle*. The cabin sported elegant furnishings, a luxurious carpet, oil paintings on the walls, and frost-covered bay windows.

"Awake in time for brunch," said Tannis Darkwolf. She wore a white pirate blouse and black pants, with a long red scarf knotted around her head and a red sash at her waist. Her rich black hair fell in rippling clusters about her shoulders.

"What are we having?" I asked, rubbing my aching head.

"Baked eggs, fresh fruit, and Neruvian coffee. But if you prefer, I can have the chef send up some raw meat."

"That's okay."

"You'd best hurry," she said, taking a mouthful. "I've quite an appetite."

For some reason, that particular comment cut through my mental fog and I realized where I was, with whom I was, and what this was all about. I sat bolt upright, which did my head no good.

"How did I get here?" I asked.

"You were drunk."

"How drunk?"

"Too drunk to be good company."

That was a relief. And yet I also felt a twinge of inexplicable disappointment. I reached for the green silk robe lying across the bed.

"You are young for a pirate captain. Particularly one so accomplished," Tannis said.

"I'm a pirate prodigy. Took my first ship at four."

"Fascinating. What other prodigal talents did you display at an early age?"

"Ahem. Nice cabin you have here."

"What is the point of winning wealth at swordpoint if you do not then enjoy the luxury which wealth can buy?"

"Good point," I said. "Good food, too."

"My chef prepares no other kind."

"Why have you brought me here?" I asked. "Not for mere lust, surely?"

"Not merely that sort of lust, no. I am the Pirate Queen. That's just a bit of self-promotion, but I would fain make it fact."

"And you think I can help you?"

"A Pirate Queen needs a Pirate King."

"Really? Unfulfilled without a man around? You don't seem the type."

"There is no end to what I could accomplish with one such as you at my side," she said, clutching my arm and locking her eyes with mine.

"Or under your thumb."

"I could never manage that. Nor could you hope to tame me. But as partners, we could take it all. Wouldn't you like to be Big Goomba?"

"Go on," I said.

"When we kill Dread and his lieutenants, we will

also kill the other captains. Then you and I will rule Rancor and the pirates."

"Big Goomba and Big Goomba Mama."

"Something like that. We could devise more euphonious titles."

"We should. But why do I need you?"

"Perhaps you don't. Perhaps you will join me because you want to." She leered suggestively. "Or want me."

"Perhaps I will," I said, laughing more to cover my discomfort than to show agreement. "On the other hand, if you're willing to share power, why not hook up with Dread? He's the man on top."

"But you should be." She paused and sucked on a wedge of orange. "Dread is a psychopath. He used to be called Pirate Joe and he was a miserable failure. He hired a PR firm, changed his name to Dread, then signed on the most brutal and cold-blooded crew available for his infamous 'Dead with Dread' tour. Granting no quarter, he rampaged from Emerald Bay to the Free Coast, then up the shores of Xornos to sack Zygra and Pylarum, slaughtering innocents, holding press conferences, and hawking tour T-shirts everywhere. By the time he returned to Rancor, he was the most widely feared pirate of all, save you. He sailed south last fall boasting that when he returned he'd strike fear in all the world."

"And when he came back, he took over Rancor?"

"Most of the captains were at sea. Once Dread was in control, he could deny us access to Rancor except on his terms. Most chieftains have joined him by now. Had you not arrived here, our group doubtless would have too. For all their talk, they are cowards!"

"So now you want to throw in with me to overthrow Dread and throw over the others?"

"Yes."

"In that event, we must not be seen together, lest they grow suspicious."

She considered my words. "You are right. Already Jacques and Louis hate you."

"I wonder why?"

"Jacques loves me. But he is a pig. I spurn him. So he is jealous. You must watch him. He will try to kill you."

"I'm not afraid of Jacques Malad. Louis either."

"I know."

"But it might be helpful if you pretend disinterest in me also. Just to avoid trouble until we're ready to make our move."

"Then you like my plan?"

"Definitely. Great plan. We'll double-cross them all."

"Yes!" she said fiercely. "And then you and I will love and revel in blood and plunder!" She lunged across the table, hooked her hands around my face, and kissed me bruisingly, the way a greedy Pirate Queen would. "Go now!" she said when she was done. "Go! Or I cannot contain myself!"

"Right," I said, dabbing my mouth with a napkin and standing. "Would you mind if I dressed first?"

"Dress. Later, my Big Goomba."

She exited. I briefly regretted I wasn't the man she thought I was. The idea of being a Pirate King and she my Pirate Queen had a perverse appeal. She was beautiful, dangerous, sensuous, and exciting. I had to remind myself that she was a notorious outlaw and that I was only playing a part. But someone else was willing to make that point clear for me.

"Swine!" raged Solana. "You leave me standing in the cold half the night while you swill rum and rut with that pirate wench! How dare you treat me so!"

"Must you shout?" I said.

"Yes! May your rotten head split open from my shouting!"

"I apologize, milady. I should have given you the

all clear signal, but in playing my part I consumed
more drink than is my wont, took leave of my senses,
and forgot about you. I am deeply sorry."

"And how did you come to pass the night aboard
the *Notorious*? Did you in your drunken stupor mistake it for the *Miracle*?"

"I'm not sure. But I assure you nothing untoward
transpired."

"I thought you a man of honor and decency! You
are nothing but a degenerate peasant! A slave to your
gross desires! The freedom of all Arden hangs in the
balance and your first thought is sating your vile lust!
You disgust me! Come not near me again!"

Solana stormed out of Skipjammer's cabin.

"Milady has quite a temper, sir," observed the sea
captain.

"That she docs. And I've unwittingly made a mess of
things, at least in that regard. But my penetration of the
pirates has succeeded far beyond my expectations."

"Has it indeed, sir?" asked Skipjammer archly.

"What?"

"Tannis Darkwolf is a nice piece of work, sir."

"Not what I meant."

"Of course not, sir."

"Oh, never mind. The important thing is that these
pirates accepted me as one of them. Indeed, as their
leader, which was a surprise. I just hope I can maintain the deception."

"You take to the role well, sir."

"Too well, it seems. By the way, that was nice work
convincing them we were pirates. If not for your performance, they might not have accepted me in my
role."

"Thank you, sir. It was not the first time I've been
in such a spot. I recall once in Portanunca, sir, when
I was locked in a burning warehouse with forty-nine
demented geese and as sorry a lot of unruly ruffi-
ans—"

A knock at the door interrupted the tale and second mate Coptris entered, spat in my direction, and said, "Captain, come quick! Zastrian troopers attack the town! We must sail at once or they will burn the ship!"

13———————————————

A hundred mounted Zastrian Blue Dragoons thundered into town on the Kielfa road. Two hundred foot soldiers followed, waving torches and spears. Not here to enjoy weekend passes, the invaders got straight to the business of killing everyone in sight and putting Nerak to the torch.

The Brythalian detachment charged with defending the town responded quickly to the assault, grabbing whatever they could and hurrying up the Fenmark road. Many ordinary Nerakians followed their example and hotfooted it for the hills. Others revived the time-honored Nerak tradition of hiding in wine cellars. The pirates ran madly for their ships.

Unfortunately for them, the average overdebauched, half-dressed, badly hung-over pirate cannot outrun galloping horses, even on a downhill slope. Few reached the docks. With the death cries of brother corsairs ringing in their ears, the pirates on the ships cast off and made ready to sail. Even the *Miracle*'s inept crew developed an uncharacteristic degree of expertise in getting under way.

However, the breeze was slight and sailing ships take longer to get moving than canoes. The dragoons sealed off the dockfront area and the foot soldiers swarmed ahead to seize the ships. They snared the *Blackguard* and the *Conspirator* with grappling hooks, lashed them to the docks, and fought their way aboard.

The *Miracle* was a good ten yards from the dock, our escape all but made, when the lookout spotted a Zastrian naval squadron at the mouth of the bay. Five war galleys rounded a small peninsula and glided toward Nerak at battle speed, their crews pedaling furiously. Two carrocks bristling with mangonels took positions to catch any ships that got past the galleys.

"They must have moved into position during the night," I said, standing at the prow with Skipjammer. "I'm all for cracking down on piracy, but I hate to get caught in the dragnet myself."

"Our night's work was all for naught, sir," mused Skipjammer. "The pirates we so carousingly befriended are in desperate straits. As are we."

"Maybe not," I said. "This might be a chance to win more points with the pirates by saving the day."

"You are actually going to aid the pirates?"

"Look, those Zastrians are killing innocent women and children as well as pirates. They're no better than the riffraff they've come to put down. When neither side stands with the angels, what do you lose by helping one over the other?"

"Little, I suppose, sir, but what can you do?"

"We'll see."

I climbed over the rail and dived into the cold water, swam to the dock, and dragged myself up the pilings. A squad of Zastrians reached the pier as I gained my feet. I called Gardion and Overwhelm from the *Miracle* and proceeded to knock the troopers senseless.

More soldiers came at me and I hit their ranks with a crash that made my hung-over head reel and split. Their swords and spears broke like crumbling crackers against Gardion and the Cosmosuit. I hurled men aside like mere nothings, casting them into the water or beating them down with my enchanted blade and shield.

Others took notice of my one-man offensive. The pirates, even some aboard the *Jaundice* and *Scurvy,* chanted my name. I don't know which the chanting hurt more, the Zastrians' morale or my aching temples. I cleared the docks around the *Blackguard* and *Conspirator* and cut the ships free. I flung over fifty Zastrians into the water, and dozens more jumped in voluntarily. I felt good about sparing my foes from Overwhelm's keen edge until I remembered that men in metal armor don't swim too well.

Out on the water, *Sea Demon* and *Deception* were away, but in the path of the oncoming pedal galleys with their mechanical corkscrew rams. One of the highly maneuverable warships veered toward the *Miracle.* Solana appeared on the deck and shouted something to me that I couldn't make out. She seemed angry. The galley *Law* rammed the *Deception* amidships, drilling through its hull with shattering force, then backing away from the crippled ship to select another target. *Equity,* the galley bearing down on the *Miracle,* burst into flame from prow to stern. Hundreds of scorched pedalers and marines abandoned ship, leaving the galley to drift toward the docks unmanned.

Miracle slipped by the galleys *Subsidy* and *Bailout* and made for the open sea, though the hardy little vessel still had to elude the waiting carrocks. *Sea Demon* also dodged the galleys. But the *Conspirator* did not and took a tough ramming from *Enforcement.*

Having failed to take the *Miracle,* the *Subsidy* and *Bailout* set their sights on easier targets, like *Jaundice,* *Scurvy,* and *Notorious,* which were still at the docks.

The *Notorious* was hard-pressed by the troopers, for the value of Tannis's head was more than any three of her fellow captains combined. The mercenaries caught the ship with two grapple lines and sought to overwhelm her defenders with sheer numbers.

Tannis fought in the forefront of her crew of cut-throats. Her gore-soaked hair hung beneath a steel skullcap. She wore a cuirass of boiled leather and wielded her bloody saber with sharp, slashing ferocity, snarling like a she-panther pumped up on serious catnip.

I battled my way down the pier, vanquishing soldiers two, four, or six at a time as I approached the *Notorious* and cut the grapple lines. The ship pulled away from the dock, and the Zastrians aboard were suddenly outnumbered. Tannis and her followers showed them no mercy at all. They savagely slaughtered the troopers, then raised their scarlet weapons to salute me.

I returned the salute, lifting my own sword high.

Tannis opened her arms to me. "Come aboard, my fierce love! Sail with me and nothing will stop us!"

"I must aid the other ships!" I cried.

"The Malads? Let them fend for themselves!"

"We'll need them later!"

I hurried down the waterfront for more feats of arms. A small knot of troopers intercepted me, holding their weapons at ease.

"I want to talk to you," said their leader, a swarthy officer. "You're Jason Cosmo, aren't you?"

"Yes."

"Living legend, son of a Demon Lord, Death's favorite cousin, slayer of a thousand men, and all that?"

"The same."

"I'm Tadzio of Cuchillo, commander of these troops. Look, could you do me a favor and perhaps sit the rest of this fight out? You're making us look bad."

"How's that?"

"Three hundred crack mercenaries and you've already defeated half of us by yourself."

"I'm sure my fellow pirates got a few of you."

"We expect that. It's a risk of the job. But we shouldn't have to deal with the likes of you. You're fouling up the whole plan. And it's a good plan, which ought to work. We swept in early, took the rabble by surprise, and by rights we should win handily. But if you're going to go tossing men around like rag dolls and such antics, we can't do our job properly."

"I'm very sorry. But I can't help it if I'm stronger and better equipped."

"Nothing wrong with that. But you should be off fighting fire-breathing dragons or cave giants, not picking on decent, hardworking mercenaries like us. President Corundum wants to clean out the pirates and annex this whole territory. How is it going to go for us if we slink back and report that we lost, beaten by a lone warrior with a magic sword?"

"Not well, I suppose."

"Not well! We'll be lucky to keep our heads! I should imagine we'd face court-martial at the very least! Cowardice in the face of the enemy, dereliction of duty. Politicians don't understand superwarriors. All they see is the numbers. Three hundred to one, they figure, ought to leave no question as to outcome. Really, what you're doing here is depriving us of our livelihoods. Some of us have got families to feed, you know."

"I didn't realize that."

"Well, you probably never stop to think about it, do you? It's just a game to you, because we can't hurt you. We're not people, just a means of keeping score. Fifty-to-one, a hundred-to-one, a thousand-to-one. You go on about 'smashing through our ranks' and 'harvests of blood' as if you're taking a stroll on the beach. You come off like the big hero, and we're just a nameless, faceless, impersonal horde of nobodies. Never mind it's not a fair fight. We don't have super strength and magic swords, you know."

"Well, I see your point, but—"

"Are you proud of what you're doing? Is this kind of one-sided slaughter anything to brag about? We're helpless! We might as well be a flock of lambs out here trying to hold off a bull elephant!"

"Be that as it may—"

"Do you care about us? Do you consider our feelings? Do you think about the pain and suffering and the grief of our loved ones when you go storming through us like the north wind through a pile of wheat chaff? Do you think our widows and orphans are impressed by such 'heroics' as that? Well? Do you?"

"Not usually," I admitted. "Do you think about the pain and suffering you cause when you burn towns and skewer women and children?"

"That's different."

"Oh?"

"We're not here in an individual capacity. We represent the government. Governments can kill all the people they want. You don't think we go around burning towns and killing innocents on our own time, do you?"

"Do you?"

"Well, most of us don't. But what do you say, Cosmo? Won't you at least give a chance to take these last two ships? Let us win or lose without your interference."

"The Malads are troublemakers," I mused.

"There! We'll be doing you a favor. You scratch our backs, we'll scratch yours."

"Still, they're pirates, and so am I. So I guess I'll have to help them. Sorry."

"You're determined, then? None of my arguments convince you?"

"I must do what I must do."

"Then no sense in more of my men getting hurt. I'll just call off the attack and save you the trouble." Tadzio shouted an order to disengage and fall back.

It took a few minutes to relay it to the front ranks, but they broke off their boarding action and assembled for further orders. The *Jaundice* and the *Scurvy* got under way.

Tadzio gave me a sour look. "Satisfied, hero?"

"You've nothing to be put out about," I said. "You've taken the town and the ships still must get past your navy."

Subsidy and *Bailout* bore down on the *Scurvy* while the galley *Law* targeted the *Notorious*.

"Right. You humiliate us and those sorry seadogs get all the glory."

"I tell you what. I'll humiliate them, too."

"How are you going to do that?"

"Is that a rack of harpoons there?"

"Looks like," said Tadzio. "Harpoons are the big spear-looking things, aren't they?"

"I thought harpoons were a kind of flute," said one of his men.

"No, that's baboons," said another. "A sort of bass flute. Looks much like a clarinet."

"Don't you mean an oboe?" said the first soldier.

"Oboe are grazing animals, you lunkhead! Like gazelle or deer or vile ilk. They eat grass and run fast."

"Now that's sloppy thinking," put in a third mercenary primly. "A classic example of the logical fallacy ipso facto. Just because oboes eat grass and then run fast, it does not follow that eating grass enables oboes to run fast. After all, cows eat grass and they don't run fast at all."

"You've never been trampled in a stampede, have you?" The second soldier sneered. "I have. Believe me, cattle can run plenty fast."

"Cattle, yes. I'm talking about cows. Fat cows in particular."

"Oh. That's different, then."

"Could someone please hand me a harpoon?" I said.

Tadzio passed me one of the heavy barbed spears. "What are you going to do?" he asked.

"Sink a ship," I said. "Attach the cable, would you?"

I hefted the weapon, got a feel for it, took aim, and cast it at the *Law,* aiming for the waterline. Propelled by my sun-charged sinews, the harpoon punched through the relatively thin hull of the galley.

"Impressive," said Tadzio.

"Thank you."

I lashed the other end of the cable to a piling. The pedalers continued toward *Notorious* at battle speed, drawing the line taut. For a moment the galley was jerked to a halt. The crew pedaled even harder and the dock creaked under the strain. But the hull gave first. The barbed harpoon ripped a long gash in the planks before coming loose. The galley took on water and listed to starboard. *Law* was out of the fight and *Notorious* was in the clear.

The other galleys were too far out to harpoon. *Enforcement* backed water and rammed *Conspirator* again, dooming her. But Toracan's crew was ready with their grapples. They lashed the ships together and boarded the Zastrian vessel.

Meanwhile, *Blackguard* came about to aid *Deception* while *Subsidy* and *Bailout* closed on *Scurvy.* The burning hulk of *Equity* crashed into the docks. The first of her crew clambered ashore, shivering violently from their dunking in the cold water.

I had done enough to help the pirates get away. The rest was up to them. My problem now was my own escape. Tadzio and his men might not want to fight me, but I wanted to get out of Nerak nonetheless. I briefly considered diving into the bay and swimming out to the ships, but realized at once that I couldn't catch them. Even fantasy heroes have their limits.

I ran up and down the dock and found a sailboat

small enough for one man to operate. I had never sailed a boat, but Skipjammer had explained to me the basic skills and principles involved, for whatever an explanation from Skipjammer was worth.

I pushed off, raised the sail, took the mainsheet and tiller in hand, and scurried around in a circle. After three collisions with the dock and nearly capsizing twice, I got the hang of it and set out across the bay.

Meanwhile, Jacques Malad came to his brother's rescue with a wild maneuver, forcing *Subsidy* to change course to avoid a fatal collision. *Bailout* ran aground. Losing the Malads, *Subsidy* came about to join the attack on *Conspirator*. *Blackguard* escorted her wounded sister ship *Deception* as she limped across the bay.

At the mouth of the bay, the carrocks lost all maneuverability when their sails burst into flame with a little help from Solana. Their crews were too busy fighting the fires to launch more than a token barrage with the slug-throwing mangonels. Thus, *Sea Demon*, *Jaundice*, and *Scurvy* had a clear run to the open sea. *Miracle* swung about to return to the bay, and *Notorious* stood to just out of range of the Zastrians' missile weapons.

I rendezvoused with the *Miracle* in the middle of the bay, climbing a rope ladder to come aboard, happy to abandon the sailboat.

"Splendid work, sir!" exulted Skipjammer, lending me a hand. "Simply amazing! Untrue as they may be, the tales don't do you justice! To fight alone against hundreds of vicious mercenary thugs! Stupendous!"

"They weren't that vicious."

"All the same, sir, you saved the pirate flotilla from being taken at the docks! If you're not careful, they'll make you their Big Goomba!"

I looked to the *Notorious*. "That they might."

Solana stormed over, livid. "Fool! You should have let the pirates and mercenary scum kill each other!

My powers would secure our escape! Are you so taken with these cutthroats that now you fight beside them?"

"Fighting beside them is the best way to win their trust."

"What need have we of their trust? You've gained nothing by our interlude here save the bed of your she-wolf of a Pirate Queen!"

"I told you nothing happened between us."

"You expect I'll believe that after seeing how you rushed to her rescue, casting aside all thought of our grave mission to play hero for your bloodstained strumpet? I'm sure Mistress Darkwolf is very impressed!"

"Why this untempered jealousy?" I asked.

Solana slapped me. It was a hard, loud slap, with a sound like a popping balloon. But I asked for it.

"You flatter yourself immensely, peasant!" Solana spat.

With that she stalked back to our cabin and slammed the door shut.

"Quite a way with women you have, sir," said Skipjammer.

I rubbed my stinging cheek. "Thanks."

14

The Spendthrift Isles speckled the Zastrian sea below Port Kylas like droplets of wine sprinkled on a polished tabletop by a tipsy god. They ranged in size from several miles across to so small you could spit from one side to the other if you worked up a good mouthful of juice. The best came with a small mountain or two, lush forested slopes, clear sparkling streams, spectacular waterfalls, and the usual pristine white beaches, romantic hidden coves, and mysterious caves that make up an island paradise. The islands like that were all taken for the exclusive use of the Zastrian upper class.

The more middle-class islands were put to many different uses. Southrop and Rockwall were the sites of strategic naval bases and weapons centers. Devilfood Island was a notorious penal colony/fat farm. Papago, Aminga, and Lesser Barbada were cesspools of poverty, neglect, and human misery papered over with an illusory veneer of prosperity and hospitality to fool the tourists. Nestegg was a bird sanctuary. Gushalo was a snail sanctuary. Many were not exactly sanctuaries, but had no inhabitants except wild pigs, monkeys, and castaways.

Zastria claimed the whole Spendthrift group, and backed up their claim with a large navy. The islanders went along with it, but looked at the situation from a different slant. Thus, what the Zastrian Senate called "collecting taxes," the islanders called "exacting tribute." What the Senate called "compliance with trade regulations," the islanders called "unfair economic exploitation." What the Senate called "developing prime real estate," the islanders called "stealing our land, throwing us out of our homes, and depriving us of our livelihoods to satisfy their rapacious greed." What the Senate called "troops on hand for your own protection," the islanders called "hostile occupation forces." What the Senate called "keeping the peace," the islanders called "foreign mercenaries running amok, brutally killing and injuring our families and friends for no good reason." What the Senate called "duly appointed territorial governors there to administer the laws and keep things running smoothly," the islanders called "petty little tyrants and incompetent buffoons who schmoozed their way into a cushy political appointment so they can sit around on their fat butts all day pawing our women and drinking our liquor when they're not busy stealing and extorting everything they can get their sticky fingers on and making our lives miserable until their pockets are full and they go home so the next bloodsucker can move in."

It was all a matter of perspective.

"I just don't get it," I said.

"What is it that you don't get?" asked Solana. We were in our cabin as the *Miracle* sailed between Oroco and Pilstan in the Spendthrifts. Solana was feeling better thanks to a special nausea-dispelling herbal tea Coptris had brewed for her with ingredients obtained in Nerak.

"Why you're acting this way. I mean, everything was going fine until these last few days. We met under awkward circumstances. There was a timely rescue. First you considered me a coward. Then you recanted and offered your friendship. We were sent on this mission together and it looked as though a romance might blossom between us. But when I pressed forward, you backed off, wanting to keep things strictly business. I respected that, cared for you when you were sick, but then you exploded over that nonincident with Tannis in Nerak and condemned me as a moral degenerate on the slightest of proof."

"You spent the night with her," said Solana. "That's proof enough for me."

"I didn't know I was spending the night with her. I was drunk."

"How manly of you."

"Let me try a different tack. You're spirited, brave, loyal, intelligent, and talented. Unquestionably beautiful. And I cannot forget the upwelling passion in your kisses."

"If you try a little harder, I'm sure you'll manage."

"We had a classic storybook romance developing, but you've stalled the process. I have no problem with you being upset about the Tannis incident. Foolish misunderstandings are an important means of heightening romantic tension. But you're taking it too far. By now you should have given me some sign that you went overboard in your outburst. Not an overt admission of fault, but just a hint that you didn't really mean all you said, that I might approach you, that we might develop more than a working relationship after all. I'd still expect to prove my soon-to-be-recognized love for you by saving you from danger and choosing you over Tannis at a critical juncture, but you ought to be laying the groundwork for our ultimate getting together. As it is, we're dead in the water. You're not doing your part."

"My part? As if this were all scripted out in advance. As if I have no will of my own. Yes, Jason, I understand perfectly what was developing between us. And I'm certain that, as you say, nothing untoward happened between you and Tannis. But nothing is going to happen between you and me either."

"But why not? What have I done wrong? Everything—"

"Everything was going according to plan. That's just it. It's all artificial. All contrived, like the way Coptris suddenly came up with the home remedy that dispels my seasickness enough for us to interact aboard the ship and do romantic things if we were going to, which we're not. I want no part of it. I'm not going to be the good little stock character, the fiery redhead that the big hero gets to tame."

"I never said anything about taming you."

"You don't have to. It's implicit in the scenario. Listen, you're a fine and noble man, Jason. I admire your heroics. I find you very attractive. But I don't think you respect me as an individual."

"Of course I do."

"No, you don't. You look at me and say to yourself, 'Ah! My romantic interest for this adventure. I can hardly wait.' You don't give any thought to who I really am. It's enough that I'm beautiful and adventurous and made my entrance early in the action. But I could just as well be Chatelaine or Devra Highrider or Megan of Cyrilla. Any gorgeous adventuress would do. It's nothing special about me that you admire."

"That's not true."

"Isn't it? I admit that I played my part in this little charade, too. I did the disdain bit and the change of heart and I enjoyed our kiss in Lowtide, but I realized I would lose all respect for myself if I played out this scenario like a good little girl. Because you know how it ends. We get together at last, and if this was an ordinary fairy tale or a romance novel, we'd live happily ever after. But it won't be like that. You'll soon embark on another adventure and find a new love interest. Heroes are fickle that way."

"I'm not."

"You've made the transition from Sapphrina and Rubis to me well enough. And don't deny you're attracted to Tannis."

I said nothing.

"So in the end, I'll be put aside, and what will it all amount to? I'll fight at your side and share danger with you and actually serve a useful function, but in the end I'll fare no better than some helpless bit of fluff you might rescue from dire bondage. The treatment and portrayal of women in these sword-and-sorcery fantasies is nauseating. And it's a nausea no herbal tea can cure."

"What do you mean?"

"We're all beautiful, of course. It wouldn't do to have a homely heroine. And most of the time we have to dress in these skimpy little costumes, parading around half-naked to gratify adolescent fantasies, a fate I've fortunately escaped, but many of my sisters do not. And do we have an important role to play? Rarely. We're just accessories to the male lead. Wenches. Wenches all. It's even a verb: 'to wench.' And we get pretty thoroughly wenched before it's all over. Used up and cast aside. The hero gets the glory, we become another notch on his scabbard."

"I haven't done anything like that."

"It doesn't matter. You're part of the whole genre. You buy into the system, you benefit from it. Just look at your whole affair with the Corundum twins. Right by the book, right up to their convenient exit to make way for me."

"They left me. I didn't leave them. I wanted to marry them."

"Both of them?"

"It's kind of complicated."

"I'm sure it is. But that only illustrates my point. They're products of this system, this whole outlook on women's roles. They play the sex kittens because that's all they know how to be. Coming from Zastria, the sex-kitten capital of the world, that's hardly surprising. Sex kittens don't marry and settle down. They just hang around and look beautiful. When you try to go beyond that, they get scared and move on."

"That's not . . . I mean, they didn't . . . well, I suppose that could be what happened. But never mind them, what about us? I'm looking for more than a pretty girl to pose with on the cover."

"Your intentions are strictly honorable. I know. But your intentions aren't the determining factor. It's the milieu that controls. And the milieu will separate us one way or another whatever your good intentions or mine. It wouldn't do for the leading hero to settle down happily with one woman. The Laws of Narrative abhor that as much as nature abhors a vacuum. The system will corrupt you and turn you into what it wants you to be—a serial womanizer."

"Never."

"You have no choice. You'll stumble over beautiful women everywhere you go. For all your noble posturing, you're a man. You won't be able to resist them all. If you did, your sales would go nowhere, because that's what the public wants. So you'll get involved, you'll help perpetuate the stereotypes, the whole degrading image. If you're not part of the solution, you can't avoid being part of the problem."

"What is the solution?"

"More women in the business would be a good start, but for you and me, why don't we try to function as partners working together on a mission and resist these plot pressures to engage in a formula romance."

"Agreed," I said.

"Just pretend I'm Prince Mercury."

"That could be difficult, but I get the idea. Now the question is what to do about Tannis."

"You'll have to decide that for yourself, hero."

*　　*　　*

"A fire devil owed you a favor?" asked Tannis incredulously.

We stood together on the deck of the *Notorious*. The pirate flotilla from Nerak scattered when we reached the islands so as to better confuse and elude any pursuers. The *Notorious* paired up with the *Miracle*. The sea had been persistently choppy and the winds inconstant, taxing the skills of Skipjammer's crew to their meager limits, so it was comforting to have another ship nearby just in case the *Miracle* finally gave out and sank. Both ships had been slightly damaged in a particularly violent squall today and we had put in at a small, unnamed island to make minor repairs.

"Yes," I lied. She had just remarked on how odd it was that several of the Zastrian ships at Nerak had burst into flame. Not wanting to reveal Solana's power, I said the first thing that came to mind.

"Flarebic was his name," I said. "I freed him from his confinement in a cursed barbecue pit in Xornos."

"A cursed barbecue pit?"

"At Leronius's Real Famous Pit Barbecue. Flarebic was trapped in the pit and Leronius exploited the fire devil's heat and flame to cook spareribs and so forth. I got bad service once, a fight broke out, and I set Flarebic free. He said to call upon him if I ever found myself in a hot spot and needed a hand. So that's what I did at Nerak."

"The elements themselves obey you," said Tannis admiringly. "Why don't we go down to my cabin and you can show me in person how you summon fire?"

A moment of truth. Desire wrestled inside me against all those higher functions that try vainly to squelch desire. As Tannis brushed against me and awaited my answer I sorted through the considerations that had to be considered.

With Solana out of the picture, I owed my romantic allegiance to no woman now and was free to dally with Tannis if I wished. And part of me did wish. But I knew there was no future with her, no possibility of any kind of real and lasting relationship, certainly no "happily ever after" on the horizon. She'd stick a knife in my back at the first opportunity.

Still, making sparks with the Pirate Queen would certainly enhance my role as the pirate paragon and thus further our mission.

But that was mere rationalization. She was a ruthless, relentless robber of the seas. I was the Champion of Rae. She stood for greed, violence, and lack of consideration for others. I stood for nobility, justice, and regard for the rights of all people. It would set a bad example if we got too cozy.

The first answer to that argument was that as far as most of the world knew, Jason Cosmo stood for the same things as Tannis Darkwolf, if not worse. So many untruths about me were in circulation that adding a sordid truth to the mixture wouldn't hurt my reputation any.

The second answer was that by long-standing tradition heroes often fell in with wily temptresses—the wayward witch, the scheming seductresses, the promiscuous priestess, the nymph gone bad. It wasn't encouraged behavior, but it was acknowledged. It was allowed for. It was even expected. It was the sort of thing that spiced up otherwise boring epics about slaying dragons and trolls and hordes of foes. The hero always wised up, moved on, and settled down with a nice girl eventually, but not before dancing down the primrose path for a while and having a hell of a good time doing it. In short, a fling with Tannis would not be beneath the standards of my profession.

But after my talk with Solana, I had to question those standards, those heroic traditions. To get involved with Tannis would be to do the very thing I had protested to Solana I would never do.

"Well, lover, are you going to light my fire or not?"

She was sleek. Sexy. Tawny. Dangerous. Exciting. She wanted me and made no bones about it. I wanted her. I had to admit it. But I didn't have to give in to it.

"Later, O Pirate Queen."

"Why do you keep putting me off?" she growled hungrily.

"I just want to make you wait," I said in my macho pirate voice. "Anticipation enhances appreciation. Eventually you'll be so hot for me that when I finally do strike a match to you, you'll go up like . . ." I struggled for a metaphor.

"Yes?" prompted Tannis.

"A white-hot sexual supernova of desire."

"I'm counting on it. But don't make me wait too long, my Big Goomba."

And with that she kissed me, another plundering pirate kiss that almost made me forget everything I had just said. With an iron effort of will, I slipped free of her embrace and staggered down the beach to the *Miracle*. Being a hero wasn't too difficult once you got the hang of it, but being a hero with integrity was a real challenge.

I spent the night in tormented dreams of passion. We finished our repairs and got under way the next day. But all the crews' work was undone within a few hours, for out of nowhere came the mother of all storms.

15

"This is a most unnatural storm!" shouted Skipjammer.

The sky was black with swirling clouds. Thunder roared, the wind screamed, frenzied rain and wild waves slashed the decks. Skipjammer ordered the hatches and ports sealed, the sails hauled in, the yards lowered, and the sea anchor dropped. Purple lightning flashed above. The *Notorious* was lost from sight.

Two sailors were swept overboard by a punishing wave and vanished without a scream. The mast broke, its upper third crashing to the main deck, then sliding across and through the port rail into the sea. The howl of the wind took on a mournful, keening note, and the air grew suddenly colder.

I ducked into the cabin, where Solana hugged her bunk miserably, the wildness of the storm having overcome the soothing effects of Coptris's concoction. The ship pitched violently as the door swung open, throwing me to the floor. A blast of salty spray followed me in.

"Sorry!" I rose and wrestled the door closed. "How are you holding up, partner?"

"Are we going to sink?" moaned Solana.

"Skipjammer says no."

"That's too bad."

"But we're both aware of his record, so there's a chance."

"We're walking home."

"Deal."

"Is the *Notorious* still with us?" she asked.

"No sign of her."

"That may solve your pirate problem."

"Maybe," I said, with only a hint of longing.

"You did the right thing in turning Tannis down. I'm proud of you."

"I didn't turn her down, I just put her off. And she's going to get suspicious if I keep doing it."

"Well, if you wench her to protect the mission, then it's for a good reason and that's okay."

"Weird morality, you've got. That would still be tacit titillation, pandering to the tawdry tastes of the masses."

"I'm glad you recognize that, Jason. But sometimes sacrifices must be made."

"Now you tell me."

A loud pounding came at the door.

"Master Cosmo!" called Skipjammer. "Are you within, sir?"

"Yes, Captain!"

"Someone would like to speak to you, sir!"

"Who?"

"We're being hailed from another ship, sir!" he said evasively.

"The *Notorious*?"

"The *Glum Reaper*, sir."

I bolted upright. "Isn't that the name of the legendary Galleon of Doom, the spectral black ship in which dark-browed Death sails the bleak seas of the mortal plane harvesting drowned souls and appearing as a terrible omen of destruction to hapless sailors caught in ferocious storms?"

"The very same, sir."

"Who exactly is it aboard the *Glum Reaper* that wants to talk to me?"

"Her captain, sir."

"I'll be right out."

"What can this mean?" asked Solana, clutching my arm.

"It means someone is in big trouble. Probably me."

I opened the door, admitting the storm. The keening wail of the wind, remarkably resonant of lost souls, was louder now. The eldritch lightning flashed madly. Skipjammer, his sea cloak whipping about him like a flock of insane crows, stood without. Wordlessly, he pointed.

The *Glum Reaper* hovered above the waves off to starboard. Her inky hull, slick with rain, reflected the flashing purple light. Her tattered gray sails flapped like tangled burial shrouds on three tall masts as somber as obelisks. Her lifeless crew wore rags that would never pass inspection in any living fleet. One undead sailor operated a skull lantern, opening and closing the jaw to flash a message to the *Miracle*.

"They're using Mortis code, sir!" said Skipjammer. "A dead signal system these days, but I happen to know it!"

"What does it say?"

" 'Attention mortal vessel! Prepare to transfer passenger Jason Cosmo to this vessel by order of Captain Death!' "

"Whatever happened to freedom of the seas?"

"I don't think that's a live issue in these circumstances! Will you go over?"

"I haven't much choice, have I? Signal that I'm ready to transfer!"

"Aye, aye!"

Skipjammer worked his way across the deck and ordered a sailor to man the storm lantern and flash a response to the *Glum Reaper*.

"Don't do this!" said Solana, standing unsteadily.

"I'll be all right! I hope! You lie down!"

I took a few minutes to don the Cosmosuit. I reemerged to see a boat launch from the *Glum Reaper*.

A skeleton rowed it through the air to the side of the *Miracle*. Cautiously, I stepped aboard.

"Don't go!" called Solana from the cabin. "Jason! Don't go!"

"Quit that!" I shouted back. "You're starting to sound like you're in love with me!"

"Oh, I guess I am! Sorry, I forgot myself! But do be careful!"

"Don't worry!"

"The Gods be with you!" said Skipjammer.

"Thanks!"

The dead man rowed us back across to the Galleon of Doom. From my aerial vantage point, I saw no sign of the *Notorious* or the other pirate ships. Whether they had sunk or been blown leagues away I did not know. The *Miracle* appeared a small and fragile toy before the awesome power of the storm.

On the *Glum Reaper*, the crew manned the rails and saluted stiffly when I came aboard. They were few in number. It looked as though Death was making do with only a skeleton crew.

An undead marine escorted me down the hatch and along a dark passage to the captain's cabin. My guide rapped the sablewood door with bony knuckles.

"Yes?" said a soul-chilling voice within.

"Cosmo," rasped the skeleton, which was quite a trick without vocal cords.

"Send him in."

The guard stepped aside and the door swung open. Hackles up and heart aquiver, I entered.

The cabin was calm and quiet as a tomb. No sound of the raging storm could be heard here. Guttering black candles set in silver sconces provided flickering light and gave off myrrh-scented smoke.

Death sat at a writing table, quill in hand. He was a fat, bald little man wearing a red dressing gown and bunny slippers. He turned and smiled and gestured for me to sit. My hackles went halfway down.

"Peppermint?" he asked jovially, holding out a bowl of candies.

"Thank you, no. Are you Death?"

"No, my hearing is quite good."

He laughed at my bewildered expression.

"Not what you expected?" he said.

"I thought Death was tall and grim and skeletal."

"And with a soul-chilling voice?" he asked in a soul-chilling voice. He laughed. "That's just on formal occasions. I'm actually a jolly chap. So be at ease, be at ease, my good fellow!"

"Thank you," I said, feeling anything but.

"Are you sure you won't have a peppermint? They're very good."

"No, thank you."

"I used to be the God of Life, you know."

"I didn't know there was a God of Life."

"There isn't anymore. I gave up that portfolio back during the Age of War. It got too depressing with all the killing going on. So I switched to the flip side of the coin, as it was. I find death far more fascinating than life, don't you?"

"I'm fond of life myself."

"Oh, yes, of course, of course. So I'm sure you're wondering why I've summoned you here?"

"Yes."

"A couple of reasons, actually. I understand you had a run-in with my Jaws a few months back."

"Yes. I did."

"I certainly would like to have them back," Death said wistfully. "You know the story, I suppose? How I lost them in a bet with Vanah, Goddess of Fortune?"

"I've heard."

"Well, those damned teeth seem to have a mind of their own. They've eluded me for centuries and I'm tired of making do with these blasted dentures. They're a nuisance when I eat poppyseed cake. Do you like poppyseed cake?"

"Never had it."

"You must try it! Remind me to give you my favorite recipe before you go. Anyway, it would be good to have my own teeth back. Perhaps you've noticed Death doesn't have the bite it used to?"

"Well, I—"

"No, of course, you're too young. You wouldn't remember. Ah, in the old days I really packed them in! Big famines and floods and earthquakes and plagues of grasshoppers and aardvarks and things. Disease. War. Suicide. Death in all its many varieties. So fascinating. So fascinating. But I can't muster things on that scale anymore. Do you know what the leading cause of death is these days?"

"No."

"Natural causes! That never used to be any higher than twelfth. Not enough violent deaths."

"That isn't so bad, is it? Less people dying, I mean."

"Perhaps not from your perspective, but The Gods have to look at the big picture. Without sufficient deaths to offset births, the population grows too quickly and outstrips the available resources of food and living space and so forth. So we need a good many deaths to thin you mortals out. Sound conservation principles, you know."

"I didn't. But it seems to me plenty of people die violently."

"It's your line of work. You get a skewed perspective. Believe me, the great masses of Arden are more likely to die in their sleep than anything else. This just can't continue. I must get my Jaws back so I can do a proper job. So then, I understand that young snot Erimandras had the Jaws and set them on you. What happened then?"

"The Jaws ate him and vanished."

"Serves him right. Making off with other people's teeth. Do you know what happens to people when the Jaws swallow them?"

"No."

"Neither do I, but I hope it's unpleasant. So they vanished. That's all you can tell me?"

"I'm afraid so."

"A pity. I was hoping you would know more. Peppermint?"

"No, thank you."

"The hunt goes on then. I must find them soon. As you know we are in the critical final years of the present Age of Hope. A long, bitter struggle lies ahead and there will be much need of Death. In all his glory." Death cleared his throat. "But that's neither here nor there. The other reason I called you here was to deliver a Divine Summons."

"A Divine Summons? What's that?"

"I'll show you." Death shuffled through the papers on his desk. "I have it here somewhere. Ah! This rolled-up parchment with the seal and ribbon. How could I miss it? Here you go, good fellow."

I accepted the document. "What do I do with it?"

"Open and read it, of course."

I broke the seal and unrolled the parchment. In glowing letters it read:

"JASON COSMO, you are hereby summoned and commanded to lay all other business aside and personally appear in the Halls of Paradise at Our convenience to testify before the Divine Ethics Committee in the matter of alleged violations of the Great Eternal Pan-Cosmic Holy/Unholy Non-Intervention Pact by Rae, Goddess of the Sun. By the authority vested in Us by Ourselves, We The Gods do command this.

Signed,
Lexis Fairplay
Goddess of Law

(On behalf of The Gods)"

"What does this mean?" I asked.

"For a legal document, I think it fairly straight-forward."

"Why is Rae on trial?"

"She isn't on trial yet, though I imagine she will be. It's a preliminary investigation for now. You are aware of the Non-Intervention Pact which ended the Age of War? The treaty forbids The Gods and Demon Lords from directly intervening in mortal affairs."

"The Demon Lords routinely violate the Pact," I said.

"But The Gods do not. At least not until recently. Dear sweet Rae has changed all that. At Rae City she went down and incinerated a demon horde. Then more recently she changed night to day to alter the course of a major battle and, at least indirectly, influenced mortal politics. You were a witness to both incidents, I understand."

"Yes. Everything she did served the cause of The Gods."

"Oh, I quite agree. But our Law Goddess is a stickler for strict adherence. 'If we can't work within the rule, we must amend it or make a new rule,' she says. 'But we must never, never bend it. If The Gods don't follow their own laws, who will?' A persuasive point."

"Maybe," I said doubtfully. "So how does this summons work? How do I get to Paradise?"

"My colleagues have got whole volumes of preachings and doctrines addressing that point. I'm just the middle-man. You should consult a priest for guidance."

"I mean to testify."

"Oh, of course. Don't worry, the Ethics Committee will transport you when they're ready. Peppermint?"

"No, thank you."

"They're quite good. Well, I expect you'll be wanting to get back to your own ship. Important mission, fate of the world and all that, I suppose?"

"Yes."

"You're doing good work. My colleagues chose well when they selected you as their Champion. Please do keep in mind the importance of upping the death rate in these critical times. Don't be squeamish, I'm saying. If someone deserves it, give it to them. Every little bit helps. And I do appreciate the assistance. Just between you and me, productive killers get a little extra time for themselves for helping me meet quota. Frequent dying bonus, you might call it."

"For mass murderers and the like?"

"Love them. They make my work a lot easier. I look out for them. Also generals, arms merchants, incompetent doctors, and cigarette manufacturers."

"Proud company."

"It's nasty work. But it has to be done. Well, nice chatting with you. For your sake, I hope it's a long while before we meet again."

16

"So where are we?" I asked.

Skipjammer looked up nervously from his charts.

"By a combined use, sir, of sextant, astrolabe, compass, dead reckoning, and other navigational aids, sir, I have determined that we are somewhere in the Hammerperk Mountains."

"The Hammerperk Mountains?"

"Just south of Highgutter Pass, I think."

I looked around and saw blue water in every direction.

"I think your calculations are a bit off."

"Obviously," said Skipjammer, throwing down his pencil in disgust. "I was never good at navigation." He scanned the horizon and tested the wind with a wet finger. "That smudge to the west must be the Heights of Knowledge on Cape Harakan, sir, which shelter fabled Everwhen Keep. And those various dots on the north horizon are more likely the Prospect Islands than the Spendthrifts. There to the southeast must be steamy Cyrilla. And from the warmer weather, we have clearly crossed the Tan Line into those waters where winter is merely an abstraction. All in all, sir, I'd guess we are less than three hundred miles southwest of our goal, past the Cape of Good Prospects and nearing the Straits of Cyrilla."

"Then the storm gave us quite a boost."

"Indeed it did, sir. And I believe we'll see Rancor before week's end."

"Good. Too much time has passed already."

"What happens when we reach Rancor?" asked Solana. "What is your plan?"

"I'll continue to play King of the Rogues and bluster my way into a confrontation with Dread. If I can take him out, I'll be the ruler of Rancor. That should make it much easier to do what we came to do."

"If Dread has the Superwand, he might not be so easy to beat."

"True. But what are the chances he'll know how to use it? If he did, wouldn't he have done so by now?"

"Who's to say he hasn't?"

"It just doesn't wash," I said. "But then, neither does the idea that a lowly pirate would find the power object which has eluded everyone, including the Demon Lords, for ten centuries."

"Stranger things have happened."

"True, but I can't imagine the Mighty Champion hiding the Superwand somewhere that Dread could get to it."

"Perhaps he hid it in a place so obvious that no one thought to look there."

"Like the purloined letter?"

"Exactly. And maybe Dread just stumbled across it. It's possible."

"Except that Tannis tells me Dread sailed south last year boasting he would come back with a superweapon. That sounds like he knew what he was going after."

"It isn't necessarily the Superwand he's got," said Solana. "We have one agent's guess to go on and he was no expert. No one has seen the Superwand for almost a millennium. Perhaps Dread located some other wand and is merely calling it the Superwand. I think that the most likely possibility. It wouldn't be the first time a knockoff Superwand has turned up."

"Then why are we here?" I asked.

"Whatever he's got, it's dangerous. And there's always that slim chance that it's the real thing. We're nearing the Next Age. If the Superwand is ever going to resurface, now is a good time for it."

The floor of shark-infested Bonerattle Bay was littered with the crushed hulls of ships and the scattered skeletons of their crews dancing jerkily in the wild current, but these were not the true source of the bay's name. That honor went to the constantly shifting rocks—the "rattling bones"—that prowled its waters like grazing behemoths and could grind up a ship like the teeth of a giant herbivore.

There was a pattern to the movement of the rocks, and only the Pirates of Rancor were privy to the secret of that pattern. Admission to the Rancor fraternity was a high honor for a pirate and was eagerly sought by most pirates not of Rancor. Membership was by invitation of the Council of Free Captains only. That invitation did not come until a corsair leader had proved himself or herself by capturing a certain tonnage of shipping and a certain amount of booty and performing a certain number of daring pirate deeds. The exact qualifications were the secret of the Council, but when they were met, the Membership Committee informed the fortunate felon of his elevation and he was escorted to Rancor and inducted into the freebooters' fraternity with great celebration and much rum guzzling.

Rarely was the invitation refused, for when a pirate captain became a Pirate of Rancor, he had arrived. Aside from the prestige and pension benefits, there was the advantage of having a virtually unassailable safe harbor in which to enjoy the fruits of one's labors unmolested by the forces of law and order. The rattling bones frustrated any large-scale naval assault on Rancor, though the fleets of Zastria, Cyrilla, Manjiphar, and Caratha had all tried at various times. Tried and failed miserably.

"Are you sure you know the route?" I demanded of Skipjammer.

"Certainly, sir! I learned it from my cousin Princess Meredith."

"Princess Meredith?"

"A mermaid, sir, of Aqualon, sir. The merfolk know all the secrets of the deep, including the ways of the rattling bones. You see, this waterproof chart bears the seal of the Royal Aqualonian Marine Survey Company."

"What does that disclaimer say? There with the fine print?"

"Just a note that every once in a while the rocks deviate from their usual pattern without warning, apparently out of a simple malicious desire to mash ships."

"What?"

"The rattling bones are a force of nature, sir. They can't be entirely predictable or it wouldn't be natural at all. This keeps the pirates on their toes, I suppose."

"Shouldn't you take the wheel yourself?" I asked, looking aft, where Nodkin the helmsman was asleep again.

"Nodkin can do the job, sir!"

"Wouldn't he do a better job if he had this chart to look at? Some of those rocks are coming awfully close."

"No need for him to consult it, sir. I'm the captain of the ship, sir. As long as I know what must be done, all is well. If he gets too far off path, I'll steer him straight, no doubt of it! I've no wish to go down in these waters again."

"Again?"

"About two years ago, sir, the rocks did indeed deviate from their appointed path and crush the *Mira-*

cle en route to Rancor. But this time, I'm sure we'll make it."

"I wish I was."

Despite my misgivings, we successfully crossed the bay and reached our next obstacle, the Gullet. This was a narrow, twisting channel enclosed by high cliffs. A lone fjord, almost. The unpredictable belching winds of the Gullet were so hazardous that sail-powered vessels had to be towed through it. And lest galleys be employed in an assault, defenders manned the heights, ready to crush invaders with catapults and prepackaged rockslides. Thus, no ship reached the inner harbor without the consent of Rancor's overlords.

An armed tug rowed out to meet us at the mouth of the Gullet.

"We must pay the tug fee, sir," said Skipjammer. "And I don't think they take credit cards."

"I'm a little short on cash. What happens if we don't pay?"

"We don't get towed and the catapults open fire."

"I'll see what I can scrape together."

The master of the tug blew his shiny whistle and hailed us.

"Hail!" he cried. "What ship be this and who be its master?"

"That would be you," whispered Skipjammer.

"That would be me!" I snarled at the tug master. "Who wants to know?"

"I'm the tug master," said the tug master. "Now identify yourself."

"I'm Jason Cosmo," I said.

"And I'm Little Boy Blue. None of this clowning now, who are you really?"

"Temper," prompted Skipjammer.

"I've told you who I am, you brainless barnacle! Now tow my ship to the inner harbor before I come over there and shove that shiny whistle somewhere you'll find it hard to blow!"

"If you are Jason Cosmo," said the tug master, "then you're not on the admit list and I can't take you through the Gullet without special permission from the Big Goomba."

"I'll give you Big Goomba!" I said, drawing my sword. "I'll blast you out of the water!"

Solana, from the cover of our cabin door, gave me a nice added effect by surrounding Overwhelm's blade and my head with a corona of heatless flame. This seemed to impress the tug master.

"No need for blasting, sir! I'm certain the Big Goomba will be pleased to receive the second greatest pirate of all time!"

"Second greatest?"

"Well, the Big Goomba claims to be the greatest, so I had to say that. Personally, you're number one in my book!"

"Good."

"About the towing fee now . . ."

"What about it?" I said with menace.

"Ah . . . it's waived! Yes, waived! An honor to tow the great Jason Cosmo in at no charge!"

"Get on with it, then!"

Threading the Gullet took hours. As the *Miracle* was pulled slowly along, word of my arrival was relayed overland to the city. Captain Dread knew I was coming. What manner of reception he would prepare for me, I could only guess. Perhaps the full might of his Dreadguards awaited me on the docks. Perhaps we would never reach the docks, but would be crushed by falling boulders at Dread's command and swallowed by the dark waters of the Gullet. Perhaps he would zap us with the Superwand.

Or perhaps there was a foul-up in the chain of communication and Dread remained ignorant of my approach, for we reached the inner harbor without incident and there was no unusual activity on the waterfront.

The inner harbor was perhaps half a mile across, hemmed in on all sides by the same high cliffs that fronted the Gullet. On the north shore a series of low stone quays jutted into the water, and there pirates from the Indigo Sea, the Straits of Cyrilla, and the Scarlet Waves moored their ships, everything from galleys to galleons, for the winter. Though some enterprising pirates worked the tropical waters off the shores of the southern continent during the cold months, most took the season off and came to Rancor if they could, lesser refuges if they could not.

Behind the quays was the city itself, poised on a rocky lip skirting the cliff face. The streets sloped upward and all the gray stone buildings were streaked with grime and smoke. Taverns and brothels abounded, as at Nerak, but here also was the Pirate Bank, where judicious corsairs invested their booty in certificates of deposit and individual retirement accounts.

Other significant structures were a few neglected temples, the Slave Emporium, and the Museum of Modern Piracy. But the Corsairium dominated all else. Carved from the living rock of the cliff at the top of the town, it was a tall and angular palace, full of pillars and columns and balconies, so that it looked like the big, stern face of an implacable pirate god.

The palace was draped with large black banners bearing a red skull emblem, Dread's sign. There we would find the Big Goomba. And there we might find the Superwand too.

"So this is Rancor," said Solana. "It stinks of blood and rum and slavery and lust."

"At least according to the Rancor Chamber of Commerce," I said.

"It looks like some of your friends from Nerak have preceded us," said Solana. "Isn't that the *Notorious*?"

"Yes."

"And there—the *Jaundice,* the *Blackguard*. And is that the *Sea Demon*?"

"Looks like. So we have Tannis, at least one Malad, Lawler, and Gypsum. The nucleus of our conspiracy survives."

"Or at least reached Rancor. Dread may have killed them all by now."

"True."

"Rancor, sir!" said Skipjammer, strolling across the deck. "As vile a den of iniquity as you will find! Rancor! A place of low cunning and black treachery, sudden violence and cruel laughter, rampant greed and gluttonous appetites! Rancor!"

"You know it well?"

"I was going to say that."

"I know. Good job, Captain. Lady Solana and I will handle things from here. But I suggest you and your crew stick close to the ship and be ready to depart at a moment's notice. We may have need for a hasty departure. Or, if you wish, depart now. I'll not ask you to risk yourself further than you have. I'm really not paying you enough for that."

"True, sir."

"Will you be leaving, then?"

"And strand you here, sir? Our contract was for a round trip and I agreed to your price! No, I'll await you here, sir. However, if you ever wish to charter me again, I'm upping my rates."

"Good enough."

We all stood and looked at each other for several moments.

"What now?" said Solana.

"I guess we go ashore. I was just waiting for something to happen to give us a sign about how to proceed."

"What sort of thing?"

"Well, a message or something."

"Message for Jason Cosmo!" called a uniformed messenger boy striding purposefully down the docks with an envelope in hand. "Message for Jason Cosmo!"

"Here!" I called, beckoning the boy as I descended the gangplank.

"Are you Jason Cosmo?" he asked, wide-eyed.

"Yes."

"Wow." He gaped wordlessly, then suddenly remembered his mission. "This message is for you."

"Thank you." I took the envelope and gave him a gold coin in exchange.

"Gosh, thanks, Captain Cosmo!"

"Stay out of trouble, kid."

"What?"

"In trouble, I mean. In trouble. Stay in trouble and maybe someday you can be an infamous pirate like me."

"Wow! Wait till I tell the fellows about this!" He ran off excitedly.

I tore open the envelope and scanned its contents.

"What does it say?" asked Solana.

"Mistress Darkwolf bids me come to her villa," I said. "She says we must act quickly if our plan is to succeed."

"That would be the plan where the two of you eliminate everyone else and rule Rancor together."

"Yes, that's the plan. Well, I suppose I should call on Mistress Tannis and see what she has in mind."

"I can guess what she has in mind," said Solana. "And I'd suggest keeping her at arm's length."

"I'll do my best," I said.

17————————————

"I thought you lost in that unnatural storm and all my hopes with you," said Tannis, twining her arms around my neck. "Dread has more mercenaries than we expected. The others turned coward, but we may carry on now that you have come."

"Good," I said, shifting in the hot tub to put as much distance between us as possible.

"Your feats at Nerak are now known to every pirate in Rancor. We can easily seize power once we kill the others." She slid around beside me and did wet, unnerving things to my left ear with her tongue.

"What about the Dreadguards?"

"We'll buy them off."

"Of course."

"Our success will be sweet," she whispered hotly.

"Naturally," I said, moving away. "When shall we strike?"

"Dread will send for you this evening to swear an oath of loyalty as the rest of us have done."

"Even you?"

"Even I, but it means nothing, being an oath sworn under duress."

"Of course."

"All the captains will be there for the ceremony. You kill Dread, then we will kill the rest together and that will be that."

"Once I kill Dread, the others will obey me. No need to kill them too."

"Better to kill them all and elevate new captains of our own choosing who will be completely loyal to us because they owe their positions to us."

"I hadn't thought of that. But didn't you imperil our whole plan by calling me here? Surely Dread is watching my every move."

"Not at the moment," said Tannis, slithering across the tub. "I went to him when your ship entered the Gullet and volunteered to seduce you, learn your intentions, and report back to him."

"I don't remember that being part of our plan."

"I improvised. But now, you see, the more time we spend together, the less suspicious he will be."

"How clever of you," I said, gently slipping away from her grasping hands.

"You seem ill at ease," said Tannis.

"You've developed double-dealing to a fine art. How do I know you won't betray me?"

Tannis laughed. "I am no fool. Dread cannot prevail against you. None of them can. And the crews worship you. You are the natural ruler of all the pirates. And I am your natural mate."

"Are you?" I asked in a trapped voice.

"Yes!" she said fiercely. "So stop eluding my touch before you drive me wild!" She dived across the tub and pinned me to the side of the tub with a great splash.

As she dragged me under, the door to the bath chamber swung open and Jacques Malad burst in, saber in hand.

"So, you lying wench!" he shouted. "I have caught you in the very act of betrayal!"

"Actually, we hadn't gotten that far yet," I said. "But I'm glad you stopped by when you did."

"Get out, Jacques!" said Tannis. "You don't belong here! Get out!"

"No, my wife! Not until I have had my revenge on you and your paramour!"

"Wife?" I said.

"He lies!" said Tannis.

"You're married?" I said.

"Yes, dog!" said Jacques.

"No!" spat Tannis. "That ended long ago!"

"Only in your treacherous mind!" raged Jacques. "I have never consented to set you free, and until I do, no other man may have you!"

"Pig!" said Tannis. "You do not own me! Now get out!"

"First I will kill this dog!"

Jacques lunged at me. I ducked under the water to avoid the thrust, then leaped out of the tub before he could stab at me again. I slipped and fell on the wet tiles, and the pirate kicked me in the ribs. I grabbed his foot and pulled him off balance. He fell backward.

Tannis exited the pool and grabbed for her own sword, only to be intercepted by Louis Malad. She struggled against him, but he clipped her on the head with the hilt of his dagger, stunning her and knocking her to her knees.

Five more pirates rushed in. I lifted the tub from its resting place and hurled it at them, then summoned Overwhelm. Jacques regained his feet and attacked. His saber snapped as it crossed with Overwhelm.

"Surrender!" snarled Louis, yanking Tannis up by her hair and holding his knife against her throat. "Or the harlot dies!"

Jacques spat in my face.

"From Coptris I'll take that, but not from you," I said.

"Who is Coptris?"

I lowered my sword, then suddenly kicked Jacques in the crotch. As he doubled over I kneed him in the face, swept his feet out from under him, and pressed Overwhelm's point to his breast.

"Idiots!" I said. "I'm Jason Cosmo, the greatest pirate who ever lived! I'd as soon kill you as look at you! In fact, I'd rather kill you than look at you, ugly as you are! Drop the knife, Louis, or your brother dies! And you'll be next! And then the rest of you slimy dogs!"

Louis dropped his knife and Tannis too. The other pirates wisely stayed on the floor where I had knocked them.

"Every man of you must be drunk out of his mind! You saw what I did at Nerak! The whole Zastrian army couldn't stop me! What chance does a pack of flea-bitten rats like you have? I'm Jason Cosmo! I take whatever I want! Ships, cities, gold, women! And that means, Jacques Malad, that if it's Tannis I want, it's Tannis I'll have. Whatever claim you once had to her, you've got none now! Is that clear?"

"Aye," he said weakly, but his eyes burned with hatred.

"Kill him!" said Tannis.

"No," I said. "No, I want these whipped dogs to slink out of here with their tails tucked between their legs! I want them to know that every breath they draw is by my good grace!"

"Idiot!" said Tannis, snatching up Louis's discarded knife and slamming it into his heart. The pirate fell, dead. "If you let them go they will betray us to Dread!"

Yet I hesitated to kill even Jacques Malad in cold blood, and in that instant of hesitation, he scrambled to his feet and ran from the room. His followers followed close on his heels.

I started after them, but Tannis grasped my arm and restrained me. She was covered with Louis's blood.

"Let them go now! You were too slow!"

"Stop them, let them go—make up your mind!"

"It is made up. Whatever Jacques tells him, Dread will not act before tonight. He already sees you as a rival and has taken precautions against you. His plan is to kill you at the ceremony, before the assembled captains, not sooner."

"Then why were you so insistent I kill them?"

"I just wanted Jacques dead."

"Are you truly his wife?"

"Once, years ago when I first began pirating. It was a mistake. He treated me poorly. I called an end to it. Yet he hounds me still."

"And that's why you want him dead?"

"Yes. However, killing his brother will satisfy me for now."

"Good."

"At least in that respect. But you must satisfy me in another." She pressed herself close and kissed me. Her kiss reeked of blood.

"Killing turns you on, eh?"

"Yes."

"Then wait a little longer, my bloodstained she-wolf," I said, pushing her away. "Wait until we are both bathed in the blood of the slaughter, the slaughter that will make us the paramount powers in Rancor. Then we shall celebrate our victory in the fashion you desire!"

"Excuse me, what happened to the ship that was berthed here?"

"What ship?" asked the old sailor sitting on a barrel, whistling and whittling something obscene.

"The caravel *Miracle*. It docked a few hours ago."

"Docked where?"

"Right there."

"Ain't no ship right there, mister."

"I know that. I'm asking where it is."

"What is?"

"The ship that was there."

"Somewhere else, I expect. Most things not here are somewhere else, usually."

"Thank you. You've been very helpful."

"Glad to oblige."

While I was with Tannis, the *Miracle* had vanished, and with it Skipjammer, his crew, and Solana. This development did not bode well for our mission.

I wandered the docks in confusion, hoping I had perhaps taken a wrong turn somewhere. But after an extensive search, I wound up where I had begun, where I knew the *Miracle* ought to be.

. The whittling sailor had moved on, but a delegation from Dread was waiting for me: a detachment of husky Dreadguards led by the pirate Mauvebeard. All wore the red skull badge. Dread apparently insisted on stylistic conformity among his followers.

"Where's my ship?" I rudely demanded of the man with the colorful facial hair. Alone in a hostile city, my role as feared pirate archetype was about all I had going for me.

"Scuttled," said Mauvebeard. "And it didn't take long. That tub went down like a lead weight."

"And my crew, dog? Where is my crew?"

"In irons, by order of the Big Goomba."

"On what grounds? Nobody puts my crew in irons but me!"

"The Big Goomba don't need grounds."

"He must have some excuse."

"Okay, on grounds of suspicion. How's that?"

"Suspicion of what?"

"Treason. Treachery. Trespassing."

"Trespassing?"

"You're not a Pirate of Rancor, Cosmo, whatever your rep. So by Rancor law, you've got no right to be here unless the Big Goomba allows it. Which he don't. So your crew is in the brig."

"I couldn't have reached Rancor if the Big Goomba hadn't allowed it. He could have had my ship sunk in the Gullet. He didn't, so that implies permission for me to be here."

"He had your ship sunk here. That implies you'd better not give me any more lip."

"Or what? I can take every man of you with one hand behind my back!"

"Maybe so, but then your crew is dead."

"What do you want then, pastel face?"

"You're to come with us to the Corsairium and swear loyalty to the Big Goomba."

"I thought that wasn't scheduled until tonight."

"You thought wrong. It's scheduled for now. When you've sworn, your crew will be released. Right now they're insurance for your good behavior."

"Do you expect me to trust you or your Big Goomba?"

"Of course not. I just expect you to do what you're told."

"This is a gross violation of the Freebooters' Code!"

"What Freebooters' Code?"

"There isn't a Freebooters' Code?"

"Not that I've heard of."

"Well, there ought to be. And this ought to be a gross violation of it!"

"Fine, fine. Are you coming along or not?"

"Aye, I'll come. The only reason I came to Rancor is to see your Big Goober, dead."

"That's Big Goomba. And his name is Dread."

"Whatever."

We proceeded to the Corsairium.

Captain Dread, Big Goomba of Rancor, entered the Hall of Free Captains and took his seat. Heavily armored Dreadguards flung open the oaken doors. A hundred mailed fists crashed against breastplates in salute. Two dozen ruthless pirate lords fell to their knees in homage. Only I failed to acknowledge his arrival with a proper show of respect.

Captain Dread was a tweedy little man wearing spectacles.

This was the Master of All the Pirates? He looked too weak and frail to command a dinghy in a duck pond. It was a wonder he could even lift the sword that he laid across his knees. This was the Terror of the Seas? His looks wouldn't frighten a shy child. His black tunic with the big red skull on the chest was too loose fitting to be imposing; it had no rippling muscles beneath it. The high back of his throne threatened to swallow him up.

This was Captain Dread?

Yet the pirate chieftains cowered around him like doves around the hawk. Jacques Malad, Lawler, Tannis, and Gypsum were there. Also Scourge, with his trademark whip, Pelga, and sharp-toothed Kakalakka of Dhurfa. Halim the Scruffy, Rubberduck, Lugnose, Vartan the Mule—it was a roll call of nautical infamy. All appeared subservient, though I knew that several held rebellion in their hearts. Perhaps the dozens of Dreadguards lining the walls had something to do with their attitude.

They didn't worry me. My only problem was deciding whether I actually wanted to challenge Dread or not. Killing him by treachery was not an option, but if I beat him in a duel, then I'd be the Big Goomba. But from the look of him, it wouldn't be a fair fight at all.

"Jason Cosmo," said Dread, in a thin, reedy voice I strained to hear. "I've heard much about your deeds. But the time has come for you to acknowledge your master." He removed his wire-rim spectacles and polished the lenses on his sleeve.

"And who would that be?"

He put his glasses back on. "Me. The Big Goomba. The absolute ruler of all pirates. The other captains have sworn to obey me without question. You'll swear too."

"They obey you without question?" I asked skeptically.

"That's what I said."

"They do anything you command?"

"They do."

"Will they bark like dogs?"

"Bark like dogs," ordered Dread.

All the pirate leaders, even my co-conspirators, barked.

"Down on all fours?" I asked.

"Down on all fours," said Dread.

The chieftains, even Tannis, dropped to all fours and continued barking. Some even wagged their tails on their own initiative.

"Amazing. Roll over and play dead?"

"Do it," said Dread. "Roll over. Play dead."

The pirates complied.

"Would they sit up and beg?"

"Sit up and beg," said Dread.

The leaders imitated begging dogs.

"Impressive," I said. "Do they do ducks?"

"Yes. They do ducks. They do whatever I say."

"And they look so silly doing it."

"They fear me. You will too."

"You may have cowed these puppies, but I'm Jason Cosmo."

"You say your name as if it means something."

"It does."

"Well, not here. Here Dread rules. That's me. And all who will not serve me must die. So just swear the blood oath, Jason Cosmo. Swear it."

"I'll swear no oaths to you! You swear one to me!"

"You don't seem to understand. I'm the Big Goomba. I don't have to swear. You do."

"I challenge your right to be Big Goomba! I'm the greatest pirate who ever lived! I should be the Big Goomba!"

"Well, that's your opinion. But as it is, I'm the Big Goomba and you're not. So swear."

"I'm challenging you to a duel of honor!"

"Having no honor, I'll pass. Are you going to swear the oath or not?"

"I swear the only blood I—"

"Before you continue, let me tell you I know all about the plot against me."

"Plot?"

"Certain of the captains here don't approve of my reign as Big Goomba and are plotting my violent removal."

"Fancy that."

"Or at least they did plot against me. My sources inform me they have abandoned their plan out of a quite reasonable fear that it will probably fail. But that's too little, too late."

Dreadguards thrust their swords into the backs of Lawler, Gypsum, and a few other captains I did not know. The conspirators crumpled.

"Then there is the Pirate Queen."

Two Dreadguards seized Tannis. Jacques laughed. Dread regarded her sternly.

"You are the worst schemer of all, dear Tannis. So for you, I decree a fate worse than death. You I give to my faithful Jacques Malad, to do with as he will."

"I'd rather die!" spat Tannis.

"I know that. That's why I'm giving you to Jacques. I did say it was a fate worse than death."

"What do you mean by that?" asked Jacques, slightly insulted.

"Nothing. Take her away now."

Four Dreadguards wrestled Tannis to the floor and Jacques snapped an iron collar and leash around her neck. It was yet another scene of degrading violence directed at women, but what happened happened. Jacques would get what was coming to him eventually anyway.

"Do something!" Tannis shouted to me. "Strike!" A Dreadguard cuffed her in the face. Jacques laughed.

I reached for Overwhelm. "Unhand her!"

"Hold that thought," said Dread.

The doors of the hall flew open and two Dread-guards dragged Solana in. She was bound, gagged, bruised, and unconscious. They threw her to the floor and held their spears against her back. The threat did not have to be spoken aloud.

"One of your crew, I think," said Dread.

"Rough on the ladies today, aren't we? You fellows aren't gentlemen."

"No, we're pirates."

"The two don't have to be mutually exclusive."

Dread shrugged.

I could save either Solana or Tannis, but not both. Had Solana and I continued our romance, this would be the point at which I would prove my love for her by springing to her side and leaving Tannis to her fate. That wasn't necessary now, but Solana was still my partner. I slowly moved my hand away from Overwhelm's hilt.

Dread smiled. "He won't be helping you, Mistress Darkwolf. He cares more for his lady friend there than for you, I think."

"Treacherous dog!" Tannis shouted at me.

"He's the treacherous dog," I said, pointing at Jacques, who thumbed his nose at me.

"Lying, filthy, stinky pig!" raged Tannis.

"Is that me or Jacques?"

"Both of you!"

Jacques tugged hard on the leash and dragged Tannis toward the door, with help from the Dread-guards, who took much abuse in the way of kicks to the shins and fingernails to the eyes.

"I find it interesting," said Dread, "that the so-called greatest of all the pirates, the infamous Jason Cosmo, would number among his crew a first cousin of the Raelnan Queen, who is also a member in good standing of the League of Benevolent Magic."

"What's this?" I said, feigning surprise. "She didn't mention that on her application."

"Oh, don't feign surprise. You know who she is. And don't expect her to get you out of this situation with a stunning spell. She has been soundly dosed with Noarcane."

"I see."

"Not yet, you don't. I know you are not truly a pirate, Cosmo. I know you are not truly a criminal at all. You are a hero. A Champion of The Gods, or at least of the Goddess Rae. You ally yourself with the League and do their dirty work. You have come to Rancor seeking the Superwand. But I don't have it. The report to the League was false. Bait for the trap."

"A trap for me? I'm flattered. What do you want?"

"I want nothing from you. I just want to rule Rancor and from Rancor the seas. Soon every ship of trade, every port will pay tribute to my coffers to avoid destruction at my hands. It is the allies providing me the means of threatening mass destruction who want something from you."

"What allies?"

"You'll meet them soon. First, remove your sword belt and take off that armored suit of yours. Hurry now, or your woman dies."

I peeled off my outer clothing and removed the Cosmosuit. Dreadguards took it from me and placed it, along with Gardion and Overwhelm, in a wooden chest. They also took the Rae medallion and the Ring of Raxx.

"The chest is made of insipid wormwood, the most highly inanimate and unmagical substance known to the world, which specifically does not run around on hundreds of tiny legs nor eat people," Dread said of the box. "But it does prevent you from summoning your magic sword by thought."

"Thought of everything, haven't you?"

"Yes," said Dread. "Everything. Now, for my amusement, bark like a dog."

"Is this necessary?"

"Indulge me."

"Woof! Woof!"

"Down on all fours."

I got down on all fours and crawled around. I sat up and begged. I rolled over. I fetched. I shook hands. I played dead. I quacked like a duck and waddled around. All for the amusement of Captain Dread and his cackling cronies. I hoped Solana appreciated all this when she came to.

"Enough merriment!" said Dread at length. "Downstairs with you! You've got an appointment with the Dark Magic Society!"

18

"Cosmo, we want the Superwand and you're going to tell us where it is," said Eufrosinia the Cruel, raking her razory black nails across my bare chest while her compatriots looked on impassively.

Chains clamped to my wrists, I hung over a gurgling pit in the bowels of the Corsairium. I wasn't sure what the pit contained, but from the sound and stench, the Corsairium had very troubled bowels.

"I don't know where it is," I said, mentally straining to connect with Overwhelm in the Hall of Free Captains several levels up. It was a futile exercise.

"Too bad. Now I get to hurt you."

"I thought you might say that."

Eufrosinia was a Dark Magic Society sorceress specializing in pain-and-torture magic. She was tall, lean, and pale, with wicked purple eyes and long hair black as a blood clot. Her taste in clothes ran to leather and metal studs. As a young girl, her favorite toys were sharp objects and injured birds.

She tapped my jaw with a slim ivory wand and every tooth in my mouth became a throbbing festival of pain, like a lifetime of dentist-chair ordeals rolled into one, complete with drills, forceps, and those nasty little metal hooks.

Eufrosinia laughed. "We are only getting started."

"How can you take such pleasure in causing pain?"

I asked, careful not to let my uppers touch my lowers and blast my jaw right off my face.

"Every girl needs a hobby."

"Ever consider stamp collecting? We went through all this at Fortress Marn. I don't know where the Superwand is."

"Have you ever had appendicitis?"

"No."

"It feels something like this."

She tapped my abdomen with her wand and it felt like I had swallowed a nest of porcupines, a cup of needles, two garter snakes, a tablespoon of ground glass, and a small saw blade.

"Hope I never get it, then," I wheezed.

"The Superwand. Where is it?"

"Didn't your new Overmaster call off the search?"

"Some of us disagree with the new policy."

In back of Eufrosinia and breathing heavily behind his mask stood Last Gasp, the so-called Prince of the Air Devils, who commanded all evil winds and foul vapors. His sky-blue robe billowed and rippled despite the stillness of the dungeon air.

The albino witch Thecia the Wan sat nearby, taking notes on Eufrosinia's technique. Previously a minor figure in the Society, her specialties were cattle cursing, crop failures, and the evil eye. Recently, she had begun dabbling in more sinister sorceries and had advanced aggressively through the ranks to join the Ruling Conclave. Her skin hovered on the visible side of translucent and her hair was like fine ash. Dark glasses shielded her sensitive and dangerous eyes.

The fourth member of the clique was Bloodstorm, who wore a dark red bodysuit covered with a grotesque network of pulsing exterior veins and arteries. He was infamous for developing the Efficient Erythrostatic Method of generating large amounts of arcane energy by removing the vital fluids of sacrificial victims with specially ionized ceremonial daggers. According to rumor, he had a gigantic erythrostatic plant in the Hammerperk Mountains, where acolytes chanted and drained victims around the clock, storing the released magic in huge arcane giga-batteries to create a pool of power that Bloodstorm could draw on at great distances.

My captors were all heavy hitters in the magical big leagues, and probably not the only ones vexed by the new Overmaster's directives. It was heartening to know the Society remained true to form by warring with itself. If the evil wizards ever truly united, Arden was theirs for the taking on sheer strength of numbers and raw power. But of course if they ever learned to appreciate mutual trust, cooperation, and putting aside personal differences for the common good, they wouldn't be evil anymore.

"You're taking quite a chance crossing Necrophilius," I said. "He's a master of death magic, you know."

"I know what he is," said Eufrosinia. "But he can die too. A new Overmaster can arise."

"You are one of the Three now, aren't you?"

The Ruling Conclave of the Dark Magic Society had four ranks: the Overmaster, the Three, the Seven, and the Twelve. When an Overmaster fell, the Three were the prime contenders to fill the vacancy. The Society had just ended the struggle to succeed Erimandras, in which Necrophilius came out on top. But all that meant was the plotting for the next change of regime could begin.

"I am asking the questions here," said Eufrosinia irritably. "Have you ever wondered what advanced arthritis feels like?"

"No, but I suppose you're going to help me find out."

She tapped me again and all my joints swelled up like twisted balloons trapped in lead pipes.

"Pretty bad," I said faintly.

"Do you ever get a pinched nerve?"

"Sometimes."

"It would be bad if all your nerves got pinched at once and stayed that way."

"Yes, it would."

"And imagine the feel of paper cuts all over your body. With salt and lemon juice rubbed in. All with one tap." She held the wand close to my chest. "Where is the Superwand?"

"I don't know."

She tapped me. The promised varieties of pain jolted me. My nerves buzzed like cantankerous hornets and my skin puckered and twitched like it was burning and peeling away.

"Are you ready to tell me what I want to know?"

"I'd love to, but I honestly don't know. You're operating on the assumption that I am the reincarnation of the original Mighty Champion and therefore have the secret of where he hid the Superwand locked inside my head somewhere. But I have it on good authority, from The Gods themselves actually, that I am not a reincarnation of anyone. They don't do reincarnations, you see. So no matter how much you torture me, I can't tell you what you want to hear. I could make up something, but that wouldn't do you any good. Why don't you save us both a lot of trouble, let me down, and we'll forget all about this? What do you say?"

"If you really do not know where it is, there is nothing to prevent me from slowly torturing you to death. I have many new techniques I want to try."

"Well, I'm all for advancing the frontiers of scientific knowledge, but wouldn't you rather let me go and instead torture some nice cuddly laboratory animals? Rub lipstick in their eyes or something?"

"No."

"Just asking."

"I think I will now let you experience the sensations

you would feel if you could actually survive all your
blood vessels bursting."

"Is this one of the new spells?"

"Yes."

She tapped me with the wand. My insides went
squish, but I didn't really notice the pain since my
nerves were at capacity dealing with the last spell.
Still, so as not to disappoint, I managed a weak
scream.

"Arrgh! Yes, I think you've perfected this one.
We're talking complete agony."

"What is it like?" she asked eagerly.

"Indescribable. I think I'll black out from the pain."

"Don't bother. I'll only revive you."

"Well, never mind, then."

"Let us talk about the Superwand."

"Let's. There are four of you. I can't see you shar-
ing the thing."

"We only want to free great Asmodraxas."

"Sure you do," I said. "You're a regular bunch of
Pup Scouts. None of you would even think of be-
traying the others."

"Do you seek to sow dissension in our ranks?" demanded Bloodstorm.

"Wise to me, eh?"

"You are hopelessly transparent. But know this,
Cosmo. We are dedicated to a higher purpose. The
Dark Magic Society was founded with one goal! One!
No less than the restoration of the Empire of Fear
and the Rule of Evil. The first Ruling Conclaves knew
that to ensure evil's triumph we must liberate great
Asmodraxas from his bondage and restore to his hand
the Superwand which the so-called Mighty Champion
stole from him with cowardly tricks. Since those days,
the Society has forgotten its true purpose. Like Necrophilius, our leaders have pursued other agendas,
sought self-aggrandizement at the expense of true
evil's cause. They betrayed the principles upon which

our Society was founded, wasted our blood and magic in mundane power plays when our every resource should have gone to restoring the King of Darkness to his throne! Not until Erimandras did we again have an Overmaster true to our cause. You stopped him, Cosmo, but we carry on his work. The Superwand will be found, Asmodraxas will be free, and the unending Age of Evil will begin! Nothing and no one can stop us!"

"Not enough that I'm captured by the Dark Magic Society. No, I've got to fall in with foaming-at-the-mouth radical Dark Magic Society hard-liners."

"Do not mock us," said Bloodstorm. "Your life is in our hands."

"So what?" I said. "Kill me and you'll never find the Superwand."

"Have you never heard of necromancy?" scoffed Last Gasp. "Even the dead can be questioned."

"Oh, are you a necromancer?"

"No," admitted Last Gasp.

"What about you, windbag?"

"Hold your tongue, maggot," said Bloodstorm.

"I thought not. Mistress Eufrosinia?"

"I will hand you your tongue on a stick," she said.

"The better to hold it. I'll certainly be able to tell you a lot after that. So I guess it's Thecia who converses with corpses."

"I never learned how," said the witch. "I've been meaning to take it up, though."

"I suppose you could always call in Necrophilius," I said scornfully.

Eufrosinia punched me in the stomach. Between the appendicitis and her spiked gloves, the blow hurt. Enough to make me vomit blood. Torture is no fun, especially on the receiving end, and I couldn't maintain this insolent front forever. I had to make something happen.

"You can't afford to kill me," I said. "I keep denying I know where the wand is and you keep insisting that I do. Maybe you're right, but you'll never get it out of me this way. If it's in there, it's hidden deep. Too deep for me to get at. Understand?"

"Torture is ineffective," said Thecia.

"You're starting to see the light," I said.

"We must employ other means," continued the witch.

"Exactly!"

"Very well," said Eufrosinia. "Have Sweetfire brought in. Perhaps watching his ally suffer will jog Cosmo's memory."

"Wait! Wait! Wait!" I said desperately. "You're missing the point! It doesn't matter who you torture, I can't get to the information you want. It's too far down in the depths of my mind."

"Then you admit that you know?" asked Eufrosinia.

"Yes," I said gamely.

"Bring the girl!" she commanded.

"I'm not getting through to you, am I?"

Eufrosinia smiled. "This has nothing to do with you, I just want to torture her for a while. She is a Leaguer and a beloved cousin of the hated Raella. But you may watch. Do you care for her?"

"Yes, you heartless witch!"

"Thecia is the heartless witch. I'm a heartless sorceress. It's a technical distinction, but an important one. Now, you care for Lady Sweetfire, you say?"

"Yes, you heartless sorceress! Don't you dare harm her!"

"You speak your clichés with such conviction. I do so enjoy making people watch their loved ones suffer. Pay close attention. It will be the last spectacle you ever see, for afterward we will strip your mind apart piece by piece and find whatever is in there. Bloodstorm, how long will it take you to prepare the Ritual of Stripping the Mind Apart Piece by Piece and Finding Whatever Is in There?"

"All the implements are laid out," said the sangui-
nary sorcerer. "I will be ready to commence by, oh
say, half past the Hour of the Horned Goat. The Dark
Pale of Midnight at the latest. Although I may not
have enough virgin's blood on hand to do a good job
of it."

"Can you get more?"

"In this city?"

"No excuses, just prepare the ritual. That will give
me plenty of time to amuse myself with Lady
Sweetfire."

Captain Dread swept suddenly into the room. He
looked like he'd had several sleepless nights in the
hour or so since I last saw him. He'd lost his spectacles
and his eyes were bloodshot and rimmed with dark
circles. His hair was matted and wild. He moved like
a paranoid spider monkey.

"Have you broken him yet?" he snarled. His voice
was deeper, stronger, and gruffer than it had been in
the Hall of Free Captains.

"Not yet," said Eufrosinia, taken aback.

"Well, what's keeping you, wench! Get to it!"

"Mind your tone, ruffian," she said dangerously.
"That could as easily be you hanging there."

"I wouldn't mind swapping places," I said.

Dread whirled on Eufrosinia like a dagger whipped
from the sheath and thrust his face close to hers.
"Don't threaten me, missy! This is my city, my palace,
and you're all here because I allow it! I'm not afraid
of your magic, but you'd be wise to fear me! Fear me!
Wise indeed!"

They locked eyes for several seconds and amazingly
it was Eufrosinia who backed down. He turned on the
others. "That goes for all of you. Dread is master
here, and don't forget it!"

The wizards made placating noises and the Big
Goomba shifted his attention to me. "You should
have sworn yourself to me when I asked, Cosmo!

Stinking do-gooder. Mighty Champion. Just like in the old days. You hate me, don't you? You always have."

"We've never met before today, but no, I'm not too fond of you."

"We've met. You just don't remember. We met a long time ago. A long time ago! That's right! You hated me then and you hate me now, but now you're the one in chains! Chains." He laughed hoarsely. "Chains, chains, chains, chains, chains!"

Dread drew his sword and waved it in my face. The long blade was exorbitantly black and inscribed with strange shifting runes.

"I have a magic sword!" he said. "Better than yours! It talks to me! Does yours?"

"Talk to you? How should I know?"

"No, to you."

"Bring it down and I'll ask it."

"No, yours stays in the box."

"Why? Do you fear it?"

"I fear nothing! I have nothing to fear! I am fear itself! I'm Dread! My very name is synonymous with fear!"

"I can't argue with you there."

"These spell spitters want to bring back the Empire of Fear. And it will be back! With me at the head as Emperor Dread! It is my destiny!"

"How do you figure that?" I asked tolerantly.

"The blood of the Evil Emperors flows in my veins! I am heir to their power! I will resurrect their empire and rule it in the name of darkness! The sword has told me so!"

"I think you've been cutting your grog too strong."

"You scoff! Everyone scoffed when I was plain old Pirate Joe. But they sang a different tune when I became Captain Dread, who takes no prisoners and leaves no witnesses. Cut 'em up for fish bait! Here fishy, fishy! Then they feared me from Xorth to Praetora. Still do. I know the power of fear, you see.

It's my destiny. That's why the sword called out to me from where it lay in the devil-haunted Tombs of the Thrice Damned. The Evil Emperors swung this sword! They hacked away the merry day with it. And their enemies, too! Hack, hack, hack, you won't be coming back!"

"You've missed your calling. You should be a poet."

"I rule the pirates now! When the springtime comes, we will sally forth and turn the seas red with blood! No port, no village is to be spared. No fleet will stand against us. By high summer, I will rule the Indigo Sea from shore to shore. The rebirth of the Empire will begin! With swords, monsters, and magic I will spread mayhem across the land! Kill! Kill! Kill some more! Kill them all from shore to shore!"

"Today Rancor, tomorrow the world, eh?"

"That's right!"

"Could one of you Society types sedate this guy?" I asked Eufrosinia as Dread danced around killing invisible phantoms with his black sword. "You've picked a real winner here."

"No," said Dread. "I picked them. I invited them to Rancor! By their arts they will pry out of you the Superwand's location. When it is in my grasp, the triumph of my empire will be assured. The Age of Evil is nigh upon us, Cosmo, and this time nothing you do will prevent it!" He sheathed his sword. "Continue the interrogation, Eufrosinia. Report to me at once if you learn anything. I must consult with my captains." He stalked out, carrying himself as if he was already Emperor of the World.

"What got into him?" I asked.

Eufrosinia cast a worried look at Bloodstorm, who returned it.

"It couldn't be, could it?" asked Thecia. "How is it possible?"

"How is what possible?" I wanted to know.

DIRTY WORK 227

"Did you notice anything familiar about his voice?"
asked Eufrosinia. "Not so much in the tone or quality
as in the cadence, the rhythm, the word choice?"

"Not really," I said. "Why do you ask?"

"Subtle foreshadowing. Never mind."

The sorcerers were obviously unsettled by what had
just happened. This was a Society operation and they
were supposed to be the masterminds pulling the
strings. But it looked like their chief puppet was set
to do his own dance, and was in fact jerking their
chains. Had Dread gone mad?

Bloodstorm left to set up his ritual and the Dreadguards arrived with Solana. She was conscious now,
but obviously drugged and unable to stand unaided.
Her hair was in disarray, her sleeve torn, an ugly
bruise marred her right cheek. At Eufrosinia's direction, they strapped her into a torture rack.

"Now, Cosmo," said the Mistress of Pain, "you will
see that I have been gentle with you. Lady Sweetfire
will be an unrecognizable bloody blob when I am done
with her. Are you ready?"

I didn't answer. Suddenly my pain was gone and so
was I.

19

"Jason Cosmo, you have been summoned to the Halls of Paradise to stand before this Divine Ethics Committee and testify truthfully and completely. Do you swear to do so, so help you me?"

"I do."

"Be seated."

I took my seat at a table facing the imposing bench behind which sat the five members of the Divine Ethics Committee. In the center was the Chairgoddess, Lexis Fairplay, who had just sworn me in. With severe hair, a stern nose, frowning eyes, and rigid lips, she presented a no-nonsense appearance.

"Master Cosmo, as you were advised previously, this committee is investigating allegations that our colleague the Sun Goddess has repeatedly violated the Non-Intervention Pact which forbids any of The Gods from directly interfering with, intervening in, intruding upon, influencing the course of, interrupting the consequences of, or otherwise impeding the natural flow of events in the mortal sphere, specifically the world of Arden. I must further advise you at this time that the inquiry in which we are presently engaged is of a purely fact-finding nature. If our findings at the close of these proceedings warrant it, we will recommend disciplinary action and turn the matter over to the Court of Divine Justice. The committee believes your testimony will be helpful in ascertaining the facts, as you were present at both of the incidents in question. Therefore, it is important that you be completely candid with the committee and answer our questions to the best of your recollection. Do you have any questions of your own before we proceed?"

"Will this take long? A friend of mine is in great danger down below."

"I had in mind questions about these proceedings," said Lexis reproachfully, "but be advised that the situation in Arden is under observation, and if, at any time, it is our opinion that your presence there is required to prevent significant disruption of the otherwise anticipated course of events, you will be transported to that plane forthwith."

"Does that mean Solana is okay for now?"

"That is substantially what I just said. If you have no procedural inquiries at this time, we will commence our questioning. The chair recognizes Goddess Varda."

At the far right sat Varda Allfrost, the implacable Ice Goddess. With her hypothermic blue skin and glacial expression, she looked as alien and hostile as the frozen wastelands of the Ultimate North. I didn't imagine she had much in common with Rae.

Speaking of Rae, the red-haired Queen of Daytime sat directly behind me on the first row of seats, flanked by her lieutenants Gloama Eventide and Eliora Dawnstar. All the solar goddesses wore dark sunglasses, giving them an air of unconcern. Rae flashed me a brief million-candle smile when I arrived, but I sensed further interaction would be inappropriate.

The spectators' gallery was filled with gods and goddesses both major and minor. I spotted Rae's gloating rival Lucinda Everfair, the Love Goddess, with her smug minions the Tempting Trio of Forna, Coquetta, and Avona. I recognized Ama, Goddess of Medicine, and her daughter Aeroba, Goddess of Physical Fitness. Lloyd, God of Insurance, was there, as was Biscona, who ruled over baked goods. History Goddess Archiva was naturally on hand to get the story straight. And Heraldo, God of Irresponsible Sensationalism, was there to get the story distorted.

Some of the most powerful deities, like Great Whoosh and Arkayne, were absent, but they could always watch the live gavel-to-gavel coverage broadcast by P-SPAN.

"Thank you for joining us today, Master Cosmo," said Varda. Her brittle breath was so cold that vapor clouds formed when she spoke. "I begin by commending you on the fine work you have done for The Gods since we placed you on the Roll of Heroes."

"I thank the Goddess for the compliment."

"I would now like to ask you about the first incident this committee is investigating, which occurred last spring in Rae City. This was soon after your arrival there. Could you first tell us why you were in Rae City at that time?"

"As I recall, Goddess, I was directed there by He Who Sits On The Porch, a minion of The Gods. I hoped that Queen Raella would be able to read my scrambled aura and tell me why the whole world was out to get me. As you know, my aura contained a message from The Gods directing me to the Shrine of Greenleaf."

"Whence you journeyed to stand before The Gods," said Varda. "But before your departure, Rae City was beset by a horde of demons. Tell us about that."

"It was a horde of bright orange flying demons. The city's air defenses couldn't stop them. In desperation, Queen Raella summoned the Goddess Rae to preserve her chosen people."

"Indeed," said Varda. "And how did she accomplish this?"

"You would have to ask Queen Raella about that," I said.

"We intend to," said Varda. "But give us your version."

"Well, a band of wizards held off the demons while Raella performed the rite of summons. It looked to me like she opened a gateway to the sun. On the other side was Goddess Rae."

"I see," said Varda. "And what was Goddess Rae doing?"

"She appeared to be sunning herself and drinking a Sola-Cola."

"Sola-Cola?"

"Diet Sola-Cola," I amended.

"She was watching her figure, then," said Varda.

Many in the audience laughed. Lexis brought down her gavel for order.

"I wouldn't speculate," I said.

"What happened next?"

"Raella told Bright Rae that demons were destroying her city."

"That was Rae City, the city of Rae's chosen people?"

"Yes."

"And what was Rae's response?"

"As I recall, she said, 'What city?' "

More titters from the audience. Lexis demanded order.

"Please speak into the microphone," said Varda. "And then?"

"Raella told her it was Rae City. Goddess Rae seemed surprised that it still existed. She indicated that she had not taken an interest in mortal affairs for several centuries."

"Nor much else," Lucinda Everfair stage-whispered to one of her cronies.

Lexis brought down her gavel with a bang. "I will have order or I will clear this meeting room!" she said, staring straight at the Love Goddess, who merely smirked.

"This is very enlightening," said Varda. "What then?"

"Raella explained that her people were in grave danger, mostly because of my presence. At this point, Goddess Rae transported me through the portal to her sunny realm."

"And what transpired in her sunny realm?"

"We talked."

"About what?"

"I told her who I was and explained my situation."

"Is that all?"

"Pretty much so," I said, not wanting to get into the business of my rubbing suntan oil on her back. "I explained Rae City's plight and pointed out that Raella was Goddess Rae's own descendant, through the line of Blaze Shurben."

"Our 'All-seeing' Rae did not instantly recognize Queen Raella as one of her own?"

"Apparently not."

"Is Raella Shurbenholt not only the ruler of Rae's chosen people in a kingdom named in Rae's honor, with a capital city named in Rae's honor, but also Rae's chief priestess?"

"I believe so."

"Yet she did not recognize her?"

"So it seemed to me. But I'm only a mortal. I wouldn't want to speculate too deeply what was going on in her mind."

"In discussing the mind of the 'Bright' Goddess, depth is evidently not a factor," observed Varda. "Did she finally recognize her own after your explanation?"

I was silent. Varda's blatant cheap shots told me she wasn't interested in merely bringing out the facts. She was trying to lead me into providing some bit of damning evidence against my patron goddess. This smacked of a personal vendetta to me. I decided not to cooperate anymore.

"Did you hear my question?" asked Varda.

"Rae did recognize Raella," I said.

"And what happened next?" asked Varda, with the eagerness of a blizzard about to bury an isolated hamlet. She wanted me to say that Rae violated the Pact by descending to Rae City.

"I don't recall," I said.

"What?"

"I don't recall."

"Did not Raella descend to Arden and incinerate the demons?"

"I don't recall."

"How can you not recall?"

"This happened months ago and I've been knocked in the head several times since then. I simply do not remember all the details of that meeting. And I did not take any notes from which I could refresh my memory."

"You recall the attack of the demons. You recall entering the realm of Rae to urge her to intercede. Yet you do not recall whether she did so or not?"

"This is correct. I do not."

"I am skeptical of this sudden and selective amnesia, Master Cosmo."

"As am I," said Lexis sternly. "Mortal, I direct you to fully and accurately answer the questions put to you or this committee will find you in contempt of The Gods, which is a major sin. Goddess Varda, repeat your question."

"Did the Goddess Rae descend to Arden and incinerate the demon horde?"

"I do not recall."

"You have been warned, mortal," said Lexis. "You will not be warned again. Answer the question."

"I have given my answer," I said defiantly.

"What more, if anything, do you recall of that incident?" asked Varda.

"The Goddess Rae kissed me, rendering me unconscious for three days. There was nothing else worth recalling."

The crowd laughed, except for Lucinda and her crew. Lexis banged her gavel for order, then pointed it at me.

"Mortal, your levity is most inappropriate! You risk grave punishment if you do not render this body the respect which it is due!"

"When she kissed you, were you in her realm or in Rae City?" asked Varda insistently.

"I don't recall."

"You had to be somewhere."

"I thought I was in Paradise."

The crowd laughed again.

"Enough!" shouted Lexis. "Master Cosmo, you are in contempt of The Gods!"

"Only some of them!" I said loudly. "I may be a mere mortal, but I see what is going on here. I can plainly hear the tone and intent of the questions put to me. This is no fact-finding inquiry. This is nothing but a kangaroo court!"

Some gods applauded. Others shouted "Blasphemy!" Lexis Fairplay turned purple.

"Bailiffs!" she commanded. "Seize the mortal and take him immediately to the Chamber of Contemplating the Error of One's Ways!"

"Madam Chairgoddess, point of order!" said Freshlord, a member of the committee.

"The chair recognizes God Freshlord. State your point."

The God of Fruits and Vegetables, in his straw hat and faded overalls, with a haystalk in his mouth, wore the aspect of a grizzled old farmer, full of homespun wisdom.

He gave a long sigh and said, "Well, ah reckon the distinguished Chairgoddess surely knows she can't send a mortal down to the Chamber of Contemplatin' without the unanimous consent of all members. And ah don't give mah consent."

"Why not?" demanded Lexis. "You heard his blasphemous utterance. He questioned the fairness and impartiality of this body!"

"Ahm just an ol' country god, Madam Chairgoddess, but it seems to me that young Jason has a point." Freshlord pushed his hat back and scratched behind his ear. "Now, we all know you're impartial, Madam Chairgoddess. No doubt about it. If anything, you're too impartial, 'cause all you see is the rules. You reckon that as long as the proper procedures are followed, everything is fair. What you don't see is that others can use those rules unfairly, follow them to the letter, and still produce a bad result. But that's your bias as the Law Goddess. You cling to the rules."

A hush fell over the room as Freshlord spoke, as calmly and casually as if he was discussing the weather or what seeds to plant or the right kind of fertilizer to use for pole beans.

"There's other biases at work here, it seems to me. Who filed these charges against Rae? Lucinda there, who's had a spite going against her for centuries. Along with her whole clique—ah won't name names, 'cause they know who they are—who have various petty reasons for wantin' to stick it to Rae. Ahm sure that Rae violated the literal terms of the Pact. She's not the first of us to do so, though ah must say her violations are the most spectackler ever committed. Changing night to day and so forth. Maybe for that reason she deserves a reprimand. But all she's really guilty of is not thinking before she takes action. That's just her hot nature at work and we all know it.

"But some among us want to use these incidents to cause her embarrassment, inconvenience, and worse. Ah have heard talk of subjecting her to the Trial of The Gods. None of this is called for and those gods and goddesses involved should be ashamed of themselves. They are lettin' their biases interfere with their judgment and their better natures. And this is not right.

"As for young Cosmo here, his bias is his sense of loyalty and fairness. He saw pretty quick what was goin' on here and he wanted no part of it. He was a farmer before we asked him to be a hero, and he's got a farmer's good sense. And he's got a hero's courage, because ah dare say there are not many mortals who would sit here in the presence of The Gods and tell us we're wrong. This boy calls a spade a spade no matter who tells him it's tuna-fish sandwich on rye. We can be thankful he's on our side. In partiklar, Rae can be proud she chose him as her Champion because ah have never seen a finer display of loyalty to one's patron than what we just saw."

Many of the assembled deities applauded.

"For all that, his outburst was ill advised. Son, you just can't talk to The Gods in that tone of voice and expect to walk off without paying a price."

"I understand, sir."

"Ah knew that you would. Madam Chairgoddess, ah move we direct a mild reprimand to Master Cosmo—ah will object to anything ah deem too harsh. Ah further move we dismiss him as witness at this time and that we call an immediate recess of these proceedings for the purpose of determining whether in fact they ought to proceed any further."

"I second the motions," said Amex, God of Commerce, also on the committee.

The vote was three to one on the motions, Freshlord, Amex, and Torrent Wetlace voting for, Varda against.

"Very well," said Lexis. "Master Cosmo, it is the will of the committee that you be reprimanded for your outburst. Therefore I hereby reprimand you as follows: For shame! Don't do it again. Do you have anything to say?"

"I apologize to the Goddess and to all members of

the committee for any comments any member found offensive," I said.

"Very well," said Lexis. "You are dismissed. This committee stands adjourned!"

She brought down the gavel and the crowd was on its feet, talking among themselves, moving about, gesturing, pointing at me.

I turned to address Rae, but Heraldo slipped in between us and thrust his big mustache and a microphone in my face.

"Master Cosmo, what are your reactions to the heavy-handed draconian tactics of the Ethics Committee? Do you feel personally outraged by their relentless and self-serving persecution of your patron goddess? What really went on between you and Rae when she entertained you in her realm? Do you deny recurring rumors of topless sunbathing and wild lesbian polygamous skinhead devil-worshiping adulterous underage racist cross-dressed kitten juggling? Can you explain the large withdrawals from the secret under-the-table private slush fund? What is your connection to the alarming increase in the statistical incidence of tattoo smudging among left-handed teenagers? Are you hiding a long-term substance-abuse problem? Who are you protecting? Who paid you to keep silent? Have you been the target of a cynical campaign of threats and harassment? Are you an Elvis love child? Would you like to be a guest on my show next week?"

"No comment."

"Beat it, Heraldo," said Eliora Dawnstar. "Or I'll hit you with a chair again."

"The people have a right to know," protested Heraldo. "Hey! The committee is leaving! Varda! Lexis! Any comment?"

He hurried to catch the committee members before they exited. They hurried to exit before he could catch them.

Rae threw her arms around me. "Jason! You were

wonderful! Of course, you need not have said all those things which made me look bad! Was I really such a silly goose? Well, it doesn't really matter, I knew I could count on you. Maybe they will call off this whole ridiculous investigation now. Don't you think they should? I didn't do anything wrong. The Pact allows personal aid to your high priestess and Raella was there both times. It's painfully obvious I was acting for her benefit and the fact I turned the tide of battle and saved thousands of other lives was purely incidental. It's not as if I was *trying* to influence events. I just have a flamboyant style, that's all. No crime in that. It's just like dear old Freshlord said. It's all spite by Lucinda and her cronies. They're jealous of me and always have been. It's very good to see you. I've been dealing with these absurd hearings since the Battle of Voripol and I've hardly had time to do anything else. Did Raella tell you she's reforming my Church? I'll have the most modern religion of all when she's done. It's very tedious with all those organizational details. I told her to just handle it, because I'm sure she will do a good job. You've met Gloama, haven't you? This is Eliora, she handles sunrises for me. I couldn't do a thing without these two. Did you get the amulet Raella asked me to bless for you? I put all sorts of interesting powers in it, I think. Gloama, dear, where are my shoes? What was I saying?"

"What a shame it is that I have to go back to Arden right away," I said.

"Oh, yes. Of course. But I should reward you first, don't you think so, Gloama?"

"Absolutely," said the Dusk Goddess. "Perhaps additional strength would be helpful."

"Something that works at night would be nice if that isn't too much trouble," I said.

"Nighttime is beyond the Sun Department's authority," said Eliora. "But Rae, you could increase his sun-supplemented strength and decree that it shall be effective whenever the sun shines, whether Jason is himself in sunlight or not. That would help him on overcast days."

"Splendid idea!" said Rae. "I so decree. And I will give you now the strength of a hundred men!"

"Too much," said Gloama.

"More than the mortal frame can bear," added Eliora. "Make it twenty men."

"Okay," said Rae. "Twenty men, then. During the day. Now, Jason, I expect you to use this new gift to perform even more spectacular deeds so I can rub Lucinda's nose in them."

"I will do my best," I said. "But if you could send me back to Rancor now, Holy Rae, I'd appreciate it. One of your people is in danger. Someone I care about."

"A Raelnan? Someone I know?"

"Lady Solana Sweetfire, Raella's cousin."

"I don't recall the name," said Rae. "But I'm sure I've seen her. After all, I see everything. At least in the daytime. When I look, that is. You like her, then. Is she pretty?"

"She was when I left."

"Whatever does that mean?"

"Rae," said Gloama. "Just send him back."

"Very well," said Rae. She waved her hand. "Back to Arden with you, Jason. Oh wait! I forgot to tell you about—"

Whatever it was Rae forgot would wait. I blinked out of the Halls of Paradise and returned to the dungeon of the Corsairium.

20_____

"Jason! Where did you come from?"

The torture chamber was as I had left it, but Eufrosinia and her cohorts were gone. Solana remained on the rack, still in one piece, now fully conscious, and obviously surprised to see me materialize out of thin air in a flash of golden light.

"Solana! Thank The Gods you're all right! Where did the wizards go?"

"What wizards?" she asked. "Where are we?"

By the nonsurge of strength to my limbs, I knew it was still nighttime. I unhitched the straps binding her rather than simply ripping them asunder.

"We're in the dungeon of the Corsairium. You were captured and drugged. No Superwand. It was all a Society trap. I guess they're out hunting me now. My timely vanishment to Paradise surely threw them for a loop!"

"Paradise? The Society? What are you talking about?"

"I'm talking about us getting out of Rancor as soon as possible! They sank the *Miracle,* so we'll have to go overland."

I released the last strap and caught her as she stumbled away from the framework. It felt good to hold her in my arms, alive and whole, if slightly worse for the wear. She clung to me tightly and we kissed, then remembered we weren't playing it that way.

"Sorry," I said. "I got carried away."

"It's okay. So did I. It happens. Plot pressure. We forget ourselves."

"I was worried sick that Eufrosinia would take out her rage on you when I disappeared," I said.

"Eufrosinia? Eufrosinia the Cruel?"

"Yes."

"Do you mean to tell me you vanished and left me here in the clutches of Eufrosinia the Cruel?"

"Yes," I said. "I'll explain later. Has the Noarcane worn off yet?"

She gestured with no effect and grimaced. "No. The very attempt of spellcasting gives me a splitting headache."

I tried summoning Overwhelm and the Cosmosuit again, with the same lack of result as before.

"They've taken my armaments, my cover is blown, Skipjammer and his crew are locked up somewhere, Tapnis is in the vengeful hands of Jacques Malad, and Captain Dread is developing multiple personalities."

"I didn't miss much, then."

"But we do have the cover of darkness. Come on. It's time to sneak through the castle."

Using skills honed sneaking into Fortress Marn, the Solar Palace at Rae City, and Castle Bloodthorn, I led Solana up through the Corsairium, retracing the path I had followed down from the Hall of Free Captains, where I hoped the box containing Overwhelm remained. We avoided all contact with Dreadguards and other palace minions. This feat was less impressive than it sounds since the palace appeared deserted.

That made me suspicious.

"I'm suspicious. I imagine if we reach the Hall unimpeded, it will be another trap," I said. "I scarcely believe that everyone is out running through the streets looking for me. For that matter it's odd that they left you unattended."

"I wasn't going anywhere."

"True enough."

As I feared, the way to the Free Captains' Hall was completely clear, the doors were wide open, the chamber brightly lit, and the box with my weapons in it sat in the middle of the floor. The only surprise was that the lid wasn't invitingly open, perhaps with my sword and armor laid out nicely for display.

"Wait here," I said.

I strode boldly into the room. According to Mercury, the best way to neutralize a trap is to spring it. As long as you go in knowing it's a trap, you won't be too surprised by whatever happens. Once you get the threat in the open, you can deal with it as appropriate and go on about your business, without having to worry anymore about what kind of trap you might be walking into or away from.

When Merc told me this, I argued that an even better way to neutralize a trap was to avoid it altogether. Merc insisted, however, that avoiding a trap you knew about only meant you would fall prey to some larger, deadlier, and more fiendish trap. He apparently believed a kind of trap karma was at work in the world and that we could buy off the nasty megatraps by stumbling into the lesser ones. I was skeptical, but Mercury was an adventurer of many years' experience, which you don't get to be by talking nonsense.

As I approached the box nothing continued to happen. I stopped short and walked slowly around it, studying the problem from all angles. I saw no trip wires, no telltale shine of contact poison, no anvils suspended above. An army of pirates did not come rushing out from behind the curtains. There weren't even any curtains.

This was indeed a devilish trap.

I gingerly touched the box.

Nothing happened. No explosion. No release of a deadly cloud of gas. No pit opening beneath me.

Perhaps it was a nasty megatrap.

I shook the box, felt the contents shift, but heard nothing. I tried to open it, but of course it was locked. Lacking the tremendous new strength Rae had promised me, I couldn't simply rip it apart. I tried lifting it, but it was too heavy. I shoved it experimentally and it shifted. I could push it out onto the balcony, lever it over the rail, and hope the fall would crack it open, but that seemed an awkward process.

"Solana, can you cast yet? If you could cut through this with fire—"

"Sorry," she said. Then: "Hurry! Someone approaches!"

"Quick! Under here!" I said.

We darted under the dais. The platform was a good two feet from the floor and the space beneath was screened by a cloth skirt.

Peering out, I saw Dread enter, accompanied by the Society wizards. He wore armor of a fancy casting, with an antique look. It was enameled in black, with skulls and demon figures traced in lines of ruby. He wasn't laughable anymore.

"If Cosmo escapes, you will all pay with your lives!" he raged.

"Everyone from the palace is running through the streets looking for him," Eufrosinia assured the Big Goomba. "We even left Sweetfire unattended."

"Do whatever it takes, but get him! I must have the Superwand, and Cosmo is the key to everything!"

Dread stomped up to the dais and sat down. His minions formed a crescent before him. What was Dread's power that even the haughty lords of the Dark Magic Society obeyed him?

"Bloodstorm! Go and prepare your ritual. Be ready when Cosmo is found."

Bloodstorm nodded and hastened eagerly from the room.

"Last Gasp! You will ward the harbor. No ship—none!—is to transit the Gullet. Use your command of the winds to make it impassable."

"Done," said Last Gasp, obviously relieved to be dismissed.

"Thecia! Your task, Wan One, is to guard the overland pass. Let no one reach the heights! He may try to flee through the Lumpwads. You must prevent this."

"As you command," said Thecia, bowing her head before taking her own leave.

"Eufrosinia! Return to the dungeon and ward the flame-haired Raelnan wench. Toy with her as you wish, but do not slay her. Cosmo will surely come back for her. You must be ready."

"Of course," said Eufrosinia, and she turned to go.

Before she left, a Dreadguard entered and saluted.

"Dread Lord, the flame-haired Raelnan wench is gone!" he announced.

"What?" cried Dread, leaping to his feet. "The flame-haired Raelnan wench gone! How can this be?"

"She cannot have escaped on her own," said Eufrosinia quickly. "Cosmo must be in the palace!"

"Find him!" roared Dread. "Find him or I will flay you alive, every one of you!"

Eufrosinia and the guard rushed out.

Dread sat once more and argued with himself. The pirate was making a last-ditch effort to reclaim his psyche from whatever thing, being, entity, spirit, or madness had possessed him so suddenly. Or perhaps the other was making a final effort to eliminate the pirate.

"I don't want to rule the world," said Dread, lapsing into his reedy voice. "I merely want gold and glory and striking fear in the hearts of my foes and paying no taxes. That's all that matters."

"Power is my destiny!" responded the maniacal

voice. "I am the scion of the ancient House of Skarri, the rightful ruler of all Arden! It is my duty and my right to restore the Empire of Fear which my fore-bears built! And I will surpass even their conquests! This time the Evil Empire will stand forever! And so will I! Or at least until my feet get sore! The Gods themselves will tremble in their alabaster halls, calls, falls—"

"What am I talking about? What is going on here? I feel like someone else is taking over—"

"The Superwand is the key. I must be free! I will be free!"

"Oh, no! Oh, all you Gods—gakk!"

"Speak not of The Gods! They are weak! They are nothing! Evil is the all! Evil everlasting!"

Dread stood and shouted that last proclamation.

As the echo died Solana sneezed.

It was a cavernous sneeze. A sneeze for the ages. A wet, messy, neck-snapping, deep-from-the-gut sneeze of sneezes. No one could mistake it for anything else.

Dread ceased his ranting and sat down.

"Come out," he said. "I know you are there."

Having little alternative, we wriggled out from beneath the dais.

"So, Cosmo, you prove as resourceful as ever. Yet you are still without your weapons." He caressed his black sword. "I am not."

"Who are you?" I asked. "You're not Dread."

"The body is Dread's, but the rest is mine. As for my identity, I am surprised you have not yet deduced it."

"Well, don't tell me. I'll get it."

"You haven't long. Your mind is to be stripped away and the refuse rooted through until I have the secret I want."

"That would be the Superwand's location?"

"Yes."

"Could I just draw you a map?"

"You jest."

"Of course."

Dread gestured, and the locks on the chest clicked open. I summoned my Overwhelm and Gardion and stood ready to do battle. Overwhelm ignited with an unprecedented blue fire while Dread's sword gave off an evil black radiance.

"What did you do that for?" I asked. "You had me dead to rights."

Dread strapped on a bat-winged helm. "I crave battle. Before you are sent screaming to the altar table to have your mind stripped away, I want the satisfaction of defeating you in personal combat."

"Okay, fine. Could I have a moment to don my own armor and make this a fair fight?"

"No. Who said anything about a fair fight?"

"Silly me."

"You have there a sword no mortal weapon can stand against. But my blade is also one of great power. Its runes were inscribed by the Demon Lord Asmodraxas aeons ago. With it an Emperor of Fear slew ten thousand foes. For an age it lay lost to memory, thirsting for what it needs most."

"Blood? Souls?"

"Banana daiquiris."

"Banana daiquiris?"

"The only way to sate this sword is to soak it in banana daiquiris. When it is not so fed, it grows angry, and when it is angry, it tends to absorb, chop, grate, mix, whip, stir, and puree souls. I haven't fed it in a while. Behold Daiquirimaker, Blender of Souls!"

An evil, eager whirring sound emanated from black sword, and its unholy dark radiance gained intensity and shifted to red.

"Fah!" I said. "You behold Daiquirimaker. I'll behold Overwhelm, god-forged sword of the Mighty Champion, who, you may recall, trashed not only the

Emperors of Fear, but their whole stinking empire and Asmodraxas besides!"

I held Overwhelm high and it glowed with its own bright light. It also made its own angry hum, which I had never known it to do. I got the impression these swords had met before and this was some kind of grudge match. Dread seemed to think he and I had met before, so there was another grudge match. Everyone and everything involved knew what was going on except for me. Which wasn't unusual.

"What's going on here?" asked Solana.

Well, Solana didn't know either, so I felt a little better.

"It looks like a climactic showdown to me," I said. "Stand back. I'm sure someone will be along shortly to keep you occupied."

"Indeed," said Dread.

"Sure. I'm a woman. Push me aside and hog all the glory."

We closed for combat. Our swords rang together explosively. Brilliant red and blue sparks flashed where metal met metal. The swords stuck to each other like the bonded poles of a magnet—the good and evil poles of a moral magnet—and bands of weird purple lightning ran down our arms. An electric burning sensation ripped through my body, and I could tell Dread felt it too.

We strained against each other hilt to hilt for several seconds until Dread gave way, then came back instantly with another slashing attack. I blocked his swing, but it was a near thing.

After that we fought in earnest. No fancy footwork or elegant moves, just gut-crunching cut and thrust. Huff and puff, flash and hum. I beat him back for a while, forcing him across the hall and onto the balcony. Solana, the only witness, stayed well clear of the titanic energies we were giving off.

Dread rallied and regained the ground he had lost,

pushing me back into the hall, around it a few times, then back to the balcony.

"You're good, Cosmo," he said. "Maybe as good as they say."

"The Gods are with me," I replied.

I know that sounded sanctimonious, but there was more to this than a simple fencing match with high-powered hardware. I felt the not-so-subtle overtones of cosmic struggle. In Rancor, of all places.

"The Gods are niggling do-nothings!" said Dread with sudden fury. "I spit on your gods!"

"Why is that?"

"What have The Gods ever given this world?"

"Existence?" I ventured.

"Oh, yes, they made the world, but care not for it. It is a mere plaything. You and I are nothing to The Gods. They sit on their high thrones in the sky and laugh at us. They'll never let mere mortals take their rightful place in the scheme of things. They're jealous! They fear us! They're afraid of what will happen when we realize we don't need them!"

"Don't we?"

Nothing like a highbrow theological disputation to spice up a death duel fought with sorcerous swords over a thousand years old.

"No we don't need The Gods!" Dread fumed. "They're not worthy of our worship! Their rules prevent the strong from mastering the weak and taking what they will, as it should be!"

"Sounds like a quote straight from the *Hellfire Catechism*. You didn't by any chance trade your soul to a Demon Lord for that sword?"

"Good guess, but not quite. I found it, as was my destiny!"

"Oh, right, I forgot. We discussed this earlier. It called to you. Object-to-person, I suppose. Or did it call collect?"

Neither of us had actually scored a hit yet. It appeared we were evenly matched.

"Do you mock me?"

"Me? Mock a megalomaniac pirate who thinks he's going to restore the Evil Empire with a sword named after a mixed drink? Perish the thought."

"You shall perish!"

As I intended, my goading enraged him. It was amazing how often that transparent tactic actually worked. He made a wild swing and couldn't recover in time to block my counterattack. I thrust Overwhelm deep into his chest through a gap in the antique armor. It was a mortal wound.

Or should have been. Dread stumbled and fell with a clatter. I breathed a sigh of relief and whirled to confront the squadron of Dreadguards who chose that moment to storm into the hall. Solana had disappeared, but I could take them alone.

Then Daiquirimaker made its whirring noises and Dread lurched to his feet again. A definite mad light shone from his eyes, which glowed as red as a feral coal in the Fathomless Furnaces of the Far Hells.

"Dread, my friend, is there something you aren't telling me?"

"I cannot die while I hold Daiquirimaker! I draw power from the souls it takes! I can increase my power beyond all imagining! Enough to defeat you! Enough to defeat The Gods themselves!"

"Gee, my sword doesn't do all that. This hardly seems fair."

"Who said anything about fairness?"

"I'm sorry to keep bringing it up. Maybe I should get my next sword at the Tombs of the Thrice Damned."

Sweeping past me, Dread fell upon his bodyguards, cutting them all down before they could even think about defending themselves. The blending noise from Daiquirimaker rose in pitch and intensity. The Dreadguards shriveled to dust and Dread grew three feet taller. The sword grew in similar proportion.

"Then again," I said. "It does seem to make you a little overaggressive."

I had a feeling Dread had not suddenly switched sides, so though it cut the odds in my favor, his move was probably a bad thing.

There was no doubt that Daiquirimaker was the key. A weapon so ancient and with such evil properties probably had an alien intelligence all its own. Maybe it was the sword itself that had possessed Dread. This was my second best guess, after the "sold your soul to a demon" scenario.

Actually, both theories were correct in a way.

Dread turned and laughed. His laughter was different now.

"Have you discerned the truth yet, Cosmo?"

So was his voice, which both soothed and stabbed my very soul with its bewitching brutality. Now I knew what Eufrosinia and the others had suspected, had feared. Now I recognized that beautiful, fearsome voice, and I cried its owner's name.

"Asmodraxas!"

21

"Aren't you imprisoned in null space or something?" I asked, my voice an octave or two higher than I preferred.

"You mean the prison you put me in?" replied Asmodraxas mockingly. His voice gave off sinister harmonics. **"Yes, I am still there."**

"You are? Aren't you here?"

"Yes and no, most hated of men."

"You're talking in riddles."

"The most sublime of mysteries must ever seem riddles to frail mortals whose minds can grasp only the tattered threads which hang from the lower hems of reality. Yes, the greater part of my substance remains trapped in the accursed nonspace into which you hurled me a thousand years ago. But never was I a prisoner entire, as you will now learn to your disadvantage."

Greatest of the Demon Lords who rule the Assorted Hells, Asmodraxas led the Hellmasters against The Gods during the mythical Age of War. His minions dominated Arden during the nightmare Age of Despair, until the Mighty Champion finally brought him down and banished the archdemon to a featureless limbo where he could harm nothing and threaten no one.

Why he didn't just destroy him, I don't know. Perhaps he couldn't. But in less than a decade, the Next

251

Age would begin. If Asmodraxas made a comeback now, he might create the Age of Evil which had eluded him last time. I had already stopped one plot to free him at Fortress Marn. This looked like another.

"You are about to horribly die," said Asmodraxas as he raised the whirring black sword.

"Let's not be hasty," I said. "What you mean is, you're about to try to kill me. But don't you want to first impress me with the depth and subtlety of your infernal genius by explaining more fully how it is that you are seemingly here inhabiting the body of an over-size pirate while claiming that you also remain confined in limbo?"

My foe laughed. **"Is it not obvious? I forged this sword Daiquirimaker millennia ago and infused it with a portion of my own essence. It partakes of my substance and is permanently linked to me. The energy of the souls it blends and purees strengthens me even in my exile, for the fundamental connection between me and the sword transcends all dimensional barriers. We are as one. You see, you pitiful speck of nothing, you never banished me completely from Arden. Even in the final moments of our climactic battle, I transmitted small portions of my power into objects and hidden places prepared as vessels for it. I have always maintained a slight influence in your world. Your victory was not as complete as you imagined!"**

"Well, it wasn't *my* victory anyway," I said. "You're confusing me with my ancestor."

"Oh, it was you, Cosmo! Do not seek to deceive the Great Deceiver. I know the stink of your courageous soul. Perhaps you have forgotten your crimes against me in that long-ago lifetime, but I have not. And you will suffer for them when I am free. How you will suffer!"

"But you're not free, are you? The crumbs of yourself you left behind haven't done you much good."

"Have they not? You know not what shadowy wheels I have set in motion. One hidden talisman let me influence the archimage Erimandras, who might have freed me but for his untimely downfall. When the pirate took this sword from the Tombs of the Thrice Damned, I corrupted his mind and urged him to spread chaos and slaughter across the face of Arden, feeding me thousands of souls to fortify me in the coming war, the final war, against The Gods. He was off to a good start until you killed him. No matter, another will claim the sword and do my work."

"Dread is dead, then?"

"You stabbed him through the heart, did you not? I animate his corpse solely to deal with you."

"Body by Dread, animation by Asmodraxas. Got it."

"Consuming your soul will be a special delight."

"I thought it was the old ritual of mind-stripping for me?"

"If I absorb your soul, the ceremony will be unnecessary. All you know and are will be mine."

"But you said—"

"Dread said that. He did not understand the full power of Daiquirimaker because I did not wish him to. I require no underlings to deal with you, Cosmo. You will be one less nuisance when I return. And I will return. The Next Age will be the Age of Asmodraxas."

"Over my dead body!"

"Are you not listening? That is exactly what I intend. Enough prattle! To it!"

Asmodraxas now had a telling advantage of height and reach. Inch by inch he forced me across the balcony again, back against the low stone railing. As I dodged his hammerlike blows a crowd gathered in the square below. Word of our duel had spread with supernatural swiftness through the city. Seemingly every pirate, slaver, trader, harlot, mercenary, and beggar in Rancor had turned out for the show with a great deal of oohing and aahing and giving of odds.

I realized Asmodraxas was not pressing his full advantage, but toying with me, as if waiting for something. What he awaited did not occur to me until he laughed evilly and said, **"Perfect!"**

"What's perfect?" I panted. I was nearly winded, for while I had only my normal strength to draw on, Asmodraxas was bursting with fiendish might. Dawn was almost an hour away.

"The crowd."

A few hundred people had now gathered below. Dread turned away from me and leaped into the air. He flew, or more accurately glided, down from the balcony, an eighty-foot drop, and landed in the thickest part of the crowd.

Amid screams of terror from men and women alike, the mad pirate whirled Daiquirimaker all about, absorbing the souls of all he touched with the sword. The blade was on high speed now, its mournful blending sounds so loud that windows shattered and the fleeing crowd covered their ears lest they be deafened. The powerful sonic vibrations made the balcony crumble, tons of stone tumbling down to add further to the carnage and panic below. And Dread's body grew— ten feet, twelve feet, thirty feet tall. Daiquirimaker grew as well.

I sprinted back into the Hall of Free Captains and hastily donned the Cosmosuit, my Rae medallion, and the Ring of Raxx. I needed every advantage I could lay my hands on.

"Solana! Where are you?"

"Here," she said, sliding out from under the dais. "Taking cover seemed the best tack until this cursed drug dissolves from my system."

"Has it? We're going to need all the firepower we can muster!"

"I'm trying for all I'm worth, but I still can't conjure."

"Keep trying!"

Below, Asmodraxas continued to sweep the crowd with his howling sword, sucking up souls and gaining stature at an alarming rate. He was passing sixty feet now, with Daiquirimaker's blade half that length. Ignoring me for the moment, he started down the slope into town, crushing buildings and scooping up handfuls of people, whom he tossed into the air and swatted with his glowing sword.

"My power grows with each passing moment, Cosmo! With every soul I whip and grate!" Dread proclaimed loudly, his voice reverberating across the city, as he neared the docks. **"Already I am far beyond your capacities! Soon I will be invincible!"**

"He's right," I said. "How are we going to fight that?"

"Deus ex machina?" said Solana.

"Doubtful," I said. "That's how I got through my last two adventures. I'd lose all credibility if I did that again."

"You'll lose more than that!"

We turned. Eufrosinia and Bloodstorm entered the hall, followed by a dozen Dreadguards.

"Quick! Behind me!" I said, stepping in front of Solana.

"How endearingly chivalrous of you," said Eufrosinia, pointing her wand. A flare of blue spiritual lightning flashed from it. I deflected the bolt with Gardion.

"Asmodraxas is among us, Champion!" ranted Bloodstorm. "The Age of Evil is at hand!"

"Thank you for that public service announcement," I said. "But in case you hadn't noticed, your Asmodraxas is pureeing the souls of everyone in sight. We're all in danger here. Let's put aside our differences and stop him. What do you say?"

"Fool!" spat Bloodstorm. "The Master of Evil

merely feeds his power on worthless cattle! He will reward his true servants as he did in former days. We have nothing to fear from him. But you do!"

"Are you insane! Look at him! Listen to him!"

Asmodraxas towered over a hundred feet now. He was skewering ships in the harbor and shaking the sailors out.

"Soon I will come for you, Cosmo! You cannot hope to defeat me and your prayers for deliverance will go unheeded, for the quaking Gods are niggling do-nothings. They will not grant you succor. There is no hope for you, Cosmo! I am coming to destroy you!"

"Well, what about it?" demanded Bloodstorm. "He sounds reasonable to me."

"To you maybe. I think he's nuts and I'm getting out of here."

"You're not going anywhere. I will personally deliver you to the Dread Master."

"The Dread Master? Clever play on words."

"Thank you."

"You show more wit than I'd expect from a run-of-the-mill stock evil sorcerer."

"Who are you calling run-of-the-mill? You're no gem of originality yourself."

"That hurts. And so will this."

I lunged across the room and slashed at Bloodstorm. He leaped back, but I severed his right hand and blood sprayed from the stump. He fell to his knees and I trampled him as I moved on to engage the startled Dreadguards.

Solana was right behind me and, though no warrior, punched Eufrosinia squarely on the jaw, knocking her back. But the Mistress of Pain quickly recovered and struck Solana with her wand, sending my partner to the floor in paralyzing paroxysms of pain. Eufrosinia kicked her in the gut with a steel-toed boot and aimed her wand for the coup de grace.

I hewed a path through the Dreadguards, Overwhelm a brilliant silver blur as I turned aside blades, pierced mail, and severed limbs, downing five warriors in my initial rush. The rest wisely fled and I pivoted to confront the sorcerers once more.

Eufrosinia blasted Solana point-blank with a soul-searing bolt of spiritual lightning. Solana screamed and writhed and foamed at the mouth as her very essence burned. Eufrosinia laughed cruelly.

I sprang to the rescue, only to be intercepted by a bloodblast from Bloodstorm. He had regained his feet and sealed the stump of his forearm with some sort of foaming putty from a belt pouch. The carmine ray of force that he projected from his right hand stopped me in my tracks, though Gardion caught most of the blow.

"You will die most horribly for daring to strike me!" frothed Bloodstorm. "You have no inkling of the power which is mine to command!"

"No inkling and no interest," I replied. "You should have stayed down where I put you."

"You'll not be so impudent when the blood boils in your veins!"

He gestured and spoke and I felt the stirring of a sinister spell gripping my body.

"The problem with most of you wizards," I said through gritted teeth as I advanced, "is that while your powers are impressive at a distance, you're pretty much useless when someone gets close to you with a sword."

Bloodstorm staggered backward, his haughtiness evaporating as he divined the murderous intent in my eyes.

"Stay back! By almighty Asmodraxas, I command you to stay back!"

"Almighty Asmodraxas is busy eating the city right now," I said. "You're on your own."

I swung Overwhelm in a bright arc that slashed

open Bloodstorm's chest, severing the network of exterior tubes and vessels that covered his suit. Sparking, shimmering blood crackling hotly with arcane energy spewed over me, sizzling and vaporizing like drops of water on a hot pan when it struck my armor. Bloodstorm's suit ignited with wild eldritch fires that consumed him as he stumbled backward. Layers of flesh peeled away into nothing, leaving only a tumbling skeleton to hit the floor. The bones crumbled to powder as they hit the floor. Thus ended the foul career of Bloodstorm.

"Impressive," I said. "I've never killed a big-time evil wizard before. You guys certainly know how to make an exit."

Across the room, Eufrosinia's relentless attack on Solana ended abruptly when Solana rolled onto her back, lifted both hands, and engulfed the Mistress of Pain with a geyser of flame. Eufrosinia, having more combat savvy than Bloodstorm, had maintained a minimal magical defense, which saved her from being toasted, but she was startled and her assault faltered.

Solana rose unsteadily to her knees, but there was nothing unsteady about the expression of hatred and fury on her face.

"Now you will taste pain, witch!" she snarled. "Your accursed bolts have purged the drug from my system! Now I can defend and avenge myself!"

She launched another flamestrike, which completely obliterated Eufrosinia's form for a full ten seconds. But when Solana relented and the firestorm cleared, Eufrosinia stood unscathed.

"Thecia is the witch. I'm a sorceress," said Eufrosinia, aiming her wand for another blast. "And many times your better, girl."

Solana, in her rage, had neglected to raise her own defenses, and so Eufrosinia's redoubled attack struck her unchecked, once more convulsing her in agony.

I slammed into Eufrosinia from behind, ramming

her with Gardion and knocking her to the floor. In an instant, Overwhelm was at her breast.

"Drop it or die," I said grimly.

Eufrosinia half raised her ivory wand as if to launch a new assault on me, then let it slip from her fingers and clatter to the floor. I kicked it across the room.

Solana was curled in a ball, vomiting, trembling, the whites of her eyes showing.

"I ought to kill you anyway, after the way you tortured me."

"Kill me in cold blood as I lay helpless before you? How heroic." Eufrosinia smiled, thin black lips over perfectly white teeth, a sinister effect.

"Kill her," wheezed Solana.

"Yes, kill me," said Eufrosinia mockingly. "I deserve it. I'm evil, without remorse. My crimes are legion. Kill me now. Carve my black heart out with your shining sword. Please."

"I will, unless you give me a reason not to."

"Cosmo," called Asmodraxas. "Come and face me now, if you dare! Come to your destruction at the hands of Asmodraxas, Lord of Evil, Prince of Darkness, Master of the Profane, Once and Future Ruler of the Universe!"

"Modest, isn't he?" I said.

"There is your reason," said Eufrosinia coolly. "You cannot hope to defeat him without help. More help than that foolish child with her pathetic flickering fires can give you."

"Why would you help me? You're a charter member of the Asmodraxas Fan Club."

"I only read the newsletter. Bloodstorm was the fanatic. The rest of us only tolerated him because we needed his power."

"What power? All he did was die well."

"A loudmouthed braggart, true, but he was good with human-sacrifice rituals. Confrontations with heroes was not his forte."

"Obviously."

"Most members of the Society would just as soon not see Asmodraxas back in power. We want the world for ourselves, not as lackeys of a demon god. Erimandras, Sinshaper, Bloodstorm, and their ilk are the exceptions, not the rule. If I got the Superwand, believe me, I'd use it for no one's benefit but my own."

"I believe you."

"We formed our gang of four to hunt for the Superwand now that Necrophilius has abandoned the official search. We lured you here to wrest its location from you."

"You launched your plot quickly. A couple of months ago you were at Castle Bloodthorn with Rom Acheron."

"So were you."

"Still, you got a complex scheme under way in just a few weeks."

"The groundwork was already laid. True masters of villainy always have a couple of schemes in the works so that as soon as one is completed or falls through, we can get the next going."

"And how did Dread figure in your plot? Did you know of his connection to Asmodraxas?"

"Had I known, I'd have slain him long before now. He invited the Society into Rancor soon after seizing power on the pretext of offering us a base of operations in return for help in his grandiose schemes of conquest. I recognized Dread's sword as a relic of the Evil Empire and suspected it influenced his mind, but not that it was a conduit for the archdemon. Dread was biddable, if somewhat willful, until your arrival, a useful catspaw easily led by the lure of power and plunder."

"But you were the true catspaws."

"Yes," she admitted reluctantly. "It is now apparent that the evil genius of Asmodraxas lurked in

Dread's mind, gnawing quietly at the moorings of his sanity and identity, waiting for his trap to be sprung. He only today began raving of dark destinies and the blood of the emperors. We were unsure how to respond, not knowing how much power was actually present. I see now I should have slain Dread sooner, but I couldn't take the chance that he had the power to destroy me for even trying."

"But now that Asmodraxas is fully in control of Dread's hundred-foot-tall body, you're willing to oppose him? That hardly seems credible."

"I have no more wish to be enslaved than you, Cosmo. Eufrosinia the Cruel serves none but herself."

"Don't trust her," said Solana.

"Cosmo, I am coming for you now!" The archdemon started back toward the Corsairium.

"How can you help?" I demanded of Eufrosinia.

"Asmodraxas is not fully present on this plane. He can't bring his full power to bear. He is limited by what the conduit of the black sword will bear and he must continue to consume souls at a rapid rate to keep the link open at all. When he runs out of souls, he is defeated."

"What's the population of Rancor?"

"Sixty thousand or so."

"It could take a few hours for him to run out of juice. Plenty of time for him to destroy us all."

"Maintaining his giant stature is a showy waste of power that consumes much energy. If we fight him, he will consume more energy. Last Gasp and Thecia will obey me. Together, we can wear him down, sever the link. He'll be completely cut off in null space again. Where he ought to remain."

"Don't trust her, Jason," repeated Solana. "Finish her."

"Where are you, Cosmo?"

Asmodraxas was near. His voice jolted the palace. I shook my head.

"Sorry, Solana. We need all the help we can get."

22_____

The Hall of Free Captains was on the upper
level of the Corsairium, overlooking the city. While
Asmodraxas sought us there, thrusting his armored
hand into the chamber like a monkey seeking to pluck
termites from the mound, I and my spellbinding allies
hurried down the stairs and through the corridors to
those portions of the palace deep within the cliff itself.

Along the way we encountered panicked pirates and
dismayed Dreadguards in groups of various sizes, from
two to twenty. Most ignored us, intent on fleeing the
danger of the Demon Lord without. Those who op-
posed us had little time to regret it, for between my
armed might and the magic of Eufrosinia and Solana,
we made short work of them.

In the dungeon, we liberated Captain Skipjammer
and his crew.

"Well met, sir! Well met indeed!" exclaimed Skipjammer as I opened his cell. "This reminds me of the
time I inadvertently offended the Royal Viceroy of
Venabulum—"

"Is everyone here? Any casualties?"

"All present and accounted for, I think. Slightly
worse for the wear, but still intact."

"The *Miracle*, unfortunately, is not."

Skipjammer sighed. "Sunk again, eh?"

"Afraid so. But come on. We'll find you another ship."

"It won't quite be the same. Fortunately, I always carry a small piece of her about my person to carry the tradition forward to the next incarnation of the *Miracle*." He drew from his pocket a small, flat block of wood.

"Maybe if you leave that here, the next *Miracle* won't sink."

"Nothing doing, sir!"

Eufrosinia leading the way, we started down an underground corridor that led out of the palace and joined with a network of secret passages under the city. It seemed every city was honeycombed with secret passages. Our plan was to follow the tunnels and emerge behind Asmodraxas, for whatever advantage of surprise that would give us.

"How did you fare with the pirates?" asked Skipjammer. "I feared the worst when the mercenaries came to seize us."

"The pirates were no problem. It's Asmodraxas we've got to worry about now."

Skipjammer and his mariners stopped in their tracks.

"Asmodraxas, sir?" he said weakly. "Surely you jest."

"No jest."

"Is it the end of the world, then?"

"I hope not. Keep moving. I'll get us all out of this alive if I can. But don't hold me to that."

I emerged from the tunnels with the rosy-fingered dawn, my armor gleaming in the cold morning light, the new strength Rae had promised surging through my limbs. Solana stood to my left, Eufrosinia to my right, as I braced myself for the most important battle of my heroic career. And the deadliest. Though able to bring only a fraction of his might to bear, Asmodraxas was the most dangerous entity in the known universe and he hated me with a vengeful passion that could only be described as apocalyptic.

My hands shook, and I wondered if my ancestor had felt such fear when he faced Asmodraxas in their final battle an age ago. He must have, for he faced an Asmodraxas untrammeled by the limitations of corpses and conduits. Armed only with the same weapons I now bore, he faced the demon god in all his awful glory.

Faced him and prevailed.

Well, he did have the Superwand. That was a significant point.

Rancor was in ruins. In his thirst for souls to fuel his rampage, Asmodraxas had reduced every building to rubble, smashed the quays, demolished the ships. The pirates and their cohorts who escaped having their souls slurped fled up the cliff paths, hid in the secret tunnels, or drowned themselves in the harbor. Many went mad and fell upon one another in their fear. That always happens to a certain susceptible percentage of the population when entities of cosmic evil are in the vicinity.

As I positioned myself near the harbor Asmodraxas was busy pounding on the Corsairium, his back to me. He seemed a little shorter, perhaps down to ninety feet, but that didn't mean much. Daiquirimaker's wild whirring echoed from the cliff walls, the sound rebounding and resonating with itself until the chips and pebbles on the ground skipped and danced and my very bones vibrated.

"Come forth, Cosmo! Come forth and face me if you dare!"

I turned to Solana. "Get his attention!" I had to shout to be heard, though she was but an arm's length away.

"Are you sure you want it?"

"Not really, but do it!"

She lifted her arms and projected a thin streamer

of flame across the city to pass within yards of Asmo-draxas's head. The archdemon turned.

"Oh, Gods," I breathed when I saw his face.

"Holy Rae preserve us!" said Solana.

"Hellfire!" spat Eufrosinia.

Dread's features were gone, replaced by the true visage of Asmodraxas, a face at once so beautiful and terrible that it inspired both fear and adoration, both a desire to fall down and worship and an urge to flee screaming with terror. I resisted both impulses.

"Ah! There you are," said Asmodraxas. "Are you prepared to die—and worse?"

"I'm ready to send you back where you belong!" I shouted defiantly.

"What was that?" asked Asmodraxas, cocking his head, as he advanced. "I hear you shouting but I cannot discern your words from across the ruined city-scape, laid low by my awesome might."

"I will defeat you!" I said.

"Some pitiful words of defiance, I suppose. It was ever your way to engage in idle histrionics."

"You're not exactly Mr. Plainspoken!" I said.

"That, I imagine, was a feeble insult. You are a trying mortal, Cosmo. But that is all you are—a mortal. Frail. Weak. Vulnerable. A mere speck of nothing before the transcendent cosmic majesty of my infernal omnipotence."

He was halfway to us and noticeably shorter, down to eighty feet or so. I turned to the left and smiled grimly at Solana. She was as shaken as I, but reso-lutely held her ground. I turned to the right.

Eufrosinia was gone.

"Where did she go?" I asked Solana.

She glanced over and shrugged. "Who gives a damn?"

I lifted Overwhelm, which burst once more into blue flame and emitted its own deafening hum.

"Come to your doom!" I cried.

"**That I heard,**" said Asmodraxas. "**Terminally trite.**"

Solana shot a fireball at his head. It staggered Asmodraxas and marred his features momentarily, but had little other effect except to make him laugh.

"**So you have a witch to help you, Cosmo? And she would assault the Master of Hell with *fire*? How absurd.**"

With that he brought Daiquirimaker down between Solana and mé. We dived in opposite directions to avoid the earth-shaking blow from the forty-foot blade. I regained my feet first, but saw no effective way to counterattack. He was too big.

Asmodraxas stepped forward and chopped downward again with madly whirring Daiquirimaker. Again I skipped to one side. I couldn't turn back his blows with my puny blade. The weight and momentum of his giant weapon would crush me if it connected. Not to mention puree my soul.

Asmodraxas swung his sword again. Daiquirimaker was the golf club and I was the ball on the tee. Fortunately, Asmodraxas wasn't much of a golfer. I ducked under the swing, then sprang away from his falling foot. And so it went, my foe advancing and me retreating like a madly hopping toad.

Solana blasted Asmodraxas again, but he shrugged off her attack and concentrated on me. At the top of his next swing I dodged between his legs and hacked at the back of his ankle. Overwhelm sliced through the thick boot leather like paper and bit into dead and distended flesh, but not deeply enough to sever the muscle or damage the bone.

Asmodraxas pivoted and stomped on me with surprising swiftness, grinding his boot into me. His foot, as big as a wagon, completely covered me. Yet he did not bear down with the crushing weight I expected and I realized that his mass had not increased to fully match his size. Dread's corpse had not so much grown to gargantuan proportions as it had been stretched supernaturally beyond its normal bounds. That was good news. It meant I would not be crushed to a pulp, just badly bruised.

"For a thousand years I have awaited this chance to grind you beneath my foot like an insect, Cosmo." Asmodraxas gloated, lifting his foot.

"I hope it was worth the wait," I grunted, rolling onto my back.

"Indeed. But now the waiting is over. And for you, everything is over."

He brought Daiquirimaker down with melodramatic slowness. The sword's wild whirring was a deafening roar as it came closer and closer. Though my limbs ached and my muscles were weary, I had to move unless I wanted my scrambled soul sucked out like a watery milkshake through a straw.

I rolled to my feet and dodged between his legs again, taking another swipe at his foot as I passed. Asmodraxas had the same problem I would have fighting a chipmunk. I was so small and quick, relative to him, that it was difficult for him to make his blows connect.

Either because he realized this, or because his accumulated soul energy was dissipating, Asmodraxas shrank rapidly down to only twenty feet tall.

Only twenty feet tall. Right.

He swung Daiquirimaker and this time I met him blade to blade. It was awkward, since his sword was twice as long as mine. It was perhaps a useless maneuver. But it sure looked heroic if anyone was watching.

"So the Mighty Champion will go down fighting, will he?" mocked Asmodraxas.

"The only one going down is you!" I said, dancing inside his swing and slashing out with Overwhelm in a two-handed swing that severed Asmodraxas's left leg halfway to the knee.

He staggered. He waved his arms. He hopped on

one foot. But he did not fall, though thickened blood rained from the stump like a scarlet waterfall and he lost another ten feet of height.

"**You were saying?**"

"How can you possibly remain standing with half your leg gone?"

"**This body is dead. It is under my control, and if I choose not to fall, then I will not fall.**"

"Yeah? Well, I'd like to see you swing your sword now without—whoa!"

I barely avoided his lightning-quick attack.

"**The dead have perfect balance.**"

"I'll remember that. Maybe this will cut you down to size."

Asmodraxas contemptuously deflected my attack on his other leg. "**That was an obvious gambit.**"

"I suppose it was. You're pretty agile for a dead guy with one leg."

Asmodraxas attacked more furiously than ever. I was as strong as twenty men, but he was at least as powerful, perhaps more. Overwhelm and Daiquiri-maker clashed and sparked, their red and blue energies melding into destructive purple and ebon flares that randomly gouged the ground, scorched our armor, or vanished into the upper atmosphere. Titanic blows rained down on Gardion, actually denting and misshaping the supposedly invincible shield. We whirled and turned and slashed. Once, twice, thrice, Asmodraxas broke through my defense and actually landed blows against my body, damaging the Cosmosuit, but not penetrating.

I would know if his blade penetrated my armor. My soul would be ripped from me and I would shrivel to dust.

I responded in kind, attacking savagely. I cut his arm, pierced his breast, dealt him a ringing blow to the head that sliced a bat wing from his helmet, rammed him with my shield in an unsuccessful attempt to overbalance him. But of what use were mortal blows against a foe already dead, a foe animated not by the chemistry of life, but the sorceries of the Darkest Depths of Hell?

Our duel raged on. Thirty minutes. An hour. Two hours. Solana watched from a distance. Her magic useless against Asmodraxas, she was helpless to intervene. Eufrosinia did not return from wherever she had fled, nor was there any sign of her compatriots Thecia and Last Gasp. It seemed Solana had been correct and the Mistress of Pain had merely played on my fears to escape certain death. Still, she had been useful in leading us to Skipjammer and the hidden tunnels, if nothing else.

Occasionally a Rancorian stuck his or her head out from a hiding place, saw what was happening, and quickly ducked back under cover. Glancing at the heights, I saw crowds of pirates gathered there to watch the duel. As the fight took us further from the dock area, Skipjammer and his crew emerged from hiding to search for anything that vaguely resembled a floating vessel.

Ten feet was apparently a height Asmodraxas could maintain without too much strain. It was enough to give him an advantage of reach—I had to risk his blade if I hoped to land a blow—without becoming a liability. He obviously couldn't transfer more of his own power or substance into the sword from null space or he would have escaped by that route long ago. That meant all the energy used to animate and expand Dread's corpse had come from his earlier harvesting of souls, from the hundreds or thousands of life forces ripped untimely from their mortal shells. My prayer was that he would use up his energy reserves before I myself tired. He had to give out eventually. If I had the will and endurance to fight on, then might I prevail despite the daunting might of my diabolical foe.

Unless he got a fresh supply of victims.

Which wasn't likely.

Not without help.

But suddenly it was raining pirates.

Hurricane-force winds whipped across the clifftops, scouring the trails clean and sending several dozen people soaring out over the harbor. The pirates screamed in terror as they were borne aloft and blown toward the city, toward hungrily whirring Daiquiri-maker.

It wasn't Asmodraxas's doing. Soaring above the scent, Last Gasp was giving the archdemon his second wind, using the air currents to bear an offering of souls to the master he had chosen to serve. My plan to run down Asmodraxas's batteries suddenly became a bad joke.

Asmodraxas laughed. **"Now your defeat is certain, fool. My resources are without limit."**

"You're just putting off the inevitable."

"I am the inevitable."

The first victims landed all around us, suffering concussions and broken bones, but surviving. Asmodraxas rushed to consume their souls. My efforts to block him were futile. I couldn't position myself between him and all of the people, not with more falling from the sky every second.

Adding to the difficulty of the feat, Eufrosinia reentered the fray—on the other side, of course. She stepped out of her hiding place and zapped me from behind with her wand of pain, delivering a giga-bolt of spiritual lightning that the tattered Cosmosuit did not entirely stop. I went down hard, kissed the dirt, and didn't move.

Solana, enraged, hit Eufrosinia with everything she had, causing a fireblast that turned a twenty-foot section of the ground into a blasted, smoking crater. However, Eufrosinia was still an arcane master of long experience and Solana was still a newly minted sub-master. Even fueled by nova-force anger, her magic wasn't enough to overcome the sadistic sorceress.

But at least she remembered to raise her own defenses this time. Eufrosinia's counterattack missed the mark, unable to penetrate Solana's mystic shields. They had a momentary standoff, but it couldn't last. Solana had foolishly expended most of her energy in her rash attack, and didn't have enough endurance to hold her defenses for long against a determined assault by Eufrosinia. She knew it and she started to sweat. Dying by Eufrosinia's hand was not a good way to go.

Meantime, Asmodraxas was gaining so much power from the rain of pirates that his borrowed body glowed with the same unearthly radiance Daiquirimaker gave off, as if Dread's animated corpse was more than ever an extension of the unhallowed sword.

I struggled to my knees, coughing and spitting blood. Asmodraxas came toward me, sword upraised to deliver the killing blow.

I tried to stand, tried to lever myself to my feet using Overwhelm as a support. I couldn't do it. My legs refused to obey my brain's commands. My innards burned from Eufrosinia's spells. My muscles ached from hours of hard battle. My skin was blistered from the excess energies thrown off by our duel. My vision blurred. Everything seemed to be happening now in slow motion.

"Yes, kneel before me, Cosmo. Bow down and worship your rightful master."

"Worship," I said to myself. I clutched the Rae medallion that hung around my neck. "Rae, Bright Goddess, if ever I have served you faithfully, aid me now. If ever I have brought honor to your name through my deeds, preserve me in my hour of need against this, the darkest of foes, the vilest of enemies, the most awful of adversaries. Hear my prayer, O Lady of the Sun! Succor your Champion! Deliver your servant! Bright Rae, heed my cry!"

I felt the amulet grow warmer in my hand and the sun jewel at its center began to softly glow. In my mind I heard a sound transmitted from on high.

It was a busy signal.

Solana's defenses failed and she was at Eufrosinia's mercy, enveloped in a twisting, shredding, piercing, collapsing net of physical and psychic agony. She screamed and thrashed, but her scream was silenced as her throat both constricted and expanded. Eufrosinia was toying with her, taking full advantage of her superiority to wring every ounce of suffering from Solana's pain-racked body that she could before she killed her.

I hurled Gardion at Asmodraxas, hoping to slow him, but the balance of the damaged shield was off. It missed the mark and failed to return. I had foolishly thrown away the only protection I had left.

I tried the amulet again. Still busy.

Asmodraxas stood over me and hefted maddeningly whirring Daiquirimaker, point toward me. The sword moaned eagerly and seemed to gloat and mock at the defeat of Overwhelm and Overwhelm's bearer.

"Good-bye, Cosmo. And good riddance."

Overwhelm.

A desperate ploy flashed through my brain and I acted on it without hesitation. With a two-handed grip on Overwhelm, I lunged upward, launching myself from the ground, my sword extended, placing my full trust in its enchantment. That, combined with Asmodraxas's surprise at having a beaten foe spring up for one final blow, did the trick. Overwhelm sliced forward, unerringly finding the gap in Asmodraxas's armor at the shoulder and striking his sword arm from his body.

The arm fell, hand still clutching Daiquirimaker's hilt. The hellsword's dark glow and blending noises faded and died as it fell to the ground.

"Damn you, Cosmo!"

"Not today. Maybe next time. You're going back to limbo land with no one to talk to and no one to play with."

I fell, now truly unable to rise.

Asmodraxas did not reply to my parting taunt. He was already sealed once more in his featureless limbo prison, cut off from contact with the rest of the universe. Dread's body imploded and then crumbled to dust. The empty black armor clattered to the paving stones.

I mentally kicked myself for not realizing sooner that separating the sword from the body would break the connection and send Asmodraxas's essence packing. Daiquirimaker was the power source, the conduit that used soul energy to animate Dread's corpse. Eufrosinia had told me that hours ago, but the fact's full significance had failed to register until that final awful moment when the grim jaws of defeat were about to gobble me down forever.

But that's when I do my clearest thinking anyway.

I had won. It was over.

I tumbled into oblivion.

23⎯⎯⎯⎯⎯⎯⎯⎯⎯⎯⎯⎯

"Awaken, Cosmo. It is time to conclude this little heroic epic of yours."

The voice that jarred me from my dreamy slumber was as dry as the desiccated tendons of a sun-bleached skeleton. It belonged to Necrophilius the Grave, Prince of the Necromancers, Mordant Grand Patriarch of the Forbidden Church of Undeath, and reigning Overmaster of the Dark Magic Society. He was stooped, thin, colorless, and had obviously been cheating Death for a long time. His robe was naturally black, as was his sablewood staff with its headpiece in the form of a grinning silver skull.

"I congratulate you on your victory," he said.

"Victory?"

Wrapped like a mummy in grave clothes, I was laid out on a bier in a murky chamber of dust and gloom and cobwebs unevenly lit by seven red candles in a tarnished silver candelabra. Necrophilius sat on a stool beside me.

"Over the incarnation of Asmodraxas. You recall that, don't you?"

"Yes. Of course. You're not going to tell me that it was all faked, that he was really just a giant hand puppet?"

"No."

"Not a dream?"

"No."

"Not a hoax?"

"No."

"Not an imaginary story?"

"That depends on your imagination."

"I'm not dead, am I?"

"Not yet."

"Then what's going on here? The last thing I remember I collapsed after cutting off Dread's arm."

"Your recollection is accurate. You have been unconscious since that moment, lost in the deep sleep of the tiger lotus."

"For how long?"

"A few weeks. Long enough for the various subplots to resolve themselves."

"What subplots? What are you talking—"

Necrophilius raised his hand. "All will be explained. This is the final chapter, in which explanations are customarily made, and I have been designated to make most of them this time. Have patience."

"I notice that these tight bandages prevent me from rising," I said. "So I suppose I have no choice."

"No, you do not."

"Am I again a prisoner of the Dark Magic Society? That's getting to be an old routine."

"No. You are my prisoner. There is a difference."

"I'll take your word for it."

"Do that."

"Where is Solana?"

"Lady Sweetfire has been safely returned to Rae City. I prevented Eufrosinia from killing her, but we will come to that momentarily."

"What fate awaits me?"

"That is entirely up to you. You must choose your fate, Mighty Champion. And you must choose wisely and well, for your choice will shape the future of all Arden."

"Your words echo the words of another. A prophet."

"I doubt we frequent the same prophets, Cosmo, but the parallel is possible, for I peer into the future from time to time, catching hazy glimpses of what is to come. I speak from the wisdom thus gained when I say you are the key to the Next Age. The Gods know this. Their oracles speak it, even the Luminous One. And do not think the Demon Lords have forgotten you. All the great ones of the universe are watching you."

"To what end?"

"You are the Mighty Champion of this age. Though you style yourself the Champion of Rae, you are truly the Champion of The Gods, all of them, the pantheon collectively, whether you realize it or not. They are preparing you for what is to come and for now it suits their purposes that you serve Rae, but I believe the day is coming when they will call you to your true station."

"Interesting speculation."

"It is speculation, I confess. But I believe it is accurate speculation. I have highly placed sources. For you see, in my own way, I too serve The Gods."

"Get out of here."

"Truly."

"Do you expect me to believe you're some kind of double agent, infiltrating the Society to destroy it from within?"

"I could be. I have spared your life on more than one occasion when I should have killed you, have I not?"

"Yes," I admitted.

"However, I make no such claims. No reward awaits me in Paradise. The Gods would not hear my prayers did I utter any. No, I fear I must be numbered among the forces of evil. But, as evil entities go, I am a moderate."

"Moderately evil?" I scoffed.

"Asmodraxas and the other Demon Lords represent

absolute evil. They would drive all goodness from the world, drag down The Gods, tilt the moral balance permanently to darkness and decadence, cruelty and fear and pain. I am moderate because I have no more desire to see that happen than you. I see a need in the universe for goodness, decency, honor, and justice. But I also recognize a need for evil, as a scourge against complacency, as a catalyst for growth and change. The good needs something against which to contend, or it is bled of meaning."

"Sounds like doublespeak to me. You're a bad guy, but since we really need bad guys, you're not so bad after all."

The Grave One chuckled. "Oh, I'm very bad, Cosmo. I am ruthless, ambitious, manipulative, and cunning. I crave power and I will have it. But I also retain a sense of balance. I see the larger picture. I see where I fit in. I see where you fit in."

"And where do I fit in?"

"As the end of this age approaches, the absolutists will produce their own Champion. Perhaps it will be Asmodraxas, despite his recent defeats. More likely one of the other Demon Lords will arise. Or maybe Dread Tsorthas down in Sanskaara will make the move for which he has spent ten centuries preparing. But there will be a Dark Champion seeking to corrupt the spirit of the Next Age and make it the Age of Absolute Evil. Your task then will be to defeat evil's Champion. That much is obvious."

"I suppose so."

"From that it follows that in the meantime you must prepare yourself for what is to come. You must gain the tools, knowledge, wisdom, and experience you will need to prevail in the final hour."

"Right. I see that."

"Well, you're going about it all wrong."

"What do you mean?"

"You're in a rut. Your adventures follow the same

pattern. Travel, survive various encounters, get captured, escape and sneak through enemy stronghold,
final confrontation with major villain, rescue through
outside intervention. Like clockwork, with only minor
variations on the theme."

"Hey, it's a formula, but it works."

"It becomes tiresome after too many repetitions,"
said Necrophilius.

"Sort of like you turning up at the end every time to
explain how you've secretly arranged everything that
happened to your benefit," I retorted. "This is the
third time in a row, you know."

"It will be the last. My participation in your patterns
only encourages you."

"I see."

"The root of your problem, Cosmo, is that you let
others direct your life and define your choices for you
rather than defining them for yourself."

"Well, if I'm an instrument of The Gods, it only
makes sense to let them call the shots."

"Don't make the mistake of ascribing too much
competence to The Gods. They are good at handling
their portfolios, but outside their narrow areas of expertise, most of them are utterly hopeless."

"That's hardly a pious thing to say."

"Can you deny the validity of the statement?"

"Er—no."

"The fate of the universe is too important to be left
in the hands of The Gods. Don't rely on them to
prepare you or all is lost. Prepare yourself!"

"How?"

"Growth comes from challenge. Seek fresh challenges! Get a new perspective. Don't sit around waiting for something to happen. Go out and look for
trouble. Wrongs to right and all that. Each victory will
make you stronger, more confident, more canny. But
don't rely on Raella or the League or wandering
prophets to point you in the right direction. All the

great heroes were self-starters and you must be the greatest hero of all if you are to win when it counts."

"Your words have merit," I admitted. "You echo some of my own thoughts. But I find it unsettling to get this lecture from the Overmaster of the Society. What's your interest?"

"I believe the Next Age will be as balanced between good and evil as this one. There will be opportunity for both sides, and I intend to make the most of that opportunity. I believe you will defeat the Champion of Absolute Evil, but I do not believe you will survive that confrontation yourself, Cosmo. Thus the Coming Age will present a level playing field. I will seek to add to my power and others will oppose me and life will go on."

"But in the meantime, you're backing me."

He smiled his rigor-mortis smile. "Let us say I prefer you to the alternative. There is no room for an independent thinker like me in a world ruled by Asmodraxas. And I value my independence, which you can protect simply by doing your job."

"You would enslave humanity as surely as the archdemon if you could," I said accusingly.

"I am no slave driver. I am most comfortable lurking in the shadows, pulling strings, arranging events to my liking."

"Why do I get the feeling I'm being arranged right now?"

"Because you are. I want to reach an understanding with you, Cosmo. I understand you. I want you to understand me."

"I understand you. Well enough not to trust you."

"That was uncalled for. I have kept my word to you thus far."

"Oh, really? You promised to take no further actions against me and Merc if we didn't bother you. Yet we were attacked at the League tower and I was lured into a Society trap at Rancor."

"You were not the target of the attack on the League tower. That was a necessary demonstration of my power, more for the benefit of my colleagues in the Society than for any strategic value. My ways are more subtle and less bloodthirsty than those of many in my profession. Some members of the Society mistake that for weakness. I orchestrated the destruction of the tower and launched a new campaign against the League to put to rest any doubts."

"You kill my friends and want me to understand you?"

"The League and Society are ancient enemies, and enemies kill each other. That shouldn't be hard to understand. And not all were your friends. Our earthquake and hellgate spells could not have reached the tower had not we had a friend of our own within the League to disarm the protective spells."

"A traitor? Who?"

"Come now, you don't expect me to tell you that, do you? Though the identity would surprise you, I think. Now, as to the other matter you mentioned, the trap at Rancor, that was not my doing, but the work of dissidents."

"You knew about their plot."

"Yes, but that is not the same as instigating it. And I also monitored the situation via my patented prying eyes and intervened at the appropriate time. There is a teleportal beneath the Corsairium. I and half a dozen of my more trusted followers arrived in time to prevent the conspirators from killing you and your companions. You are here, alive, in this Hidden Chapel of Undeath. Eufrosinia, Last Gasp, and Thecia are in my custody elsewhere, contemplating the error of their ways. Captain Skipjammer and his crew were set free. And Tannis Darkwolf is now the Pirate Queen in fact as well as name."

"Tannis?"

"Promising young woman. During the confusion,

she strangled Jacques Malad with the very chains that bound her. Organized her surviving followers and did away with all her rivals before they knew what hit them. Naturally, I offered her an alliance and Society assistance in rebuilding the city. The new Rancor will be more impregnable than ever and an important base of operations for my organization. I didn't overlook anything, did I?"

"Do you ever?"

"No. Details win. A simple truth which eludes many. Now. Shall we bargain?"

"What if we don't?"

"You will die here and now."

An eerie purple phosphorescence outlined his staff and the silver skull at the tip opened its mouth.

"After all the nice things you've said about me?"

"The Gods can always find another Champion if they must, Cosmo."

"Let's deal. What's your offer?"

"I am in the process of purging the Society of absolutists. In this our interests coincide, for my enemies are your enemies. You will be provided with the names of those I would not mind seeing come to an unfortunate end. You may act against them with impunity. That is, without fear of organized retaliation from me and my loyalists."

"Fair enough."

"I am also doing all I can to discourage searches for the Superwand. This also is in your interest."

"Go on."

"I will also continue our earlier pact. If you take no action against me and my loyal followers, we will take no action against you."

"Fair enough," I said. "But we both realize that a truce can't last forever."

"Agreed. But I am willing to wager you will find other foes more worthy of your attention for the near future."

"Next."

"I am going to release you, but without Overwhelm and without your fabulous armor and shield. The ring and medallion you may retain. I do this not to weaken you, but to strengthen you."

"What are you talking about?"

"I have watched you, Cosmo. I think you rely too much on those props. You must learn to be more self-reliant."

"The Gods gave me those relics! They belonged to the original Mighty Champion!"

"I know their pedigree. And I know that you will need them at the appointed time. Until then, I will keep them. And don't bother trying to summon them—Dread's insipid wormwood box has a new owner. Believe me, this is for your own good. You'll be a better hero for it."

"Of all the arrogant—"

"Yes, yes, I know. Look, even though we're forming this covert alliance—"

"Nonaggression pact."

"Whatever. Even so, it serves me to see you weakened. You'll get them back when the time is right, but in the meantime you won't be able to do quite so much damage to my operations should you take a notion to do so. Which you might. Heroes are like that. But please don't start questing for the things as soon as I release you. Find new interests. Explore some alternatives."

"Are you a villain or a guidance counselor?"

"A little of both. I've got a lot riding on you, Cosmo, whether you like it or not."

"Not."

"As I thought."

"So I get my life, my freedom, and a hunting license to dispose of your enemies for you?"

"Yes."

"And you get the relics of the Mighty Champion."

"That's it. Or I can just kill you now. Do we have a deal?"

"I dislike this, Necrophilius. I don't trust your subtlety. But it appears I have little choice."

"What kind of ending is this?" I demanded, sipping my hot coffee. The warmth felt good.

Merc had no answer.

"Bundled up in bandages like an intensive-care patient and dumped ignominiously in a refuse heap in Slumville in the middle of the night! If the watch hadn't found me, the rats would have eaten my face off. It was the only part they could get to. Of course, if it had been much longer, I'd have frozen so solid even their fangs couldn't pierce my skin."

"That was in poor taste," said Merc. "But you're in the Solar Palace now. No rats here. At least not on the upper levels."

"Overwhelm, the Cosmosuit, Gardion—all stolen! A fine hero I am. I lose my trademarks, my signature weapon. The relics of the Mighty Champion lie moldering in a box of wormwood."

Merc shook his head. "Do you recall our discussion in the sewers of Caratha? When you become too invincible, you cease to be interesting. All the drama evaporates."

"You agree with Necrophilius?" I sipped my coffee.

"To a certain extent. It might be good for you to do without the props for a while. You've still got your incredible strength, of course, but strength alone has its limits. Loaded down with all your divine hardware it's too easy for you to hack and slash your way through problems. Haven't you noticed that the really interesting things only happen to us when we've temporarily lost our magic goodies?"

"Hmmm."

"Your life will be much more interesting without all that clutter."

"Perhaps so."

Raella, clad in a gold nightgown, entered the sitting room and embraced me when I stood. "Jason! We thought you dead! You've been missing for weeks and Solana had no clue of your fate."

"Where is Solana? Is she all right?"

"Mostly recovered from her injuries. She is abed upstairs, but I have sent word of your arrival. She has been most worried about you. The most worried of all, I think."

Raella sat carefully in an overstuffed chair and Merc moved to her side with a look of mild concern. As if on cue, both turned their gaze to me and I got the feeling that I was being cued in turn. But for what I wasn't sure.

"Is there something I ought to know?" I asked.

"Ahem!" said Merc. "Did I neglect to mention that the heir to the throne is on the way?"

I scrutinized Raella. Now that he mentioned it, she did seem a little thicker around the middle.

"An heir? A child? You? Raella?" I stopped sputtering and got my flapping tongue under control. "Congratulations!"

"Thank you," said Raella.

"When did this come about?"

"We did not learn of my condition until soon after your departure," said Raella, "or we'd have told you sooner."

"As it is," said Merc. "This makes for something of a surprise ending. Not that it has much to do with your adventure, but the news adds something in the way of human interest to the tale."

"I'll say! This is great!"

"Having reigned for ten years without a husband," said Raella, "this was a royal duty long neglected." She clasped Merc's hand. "And cheerfully performed."

"Yes," I said. "You're positively—"

"Don't say it," said Merc.

"—glowing," I finished.

"Thank you," said Raella.

"When are you due?"

"Another six months. As you can imagine, this makes prosecution of the war with the Society more harrowing. I am their prime target. But now more than my own safety is at risk."

"I am your Champion as surely as I am Rae's, Your Majesty," I said gravely, kneeling before her with my hand to my heart. "My sword, if I still had it, would be pledged to your defense and that of the unborn life you carry. I have misplaced my sword, but I can still pledge my body and my life."

"Thank you, Jason. I could ask for no finer guardian. Nor could your future godchild."

"Agreed," said Merc. We all clasped hands solemnly.

At that moment Solana entered. "Jason! I can scarcely believe it! I had lost all hope!"

I rose and embraced her. "It's good to see you, milady."

Without warning, she kissed me.

"What was that for?" I asked.

Solana smiled. "For you, foolish man."

"Foolish?"

"Foolish to leave me thinking you were dead."

"It wasn't my idea."

"We'll be taking our leave now," said Raella. "I need my rest and I'm certain the two of you have much to discuss."

"Good night," I said absently, not taking my eyes from Solana's.

"I have been thinking," she said, "that perhaps the plot pressures were not so far off the mark."

"Meaning?"

"Meaning I squelched our budding romance to assert myself against stereotyping forces, because I didn't want to simply conform to my expected role."

"Yes?"

"But it has since occurred to me that you were—are—a man worth a second look. Now that the pressure of the adventure is off and we can make our own decisions. That is, if you think it's worth looking into."

"Oh, I think so."

"Well. Good. I'm glad."

I kissed her again.

"Now *this* is an ending."

All Pan books are available at your local bookshop or newsagent, or can be ordered direct from the publisher. Indicate the number of copies required and fill in the form below.

Send to: Pan C. S. Dept
               Macmillan Distribution Ltd
               Houndmills Basingstoke RG21 2XS
or phone: 0256 29242, quoting title, author and Credit Card number.

Please enclose a remittance* to the value of the cover price plus: £1.00 for the first book plus 50p per copy for each additional book ordered.

*Payment may be made in sterling by UK personal cheque, postal order, sterling draft or international money order, made payable to Pan Books Ltd.

Alternatively by Barclaycard/Access/Amex/Diners

Card No.

Expiry Date

Signature:

Applicable only in the UK and BFPO addresses

While every effort is made to keep prices low, it is sometimes necessary to increase prices at short notice. Pan Books reserve the right to show on covers and charge new retail prices which may differ from those advertised in the text or elsewhere.

NAME AND ADDRESS IN BLOCK LETTERS PLEASE:

....

Name _____

Address _____

_____

_____

_____

6/92